The Celestial Beings Trilogy

PNĔUMÄ

Book One

Eli Liszt

ELI LISZT

Excerpt from THE DIARY OF ANAIS NIN, Volume Five: 1947-
1955. Copyright © 1974 by Anais Nin. Used by permission of
Houghton Mifflin Harcourt Publishing Company. All rights reserved.

ISBN 978-0-578-68056-9
eBook ISBN 978-0-578-69713-0

Cover design by Daniel Lieske

To my lover and our children: Thank you for your infinite support.

"We write to taste life twice, in the moment and in retrospect." ~ Anais Nin ~

Acknowledgments

First and foremost, I want to thank:

God for giving me the courage and strength to pursue my passion that I thought was out of reach. This story started off as a simple journal five years ago. Anytime I had an idea, thought, or dream I would jot it down. At first it was more of a hobby in a therapeutic sense, but as time passed, I found that I rather enjoyed writing and then it turned from a *want* to a *need* which slowly progressed into this novel.

To all my sci-fi readers and supporters, I am honored that you have decided to take a chance on my book when there are so many other options. It has been a long journey and I hope that this story has captivated your imagination as much as it did mine.

There are a handful of intimate friends that influenced the camaraderie of my characters. Sabrina whom I've known since I was six; Linda and Haide whom I met in middle school – our lasting friendship and solidarity has been essential in creating the bond that my characters share. I want to thank each one of you for remaining a constant in my life through good and bad times.

Sisterhood is instrumental in shaping who we are as women and for that reason I want to thank my sisters Luz, Angelica, Jessica, and Diana for keeping me motivated and grounded even when I was not so inclined.

To my loving parents who created me: my father Ernesto, may he rest in peace and therefore is not able to witness my accomplishments and mother, Ana for raising six children - without your bravery, I would not have had this wonderful opportunity.

Last but not least, I want to thank my devoted husband and lover Omar for being patient and exceptionally supportive. There were times when I did not want to do anything but write all day long and you never once made me feel bad about it. To my children Yvonne, Ozzy and Carmelo, my goal is to inspire you in pursuing your dreams no matter how impossible the goal may seem. The sky is not the limit, and nothing is out of reach so long as your heart aches to get you there.

Chapter One

~Fervor~

It's eight twenty in the morning as I'm running down the porcelain stairs in a startled rush. I manage to grab my light blue sweater from the chaise lounge and dash out into the bitter crisp morning.

The sun is bright, beaming with intensity as its warmth reaches my face while I skid to a halt in front of my sedan. Its Tuesday, my first day back at the University and I'm already running late. I notice that my sisters parking space is vacant, leading me to believe that she is overly eager to be punctual.

Pulling the door handle to my blue metallic sedan I quickly throw my satchel onto the leather seat and start the ignition while closing my door. As the engine springs to life, I pull down the sun visor and attempt to straighten my wavy hair in the small mirror. My rough hand slightly skims over the beard stubble that has begun to sprout on my chin and cheeks. Deciding that my appearance is of non-importance I settle on a mussed look instead and slam the visor shut.

With Jack Garratt playing in the background, I sit back into my seat exasperated and begin to reflect on my past and the impending future. So many thoughts are crossing my mind at once that I quickly become overwhelmed and find myself in a resentful state.

I hate being in this predicament, where I must do what is asked of me, otherwise I risk being labeled as *unadaptable*. Against my will, I have acquired certain undesirable responsibilities that one day will hold me accountable for leading all five tribes. This prophecy was delivered unto my family by the tribe's seer the moment I became of age. And once the divination is presented, there is no getting out of it unless the chosen has perished.

At first, I didn't understand what that duty entailed but learned early on that it wasn't something that I wanted to be a part of. Being watched from every angle with no room for faults or slipups places a tremendous amount of pressure on a young leader who is still trying to figure out who they really are. It's like they are waiting for me to screw up; always criticizing my actions without ever providing guidance or support. Someone is always present, ready to bark orders on how I should conduct myself, what I should or shouldn't be doing or when I should be doing them.

The burden soon became far too great which eventually caused me to flout and placed me directly towards a path of destruction. Being pulled in every direction turned out to be hazardous for myself and everyone around me. I almost condemned myself to *the shadows* for my ruthless behavior when I nearly carried out a threat that no one thought possible, not even me.

My temper was hanging on by a thread so even the slightest presence of ridicule would send me over the edge. The final straw that landed me in the hot seat was when a member of the Nadöb tribe was being overly aggressive to my younger sister.

We had traveled to Brazil to meet with the elders and council members one summer. While the adults were in the assembly room discussing business matters that we were not privileged to, the young adults gathered outside in the garden terrace of the gated mansion.

Surrounded by music and familiar faces, we all indulged in food and drinks while enjoying each other's company. Just as I'm about to take another sip of my drink, Titus my younger brother walks over to me with urgency. His infuriated expression stops the glass from reaching my lips as I slowly lower my hand to the side.

"Is everything ok brother?"

"No!" He exclaims while running his hand through his hair, agitated and full of anger.

"What is it?" No response as he begins to pace back and forth. Stepping in front of him I place my free hand on his shoulder and speak words of ease. "I'm sure we can resolve whatever has brought on this foul mood." After a few seconds, he stops fidgeting and looks directly into my eyes finally revealing his burden.

"For the past ten minutes that jerk over there has been pestering Clodia. I wanted to approach him without making a scene, but I'm afraid that he will not be as inclined. How should I handle the matter without insulting the elders?"

Suddenly, from the corner of my eye I could see my sister trying to yank free of a male's tight grip around her upper arm. He seemed to be cornering her while whispering into her ear as she looked away, disgusted by his touch. His advances were unwelcomed as she scanned the crowd looking vulnerable and seeking help. His actions bothered me in more ways that I could count. Deciding to intervene I find that my anger has spiked to a new level of insanity.

Without another word, I place my drink down onto a nearby table and carefully stroll over to my sister's defense. Quickly recognizing the perpetrator, I try to reason with him to avoid a full out brawl. Standing between them, I place my hand over his while politely asking him to release her.

"I would strongly advise that you let go of her before you draw unnecessary attention to yourself." My smile reaches my eyes, but my voice is laced with malice as I make promise to my warning. He seemed surprised to see me but wasn't alarmed by my declaration.

"This is between me and Clodia. Isn't that right baby?" He hisses and quickly turns his gaze to my sister while tightening his grip on her arm. My eyes never waver as I hear my sister whimper out of pain beside me.

"Let go of her, NOW! That is if you want to avoid embarrassment." I mutter silently so that only he can hear me.

"Is that a challenge?" He retracts his gaze from my sister's face and focuses on my reaction.

"It most definitely is. Now remove your filthy hands from my sister's arm before I break it and shove it up your ass!"

He then purposely yank's on Clodia's arm and pulls her body closer to his while speaking directly into her ear, "Let me remind you Jovianus, that I don't take too kindly to threats," cautioning me that he could hurt her at any given moment should I decide to proceed with this brazen confrontation.

"Then you should know that I have never made an idle threat."

I can sense his anger spike as he swiftly shoves her body onto the concrete floor. Bad idea, for him anyway. It all happened so fast that I didn't have time to think it through. Without hesitation, my fist immediately connects with his face, striking several unexpected *blows. He tries to swing back in defense, but I quickly sidestep his advance. Moving into the fight he attempts to step forward and regain his posture as I land another powerful punch to his torso causing him to lose balance. His body crashes against some medal chairs as I begin to close the distance between us like a lion encircles his prey.*

He stands, recovers from his fall, and moves his fist upwards to protect his face but it doesn't make a difference. I'm too agile and proficient in combat for his liking as I decide to end his embarrassment when I flip his body backwards and he lands on top of a table. The wood breaks in half as I place him in a lethal headlock and his body begins to squirm underneath my grip.

At this rate, I couldn't be reasoned with because I allowed my anger to prevail which in turn clouded my judgment. Swiftly grabbing a blade from my waistline, I hook the knife onto his top lip with excessive pressure and slash it down to the center of his throat. Blood spilled everywhere causing hush gasps among the guest. I thought I heard a few pleas to stop but wasn't sure and didn't bother to investigate. I was so caught up in the moment and fuming with rage that I didn't realize the consequences of my actions when I dropped the bloody knife, positioned my palms over his face and attempted to break his neck.

That's when a blurred male figure stood before me, placed his hand on top of mine and began to plead for this male's life, "That's enough brother! He isn't worth it!"

As I try to regain my wits, I notice that a crowd has already begun to huddle around us. Not wanting to draw anymore unnecessary attention, I release my death grip and wipe the specks of blood from my face as I stand. But before leaving the scene I deliberately spit on the perpetrator and provide a harsh warning to the bystanders that the next usurper who tries to disrespect my sister will have signed his own fate.

Hushed murmurs resonated throughout the crowd as I graciously walk over to Clodia and help her to her feet. Had it not been for my brother, then I would have taken his life and ended up condemned to the shadows until my natural death. It was clear that he was no match for me but still I proceeded with the attack, feeling provoked.

With a stroke of luck, he survived the assault thus sparing any long-term judgment against me however, it caused much scrutiny among the tribe leaders while the elders began to label me as toxic. Soon everyone from all five tribes caught wind of the scenario and questioned my ability to rule our race. To say that I put my parents through hell would be an understatement. Talk about bad karma!

So here I am, three years later trying to play my part and hopefully become the prodigal son and future leader that my tribe desires by living among our natural enemy, the humans.

The plan is supposed to be simple. Live alongside your adversary. Blend in. Observe. And learn about their weaknesses. I'm not entirety sure how much longer I will be able to maintain this charade of compulsory socialization.

It is because of them that we are unable to reveal our true identity. Because we are different and by different, I mean a noble breed, they would feel threatened by our capabilities and probably cage us up like animals.

In my opinion, the best way to live among the mortals is to continue living apart from them, in our own land, secluded, with minimal interaction, however the tribe leaders and elders believe otherwise.

"It is essential to our survival", were their exact words, "so that we may acquire the necessary knowledge, skills and abilities that will enable our species to continue to flourish while utilizing the planets resources efficiently".

Blah. Blah. Blah! A bunch of nonsense mixed with politics that I could care less about. This facade is pointless. I'll just keep telling myself to endure one more year and I'll have my undergraduate degree which will take me far away from these wretched creatures.

Since defying and disappointing my parents for the millionth time would not be wise, I decide to cooperate and sluggishly descend to the main road and out into traffic. A light drizzle takes over as I turn on North Highland Avenue.

Twenty minutes later I arrive at the campus parking lot which is unusually overcrowded. I'm already forty-five minutes late and class will be over soon, so I decide to ditch my Structural Geology lecture. My next lesson starts in about fifteen minutes; this one is not as important, but I had to fill my daily schedule and an art course in ancient empires sounded quite intriguing.

Feeling aggravated and forlorn I shift my gear to park, reach for my leather satchel and swiftly pull the sweater over my head as I exit the vehicle. Stuffing the keys into the front pocket of my blue jeans, I take notice that I've parked on University Drive right by the Research and Development Center which plants me directly across from the Frick Fine Arts building. Damn, what are the odds?

The drizzle hasn't led up, but it hasn't started to pour either as I take measured steps towards O'Hara Street. The wind has picked up in tempo causing the loose leaves to skip and dance along the brick concrete floor. The sidewalks are jammed with mostly new and confused faces aka *the freshman*. Some students are on bicycles while others took public transportation to get here. Everywhere I look I either see friends huddled together in their own little circle sharing casual conversations or couples holding hands, lost in their moment.

Frowning, I have a brief moment of what, remorse? Guilt maybe? Shouldn't I have some type of emotion or reaction to their bond? I ought to feel happy for them or even sad for myself that I don't have that type of relationship, but the truth is, I don't feel anything anymore.

It has been ages since I had any true feelings or emotions about anything or anyone for that matter. It's my own fault really because for the past few years I have made it my mission to ignore every human being that I've come across. Only speaking to them when necessary and for the most part, it hasn't been necessary.

I'm here against my will, following orders or protocol in a manner of speaking. It doesn't mean that I must enjoy myself while I'm here, stuck with these miserable mortals. They are always moping or complaining about something but never propose a solution to their problems. It gets boring really and I don't have the patience to deal with such insignificance. Why bother investing my quality time on a human or humans for that matter if I will never see them again? This is only temporary, and my time here will be up soon.

Shaking the negative thoughts from my head, I scurry through Benedum Hall and begin to fish for my blackberry, vaguely unaware that I'm walking into a mob of idiots who refuse to stay out of my way. As I'm dashing through the crowd with my head down trying to avoid eye contact, my body accidentally slams into a dark brunette. Halting to a complete stop, I suddenly feel the rage boil over and consume me once more. Irritation swiftly shoots through my veins and my muscles tense as heat begins to course within me.

"You have got to be kidding me!" My harsh thoughts tumble right out of my mouth before I could stop them.

Inhaling deep, I close my eyes and attempt to control my anger. Seconds pass when I finally blink open my eyelids and inspect the scene before me.

The senseless female has already began retrieving her items from the filthy concrete floor. Her long dark brown hair hangs over her shoulders concealing her face as she begins to gather her books into a stack. I've managed to knock her purse off her shoulder along with three hardbacks, a notepad, and some pens. Crammed bodies continue to breeze by us while maneuvering to avoid collision. No one cares to stop and offer help as gazes linger out of curiosity. I just stand there, staring, unsure what to do.

Shit! Should I help her? Damn it, if I don't then I'm the asshole, right?

Without further hesitation, I lean over and hold my weight on my tiptoes as I bend down and grab two of the remaining articles from the floor. Sighing along the way, we both stand at the exact same time. As I begin to hand her the notepad and book, our gazes carelessly collide which promptly stops me in my tracks.

Because in that moment, something happens to me, something unknown and unfamiliar, causing my pupils to dilate as all my senses are suddenly attuned to her presence. It's a strong force of attraction like no other. An undeniable bond. Unquantifiable in every way possible.

My insides twist and contort but not from agony or pain; it stirs, rocking me from my slumber. Yes, the very slumber that I've devoted most of my adulthood to; imprisoned by my own resolve and unwilling to escape.

I feel possessed as I continue to gawk at this beautiful creature that has managed to secure my undivided attention. Her hazel eyes remind me of a tropical rainforest; warm, vibrant, and full of mystery. And those pink pillowy lips, imploring a foray as they stand out against her copper complexion. Long dark lashes blink at my startled reaction as she takes the articles from my hand and smiles politely.

"Thank you."

Goosebumps rapidly form on my skin catching me by surprise. My foul mood subdues and is replaced with bemusement. The anger that once coursed through my veins has vanished as a mellow ambiance consumes my thoughts. In this moment, it's just me and her, no one else exists or matters. I just stand there with my empty hand mid-air, unable to formulate words like a foolish little boy. What's going on here, I question myself?

She notices that I haven't removed my hand and takes this as an invitation to introduce herself by placing her free palm into mine and begins to shake it.

"Hi, I'm Simone."

Her delicate voice pierces my ear drums as her touch sends electric currents throughout my body. Confused and disoriented I deliberately command my hand to drop but it betrays me and before I know it my fingers have curled around hers and returns the hand jester.

"Hi," is all I could manage to say without ever breaking eye contact. I think my mouth is open, not sure but it's starting to feel dry and scratchy. She stifles a laugh and reveals a devilish smile that curves onto freckled cheeks, exposing diminutive dimples that only heightens my attraction towards her. Damn. Who is this mortal?

Still smiling, revealing perfectly pearly white teeth she somehow summons the courage to continue speaking to me as if I've been so inviting.

"So... do you have a name?" She coaxes for information with our palms still intact, causing my blood pressure to rise with each passing moment.

My curiosity is piqued, and I can no longer contain this new-found bliss that has suddenly blossomed within me.

"Yes." I respond instantaneously and gently retrieve my hand while shaking out of my reverie. "Hi, uh my name is Jovianus. Jovianus Moreau."

Did I just tell her my full name? Oh why? I find myself smiling like a nerd who just answered a math question that no one else could figure out. I continue talking, well babbling really because at this point, I feel like I'm unable to contain my inquisitiveness.

"Apologies for my rude behavior and for knocking down your books, it was foolish of me."

Confusion settles into my consciousness while I fiddle with my temper. Since when do you need to apologize to a human?

She tucks a lost strand of hair behind her ear revealing a pierced earlobe that is lined to the top with tiny bright studs. Looking down shyly, she begins to fidget and sway from side to side. I was so affixed on her face that I never bothered to look at her physique. She's wearing fitted denim jeans that are slightly torn from her thighs all the way down to her knees. Her plain white tee is accented by a dark red scarf that drapes lightly around her neck and a black lose jacket that looms over her small frame. Black ankle boots with a gold buckle hug her feet. I am taken aback by her appearance as she is a sight to see.

"Aww, it's ok. It's actually my fault. I wasn't paying attention. You know, caught up on reading my schedule and trying to find my class."

I notice that she is swinging a piece of white paper with bold letters in the air. Completely caught up in our conversation, I find myself drinking in every word she says and detect a loophole to continue interacting with her.

"Maybe I can help. I'm no stranger to this school and fully acquainted with the campus." Why am I offering to help her? Since when am I nice to anyone, I huff!

I catch her looking at her watch before she turns her attention back to me, "Um, I'm looking for the art building and my class starts in about four minutes."

"Well, you're in luck. I was just about to head that way myself. We can walk together if that's alright?" So now I'm offering to walk her to class? What in the world are you doing Jovi?

"That would be great!" I wait patiently as she flings her purse onto her shoulder and attempts to balance the few hardbacks, pens and a notepad between her arms but somehow manages to drop yet another item.

"Let me get that for you." I bend down quickly and grab the chemistry publication from the floor.

"These books can get quite heavy." Reaching out, I grab another volume from her arms and place it into my own. She doesn't object which is comforting.

I signal for her to follow suit, "Come. The Fine Arts building is just here to our left."

"Ok." She smiles bashfully as we begin to walk side by side in silence, down a hallway and towards some double doors.

The halls are noisy and occupied with hordes of students who are also rushing to their next class. I can feel her warm presence within my reach as the sound of her breathing creeps into my ears. A tortured longing to hear her voice once more engulfs my thoughts and I find myself distracted.

What should I say to her? Should I wait for her to speak first or should I interrupt this deserted affair that has settled upon us like a dark cloud? But before I'm able to formulate any thoughts and possibly embarrass myself some more, she decides to break our dreadful silence by a way of observation.

"Anisocoria?"

A confused frown immediately forms on my face as I try to clarify her statement. "Excuse me?"

I then notice a smile form on her lips as she continues speaking, "Anisocoria. The reason why your eyes differ in color. Am I right?"

Caught off guard by her candid remark, I only manage an, "Oh."

As I turn to look at this incredible being that is haphazardly rewiring my brain, I come to realize that deceit is not something that I'm capable of accomplishing while in her presence. So instead of changing the subject or walking away, I decide to provide a detailed explanation of a rather personal and common trait that is only found within our male species.

"Um, no. Anisocoria is when the pupils are not the same size. My condition is known as complete heterochromia, meaning that my iris's differ in color. In my case, I have one blue and one brown iris."

She then comes to a complete stop and turns to face me. With her sight carefully affixed onto mine, she begins to describe the mutation in my eyes as if they were a wonder.

"I see. So, sapphire blue like the depths of the Caribbean Sea and golden-brown similar to autumn leaves."

This mortal is clearly oblivious that her voice has a spellbinding effect to those around her or is that just me? Swallowing hard, I somehow manage to respond.

"Yeah, I guess. If that's how you'd like to describe my incongruous disorder."

I'm struggling to remain composed as our eyes remain affixed onto one another. My mind has detached from reality while my evil twin begins to question my motives. She then suppresses a smile, breaks eye contact, and continues walking while describing my half-truths.

"Well, your *incongruous disorder* is eccentrically beautiful so don't ever let anyone tell you different."

Unsure how to refute the false pretext about my appearance, I decide to overlook her courteous demeanor and resume walking by her side through the halls. She seems content in my presence which is a bit unnerving given that I've never spent time with a human being before.

My thoughts are misplaced with images of her lips crushed against mine when she interrupts my moment of solitude.

"I appreciate you taking the time to help me. I haven't come across many friendly faces as everyone seems too busy to help the newcomers." Her voice is like a sweet melody, luring me to my impending death.

"Then I am glad that we ran into each other." Am I seriously flirting?

"So, are you a junior?" She glances over in my direction, smiling so big that it becomes infectious.

"Oh, um no. I'm a senior this year and hopefully graduating in the spring."

"What are you majoring in, if you don't mind me asking?"

"No, I don't mind at all." I slow down a bit so that I am able to make eye contact while giving her the attention she deserves and that I so desperately crave.

"I'll be receiving my undergraduate degree in Mining Engineering within a three-year span and it's kind of expected of me so..."

Why am I providing her with privileged information? Stop before you put your foot in your mouth you idiot!

"Oh, your parents must be pleased." She remains polite and engaged in spite of my previous unruly behavior.

"What about you? I know that you're either a freshman or transfer student seeing that you are not familiar with the campus."

"You are correct. I am a freshman and for the next four years I will focus on the history of art and architecture." She states as a matter of fact.

"So, you're an artist?"

"Yup. I'm particularly fond of sculpting." She confesses as we arrive at the grand memorial fountain known as *A song to nature* in honor of Mary Schenley.

"You must show me some of your pieces sometime."

I slow to a stop and turn my body to face her. The light drizzle continues to trickle, causing white flecks to formulate on our hair and clothes.

Shaking her head and blushing, she agrees with my request, "I would love to."

"Ok so, here is the famous Frick Fine Arts building. Do you think you can find your class from here?"

"I'm sure I can manage." Mesmerized by her mere presence, I become disappointed that our interaction has come to an end.

"Cool, here are your belongings," I gently place the publications back into her arms, making sure she has a handle on them before I let go.

"Thank you for um.. walking with me and carrying my things." Her shy smile reaches her eyes making her dimples reappear.

"Anytime." Anytime? Really Jovianus? What has gotten into you?

She waives, "Ok. See you around," and pivots around the fountain, towards the entrance of the building.

I stand there like a total creep, gawking and unsure of what just happened. At this point I'm scowling at myself while running my hand through my hair out of confusion and uncertainty. I can still smell her sweet scent on the palm of my hand; something that I'm sure will torture the rest of my afternoon.

Looking up again I watch as she disappears behind the double doors and I quickly follow suit. Entering the lecture hall, I notice that almost all the seats are taken as the professor begins to jot his name on the dry erase board, MR. NEUMANN in capital letters. Looks like I am the last student to enter as he rushes over and closes the door behind me.

"Please take a seat, we are about to begin." He smiles tentatively causing his eyeglasses to move further down his narrow nose as he swivels back to his workstation.

His desk is covered in papers and several empty cups of coffee as he begins to read the agenda for today's lecture to himself. I don't bother to return his polite gesture; it isn't in my nature to be pleasant or courteous to humans and decide to defer my cruel reactions by a way of silence.

The room already feels stuffy and reeks of fresh paint, faintly mixed with a familiar scent that unexpectedly attracts my attention. My head snaps up as I begin to briefly scan the space before me, hoping to identify its source but I'm swiftly met with disappointment when my sight deceives me and reveals nothing.

Puzzled and frustrated I slowly begin to make my way up the steps, searching for an empty seat while I pass row after row. Everyone is still getting settled as hush murmurs and mild banter fills the air. Faint light beams escape through the window blinds, bringing life into the dull room.

I take notice of an odd-looking human slouching in his chair as his eyes are half closed, mouth open with his head leaning towards a young woman next to him. An abrupt loud snore escapes his throat that causes him to wake from his catnap as he swiftly straightens up in his seat. A few females begin to laugh while covering their mouths to suppress the noise. He seems to notice but doesn't care and grins instead while giving them a thumbs up. What a waste of space!

Making my way further up the steps I continue to search for a vacant slot when I hear a silky voice purr my name from above, *"Jovianus."*

I'm instantly immobilized and my body responds reluctantly as I am suddenly attuned to her presence once more. The knots in my stomach resurface but with a brute intensity that instantly becomes unbearable. My knees begin to quiver, and the remnants of my heart quickens to a silent beat.

There in the far back corner sits the exquisite creature that I ran into in the hallway earlier. The moment our eyes lock I feel the same pull again, disturbing my abandoned state. A slow smile forms on her lips that sends me into overdrive. The need to be in her presence is exceedingly overwhelming as my feet embark on a mission to reach her.

Without ever breaking eye contact she motions for me to join her as there is an empty seat to her left. What are the odds? Returning her courteous behavior, I smile back and begin making my way through the row, anxious to reach the glowing ember that has abruptly sparked a new flame in my dying soul. But how could this be?

At that moment, a silent vow is meticulously arranged without her knowledge. I was vaguely unaware that this would be the beginning of my resurrection and a new chapter that would change the course of my life, forever.

Chapter Two

~Jealous~

Aemilia's strained voice is cloaked by the loud and energetic music radiating from the live band as we sway to the alternative rock tune from our table. She casually takes a drag from her cigarette while swinging her hips to the cover song *Do I wanna know* by the Artic Monkeys.

As she lifts her arms in the air and mouths the words to the chorus, a sense of envy washes over me. She carries herself with such poise and certainty, commanding everyone's attention upon contact. With her dark blonde hair, light brown eyes, and a slender figure, she is the equivalent of a supermodel that has yet to be discovered.

I on the other hand never had that type of self-assurance, always doubting myself and worried about what others perceive of me. I'm an introvert and find it difficult to make friends or even attract any being from the opposite sex whereas Aemilia is a livewire. She can have any male eating out of the palm of her hand at any given moment. The disturbing part is that she knows it and uses that fact to her advantage, with the exception of Ethan of course. They're both exactly the same and are constantly at odds with each other, *or at least that's what they want us to believe.*

I roll my eyes at her flirtatious demeanor as she toys with the beer bottle with the tip of her lips while the two males across our table salivate. One of the men has glasses thick as jam jars paired with a round middle section that is struggling to maintain inside his shirt. The other one has several threads of gray hair and teeth like a horse that becomes painfully obvious as he attempts to smile at the sexy yet ill-mannered female to my right.

And what's worst is that her intentions are more for amusement, like pretending that she is interested when she actually isn't. She reels them in, gets what she wants and brutally cuts them off. It's a cruel notion but they fall for it, time and time again. I'm sure we'll get free beers for the rest of the evening or at least until they figure out that she is full of herself.

Ignoring her vulgar tactics, I begin scanning the scene and take in the ambience of the place. The venue at the strip district is crammed with strangers, all of which are waiting for the next band to hop on stage and start their session. I'm beginning to feel a little insecure with myself while I sulk with the thought that he might have stood me up.

I invited Jovianus on a whim tonight, hoping to finally introduce him to my friends given that we have been spending a lot of time together these past few weeks. All of them were excited to meet this mystery male that has manage to capture the attention of my mundane personal life which lacks social companionship outside of our circle, however Ethan was not as inclined.

He was a little distrustful at first but then finally agreed to be on his best behavior if he felt Jovi was worthy of it. His approval means everything to me given that Ethan is somewhat family. We have known each other since middle school and have remained close friends ever since, so yeah, he's like my big brother so to speak.

It's a little past 10:30 and I'm growing anxious by the minute as I continue fidgeting out of habit. Doing a quick look over of my attire, I place my hands on my stomach and smooth out the imaginary wrinkles of my emerald button-down shirt. Pulling my wavy locks to the side, I twirl my hair in circles to keep it in place and away from my face.

Our waiter comes over and hands us our second round of drinks, *courtesy of our two new male friends* as we patiently wait for the rest of the gang to show up. With a beer in one hand and my cell in the other, I lean in closer as Aemilia continues mouthing inaudible words, "I can't hear you. What did you say?"

She pulls a slow drag from her cigarette and exhale's all while keeping her doubtful gaze on mine, "I said when is this imaginary friend of yours coming? Or did he sell you out?"

Her condescending remark about his character catches me off guard and unintentionally lights a fire in my ass. Does she really think I made him up? Because concocting an individual's mere existence would benefit me how?

Unknown to her, I'm already on the edge tonight coupled with insecurity and the fact that my *date* has yet to arrive. Well, I consider him my date although he more than likely just considers me a charity case. Great, so I've been placed in the friend zone and there is a high probability that I will remain there until I no longer am.

How could he ever really see me as something more? I'm not Aemilia. I can't just throw myself at him or anyone for that matter. The thing is that he has never been rude or discourteous towards me. If anything, he has been nothing but a gentleman which is more than I could have hoped for.

There is a high probability that he finds me repulsive but doesn't know how to let me down easy. Or maybe he already has a special someone back home and doesn't want to hurt my miserable little feelings. Regardless, I allowed my emotional state to get the best of me.

Placing my beer bottle down onto the table, I narrow my eyes and take an aggressive stance on this rather sensitive subject. Unable to contain the unkind thoughts that formulated in my brain, they come flying straight out of my mouth without hesitation.

"What's it to you anyway huh? It's not like you're here to support me." I scoff and continue the unwarranted attack. "You only agreed to accompany me because you're hoping to have a run in with Ethan for another meaningless sexual encounter that you both will likely regret in the morning!"

There, I told her! My body is bursting with heat and I feel disturbed beyond measure for reasons unknown. As I narrow my eyes on Aemilia's face, I notice that her lighthearted mood has shifted to a more serious tone.

With a confused frown, she carefully places her unfinished cigarette in the ashtray and takes a step forward.

"Whoa. Slow down hon. That comment was totally uncalled for. I was only teasing and didn't mean to offend you. What is it with you tonight?"

Blindsided by my harsh reaction, I realize that I'm not upset with her but rather annoyed with myself for thinking that my friendship with Jovianus could develop into something more. My tense body relaxes, and the irritation drains from my face which is promptly replaced with a sheepish grin.

"You're right. I'm sorry. I didn't mean to lash out at you. I'm just nervous that's all."

A cheery smile appears at the corner of her mouth as she leans over and rubs my shoulder in a soothing manner, "It's ok, I know you didn't mean it. Just try to relax and remember that he's the lucky one and not the other way around."

I enthusiastically return her polite gesture and realize that I totally overreacted for no apparent reason. This is certainly out of character and I'm not the only one who noticed it. Trying my best to erase the brief lapse in my judgment, I attempt to pick-up my beer when I'm intercepted by a firm grip and my body is slightly dragged backwards. The masculine cologne gave away his identity as I turn around to meet Ethan's gaze and he plants a hard kiss on my forehead.

Giggling out of habit, I slide out of his hold and turn to face him, "So, I see that you finally decided to grant us with your presence your royal highness." Poking fun at his late arrival, I bend my knees, bow my head, and curtsy all while laughing.

He quickly joins in on the mockery and motions with his hand, "You may carry on." I swat him on the shoulder as he pulls me in for an affectionate embrace and that's when I notice his unsolicited guest, Franco Alves. Ignoring his presence, I release Ethan and focus on our other two arrivals, Derek, and Leona both of which were invited by *yours truly*.

Reaching towards the endearing couple, we hug and exchange a kiss on each other's cheek. They quickly move onto Aemilia who has somehow managed to guzzle down her second beer.

As the trio embark on a lengthy conversation, Ethan awkwardly moves in with his back turned to us and whispers something into Aemilia's ear. Her eyes go wide, but she never breaks character and continues chatting with both Derek and Leona as if he didn't just promise her an eventful evening of cat and mouse.

And in case you missed it, she is the cat and Ethan's the mouse in their peculiar tale. Meanwhile, I can feel Franco's stare burning a whole right through me. I knew my solitude wouldn't last as he takes this opportunity to swoon in and commence his endless pursuit of infatuation.

Slowly walking over with one hand in his pocket and the other to the side he leans in and murmurs, "Still looking beautiful as ever Simone."

I don't say anything and settle on providing a polite smile that is more forced than natural. Looking away, I try my best to avoid eye contact and remain hopeful that someone will come to my rescue. But sadly, to my dismay, help doesn't arrive. So, I guess I'll have to endure this inevitable conversation about me being single and available and why aren't we together.

Don't get me wrong, Franco is drop dead gorgeous and charming as ever, but he is also arrogant, conceited and not to mention a ladies' man. I met him through Ethan as they both live in the same neighborhood. We would constantly run into each other given that me and Ethan have been inseparable. And the only reason he continues to harass me is because I'm the only one who has not given him the time of day.

I'm just not attracted to him in that way regardless of his obvious charismatic traits. Since I failed to respond, he takes it as an invitation to continue his torment. Don't make eye contact. Don't make eye contact. Damn, there goes my eyes.

"So, tell me, what does a single and stunning female such as yourself look for in a man?"

Reaching for my beer, I take a quick drink, clear my throat, and pretend that I'm not thinking about Jovianus.

"Let's see. Well, I haven't really put much thought into it. All of my time and energy is focused on school, so I don't have room for any distractions at the moment."

He then lifts his hand to his chin like he is thinking.

"Or maybe it's because you haven't found the right one." Feeling a little annoyed with his persistence, I decide to give him a taste of his own medicine.

"You know what Franco; I agree with your assessment."

"Really?"

"Absolutely. I don't believe I have found the one because he has yet to make an appearance but when he does, I'll be sure to introduce you to him." His mouth then goes from a soft smile to a huge grin and he begins to chuckle.

"So, I see that you like playing hard to get. Ok. I'll play along little dove and..." He gets cut off by Ethan who has now decided to come to my rescue.

"What were you ladies drinking?" He looks between me and Aemilia who is now standing to my left.

Snickering out of amusement I respond with a mocking tone, "Oh, Michelob Ultra."

His eyebrows go up in hilarity, "Interesting. Fake Id's," which caused Aemilia to interject.

"Not even close." She then places her hands on her hips and inches closer to his face as she continues to antagonize the one male who remains a constant in her dramatic life.

"Who needs fake id's when there are so many gentlemen at our fingertips?"

With a huge grin on his face, he finally manages to pry his eyes off of Aemilia and addresses the rest of the group.

"I'll order another round for the table then."

"No need," Franco interrupts, "this round is on me. I'll just go find a waitress that can keep us entertained for the rest of the evening."

With a wink he pivots and begins making his way towards the bar. Well, at least he isn't here ogling my every move and making me feel uncomfortable. I then feel everyone's eyes focus on me.

"What?" I shrug my shoulders and then Aemilia starts laughing with Leona and Derek joining in. What is it with everyone?

"Be nice Simone." Ethan's eyes narrow in on mine as he steals the beer from my hand and takes a long drink.

"When am I not nice to him?"

"Hmmm, I can think of a few less fortunate occasions when you weren't being yourself." I give him a scowl and retort his statement with a less than friendly attitude.

"Please spare me your criticism Ethan. The last thing I want to think about is his crazy obsession that we somehow belong together. Can we please focus on something else? I've had a long week and just need to unwind."

He swiftly lifts his palms in the air in surrender and provides a tentative smile, "Alright. Just saying, there's no need to shout."

He then reaches over and lightly nudge's my arm to call truce. While exchanging a friendly smile, Leona decides to question me about Jovianus and his whereabouts. It takes all of my patience not to snap at her inquisitiveness because now I'm more irritated than before. But unlike Aemilia she means well and is genuinely curious, nothing more.

"So, where's your date Sim?"

"Oh, it isn't a date. He's just my friend and he's running late. Got held up at practice but should be here soon."

"Practice? What's he practicing?"

"Oh, um...he plays hockey for a mid-level professional league." Her eyebrows move up in wonder while Derek makes a whistling sound with his mouth.

"Say no more, I like him already. Any man that can play a rough sport like hockey has my stamp of approval."

Both Ethan and Derek give her a nasty look like their feelings were just crushed by her comment and we girls launch into laughter. Unfortunately for me, my moment of happiness is short lived when Franco reappears at our table with a striking female who is holding our drinks. She hands them over to us while being extra flirty with Ethan.

As he entertains her advances, we engage is some much-needed banter when the ever so relentless Franco walks up beside me and gets rather close for my liking. I display to Aemilia the *help me* gaze, but I can sense that she is already aggravated with Ethan's not so attentiveness and decides to ignore my plea. Damn her. Looks like I'll be on my own for this one.

Looking down at my phone, I validate that it's a little after 11pm and not a single text message from Jovianus has magically appeared in the last hour. I can't even be mad at him because it's not like he actually agreed to meet up tonight. He said he would *try* because practice can sometimes last longer than expected.

What was I thinking when I invited him? He has more pressing matters to attend to and I am the farthest from that list. Coming to terms that he will not be meeting my friends tonight; I turn my attention to the sinister male that can't seem to take *no* for an answer. This is definitely going to be an interesting evening.

With his gaze glued to mine, he proceeds with his unyielding antics. "So, are you enjoying yourself?"

I was enjoying myself up until he opened his mouth, but now that Jovianus isn't showing up I have decided to leave and end this dreadful encounter.

"Yes, I was, but I'm afraid that I'll be leaving soon."

Confused and caught off guard by my declaration, he stands up straight, squares his shoulders and turns serious as he embarks on a mission of persuasion.

"Where are you going?"

"Home. I have some assignments due in the morning that I haven't had a chance to start."

"How about a dance before you go then?" He takes a step closer causing his face to remain inches from mine. Geez, this guy is bold and extremely confident; however, he still lacks one important trait that every woman seeks in a man but fails to find. Chivalry.

I quickly turn my face away from his in case he decides to make a move, "I don't think that's a good idea."

His voice drops to a low sultry tone which does nothing to improve his chances on seducing me.

"Why not? I'm single. You're single. We are both young and obviously attracted to one another."

I cut him off abruptly, "Look Franco, you're a nice guy but I feel that I should be honest with you." Taking a step back, I attempt to explain the dynamics of impartial emotions. "I'm not interested in what you have to offer. I'm sorry. I don't want to hurt your feelings, but I have a lot going on and it's just a bad time for me."

He takes another step forward and closes the gap between our bodies, making sure there's no space between us.

"Are you telling me," he pauses and then lifts his hand to my face and moves a strand of hair to the side, "that I have no effect on you whatsoever?"

I can feel his breath so close to my lips that I'm starting to worry what will happen if I don't look away.

"You can't deny that there is something between us." Reaching down, he takes my hand into his all while keeping his eyes glued to mine.

My body feels spellbound like I'm being lured by the sound of his voice or maybe it's the two beers that are finally taking effect. In spite of this, I finally come to my senses and pull my hand out of his hold.

"Franco, please understand that I am in no position to offer anything more than just friendship."

As I attempt to turn and walk away, he forcefully takes my hand and stops me from leaving, "Just one dance is all I'm asking."

I attempt to remove my hand from his grip, but he decides to tighten his hold which causes my temper to unexpectedly spike.

Turning to face him once again I snarl, "Please. Let. Me. Go."

What happens next was so unexpected that it caught us both by surprise when a male's stern voice interjects.

"Surely you can understand the meaning of *no*, but in case you missed it, she isn't interested in your insipid pursuit." His tone is commanding and full of conviction, making it difficult to ignore.

Instantly recognizing his husky voice, I immediately turn around and almost land directly into his chest. Jovianus is already standing next to me like my own personal bodyguard, towering over the lone male who has now lost the upper hand. Within seconds I feel his fingers gracefully skim along my lower back and land on my hip as he pulls me in closer. My body instinctively responds to his implicit request and before I know it, we are both staring into each other's eyes.

The music has dulled to a silent beat and all I can hear is a whisper escape his lips, "Hi."

Jovi is no longer addressing the stranger to my left who has gone completely still, possibly caught off guard by our rather friendly interaction. Staring into those fascinating eyes, I respond with a soft tone.

"Hi." He doesn't take his eyes off of me while we continue this innocent display of affection. "I'm sorry for being late."

I slowly lift my hand to his face and gracefully glide it over his beard stubble that has started to appear which gives him a rugged look. "It's ok. You're here now."

Placing his free hand over mine, he moves it down to his mouth and plants a soft kiss on my knuckles. His sight never waivers as he laces our fingers together and makes a gracious bid. One that I am all too eager to comply with. "May I please have this dance?"

My response is instantaneous, "Yes," and well received as he dashes me off into the crowd. The last thing I hear is Franco asking who the hell is this male. Ethan's voice is full of bewilderment when he responds.

"That my friend, must be Jovianus."

I don't bother to look back as we push past the horde of people and away from prying eyes.

*****

As we make our way to the front of the stage, I begin to question this thoughtless decision to see her again. Coming here tonight was definitely a mistake. A reckless oversight on my part. What was I thinking? Well, that's the problem, I wasn't. I can feel a sense of possessiveness engulf my thoughts as we come to a complete stop near the dance floor.

The band changes their tune to a softer melody as the vibration of an acoustic guitar begins to strum lightly in the background. Within a matter of seconds, the sound of a male's voice croons over the microphone with such intensity and emotion that it causes the audience to shout and praise in approval.

As the words begin to flow, I quickly recognize the cover song, *Wicked Game* by *James McMorrow.*

Feeling unsure of these overstimulated emotions, I mentally make a hasty decision to leave, however, I never get the chance to carry out my actions. Because in that moment of doubt, she decides to gracefully caress the back of my hand with her thumb. That guileless touch was my undoing.

With our fingers securely intertwined, I turn to face her and instantly become immobilized by her spellbinding gaze. I carefully slide my free hand onto her waistline and she quickly follow's suit. With our eyes affixed on one another, I gently pull her delicate body close to mine and begin to sway to the sensibly orchestrated ballad. Any doubts that had begun to settle have now diminished as the need to remain in her presence becomes unbearable.

I find it difficult to concentrate as her warm breath grazes the skin on my chest. And although I remain a foot taller than her, I'm still able to detect a delectable aroma radiating from her small form. As I struggle to remain composed, it becomes abundantly clear that my weak heart is unable to compete with her uncompromising demands.

After a few moments, I lean down and murmur into her ear, "You look lovely tonight."

I can feel hesitation in her response when she utters, "Thank you."

We continue this slow and gentle exchange; powerful in so many ways yet it's still innocent to the touch. As the song comes to an end, we reluctantly part from one another but not before I plant a soft and very sensual kiss on her cheek, *or at least it felt that way to me.* A blinding smile forms on her lips causing me to lose my train of thought.

Quickly letting go of her hand that I didn't realize I was still holding; I decide to launch into interrogation mode to distract myself from this forbidden curse.

"What am I going to do with you?" As I shake my head in a mocking manner, I cautiously move her against the wall to avoid collision with the swarm of party goers that are passing by while positioning myself directly in front of her.

With a confused look on her face, she gives me a harmless smirk that only heightens her beauty. "What do you mean?"

Moving in closer, I place my hand against the wall to hold my weight and lean down close to her face so that she may hear me.

"For starters, how am I supposed to defend you from unwarranted attacks by possible male stalkers when I'm not around?" Her innocence knows no bounds.

"His name is Franco and he isn't a stalker. Ethan invited him."

I can feel my anger double down at the image of his unwelcomed touch as she pleads for him to release her. His vulgar conduct unexpectedly caused old memories to resurface. That scumbag is lucky that she was standing between us otherwise he'd be nursing a dislocated arm right about now. I'm momentarily taken aback by these newfound feelings which are foreign to me, however, it doesn't stop me from expressing my annoyance with this outsider whom I've never met.

"His name has no significance to me. That aggressive behavior almost got him into a lot of trouble."

She stifles a laugh before responding. "Well, I'll have you know that I once upon a time was a champion in kickboxing, so I do know a thing or two on how to defend myself should the occasion arise."

I then turn around and lean my body against the wall with one foot up and both of my hands stuffed in the pocket of my jeans. Staying close enough to hear her but not too close that I would be invading her space.

"I have no doubt that you could defend yourself, but the point is that you shouldn't be placed in a position where you would have to."

"And why is that?"

"As a male, there is an unspoken oath that we should always exercise control and respect towards a female regardless of her outlook on the matter. He clearly failed at both when he forced his advances and refused to take *no* for an answer." I can tell that my response has captivated her interest which only prompts more questions.

"So, tell me, how would you have handled my rejection if you were in his place?"

"Well, I've had my fair share of rejections," I chuckle to myself as I envision her dismissal, "however, it's in the manner of how we conduct ourselves under strenuous situations that defines who we are as individuals." With a smile and a little confidence, I keep my gazed affixed to hers as I continue speaking. "If you would have rejected me for whatever reason then a polite *thank you for your time* followed by a smile would have slipped through my lips."

"And just like that," she snaps her fingers in the air, "you would let me be?"

"Yes. Any being with an ounce of respect would have done the same." She crosses her arms over her chest and leans her shoulder against the wall, conflicted with my honesty.

"You are by far too courteous."

Her shirt hikes up a bit revealing the side of her stomach which outlines her curves below the waistline that only distracts me further. First, I act like she belongs to me and almost send the scrawny human to the hospital. Then I become possessive and pull her away from her friends so that I could have her all to myself.

And as if that weren't bad enough, I purposely kiss her and at the last minute decide that the cheek was my best option. So yeah, I'm a wreck and she is clearly unaware of the effect she has over me.

"Only with you, but right now I find myself at odds with being courteous."

"Are these feelings geared towards my association with Franco or directed at him?"

As she shifts positions and moves closer to me, I become fully aware that I am powerless around her. So instead of lying and stating that I'm just a concerned friend and not jealous of her interaction with this dimwit or any male for that matter, I tell her the truth. But this reality does nothing to set me free of my own guilt because I'm not even sure that I truly understand what I'm feeling.

"I've never encountered this type of emotion before but if its anything close to what I am feeling now then I believe it would be a sense of jealousy as it relates to your kinship with him."

She then takes a step closer to me with a serious yet controlled tone. "Well, you don't have to be."

Her candid response only solidifies that our friendship is no longer harmless as we are drifting onto dangerous ground. I cannot allow myself to entertain these notions because it would be disastrous for us both. She is but a human. A mortal whose life is worthless and insignificant to our kind. And I am a celestial being. An eternal creature who has and continues to live among the human population in secrecy.

Our races have the means and capability to socialize in order to secure our survival but under no circumstance are we to ever amalgamate the two species. Doing so would be like signing my own death warrant as well as hers and I'm not about to place her life in danger for an indecisive emotion.

Knowing that nothing good can come of this, I decide to offer an alternative solution to our complicated dilemma and extend my hand to her.

"Come, let's go meet your friends."

Without hesitation she curls her soft hand into mine as we begin making our way back.

Chapter Three

~Quarrel~

As we approach the area where her friends are casually interacting with one another, I decide to avoid scrutiny by introducing myself first as opposed to waiting. First impressions are rather important for mortals and I can almost guarantee that mine was not well received when I decided to act like a caveman and run-off with their friend.

Carefully releasing her hand and motioning for her to walk in front of me, I approach a male with dark blond hair that has a mustache and a clean-cut beard.

Given that he has been cautiously watching me since my arrival, I assumed it would be wise to start with him. I initiate first contact by extending my hand out in a goodwill manner, "You must be Ethan. I'm Jovianus. Jovianus Moreau."

My voice is firm and controlled while my unwavering eyes remain affixed onto his.

His expression says it all; from his blank stare to his indifferent attitude as he tightens the grip of his drink with one hand and moves the other behind his back. So, this is how it's going to be. I knew the odds of us hitting it off were not in my favor and I do understand that if I want to remain in the presence of Simone then I would have to win over her friends as well. This was a given, however, I'm not one to implore.

As my hand remains mid-air, waiting for our intense interaction to end, his reluctance fades as he decides to down the remaining amber liquid from his glass. Once his task has been completed, he then places the empty tumbler onto the nearest table and greets me with a forced smile.

"It's a pleasure to finally meet you."

He emphasized the word *finally* with a derisive undertone while raising his eyebrows in a patronizing manner. His grip is firm and excessively pungent but then again, so is mine.

A hint of displeasure settles upon his face and after a few seconds of tasteless observation, we both release our grasp and take a step back at the same time.

I can sense tension exuding from his form; luckily for him, I'm not affected by this cold display. If anything, I can understand his lack of decorum towards a male stranger who happens to have an unclear interest in Simone. He knows nothing about me; doesn't know if I'm a stalker, a murderer or if I come from a highly educated and humble upbringing. If I'm being honest with myself, he probably doesn't give a damn either way. Ethan's sole interest is her wellbeing and he'll do whatever to whomever to protect her. That, I can respect.

Surprisingly, her other friends do not share his sentiment when a highly energetic female step's in front of him and introduces herself, concluding our male arrogance.

"Hi. I'm Aemilia. Simone's best friend." She reaches for my hand before I could respond and begins to shake it. "I'm sure she's mentioned me somewhere."

A low chuckle rumbles in my throat as I try my best to remain sociable.

"Yes um, Simone has told me all about you."

"Has she now," she then turns to face Simone and begins to tease, "I hope she hasn't painted me as some villain."

Removing my hand from hers, I tuck one of them in my pocket to avoid any further contact and refute her remarks about Simone's perception.

"Rest assured, she has your best interest at heart."

She takes a step closer and counters my comment all while staring into my eyes.

"I'm sure she does. So, where are you from? I can't seem to place that accent."

This mortal is downright outspoken and wastes no time in concealing her objective. I'm not used to interacting with humans on any level *with the exception of Simone,* let alone having to answer intrusive inquiries about my appearance or origin.

Irritation quickly follows suit and I suddenly feel out of place. I knew this was a bad idea but against my better judgment I went ahead and agreed to meet them. So instead of displaying a foul demeanor, I decide to remain courteous and acknowledge her probing request. "Oh, – Canada."

However, the questions won't stop there – no, that would be far too easy. They will continue throughout the evening unless someone decides to put a stop to it. And as much as I want to be that individual, I won't because this is my one and only shot to make things right.

"But you have a British accent. Did you move from England to Canada?"

"No, I've lived in Canada my whole life. I'm Anglo-Canadian, meaning that my ancestors have English roots."

"What province?"

"Quebec."

"Does that mean you speak French as well?" She seems overly intrigued as if she's never met anyone from Canada or from a different country for that matter. It's hard to tell if she is being sarcastic or if she is trying to flirt. Whatever the case might be, her behavior has no influence on me.

"Yes, as a matter of fact I do. French is the predominant language in Quebec." Unknown to her I am fluent in four languages including Latin; however, I'll keep that tidbit of information to myself in order to avoid further scrutiny.

Simone then kindly interjects and halts further interrogation. "Aemilia, please don't pry and try to be a little less cheeky."

Exasperated, she grabs my hand and pulls me towards a couple that are off to the side. Both of them are standing near a table that is lined with a variety of alcoholic beverages.

The tall dark male that's sporting a stylish fohawk places his drink down and moves towards us while offering a welcoming smile. I can hear Aemilia complaining in the background as Simone launches into affable introductions.

"Jovi, this is Derek and Leona, my other two friends that I've known since high school. Derek, Leona this is Jovianus."

Both Derek and I shake hands and engage in light conversation about my eyes which seems to be a hot topic among humans. Leona joins in as Derek launches into a spew of facts about my condition and its rarity in humans.

Turns out, Derek is pre-med, going on his third year at the University and Leona is on her second, working towards an engineering degree in case the whole model career doesn't pan out. In mid conversation about the underlying causes of this so-called *inherited disease*, I hear someone clear their throat loud enough to capture our attention. As I turn to face the culprit, I'm greeted with an unlikely antagonist.

Standing there behind Simone, holding two drinks in his hands is the schemer Franco. I had forgotten about him since he wasn't present when the introductions where being made. As she turns around to acknowledge the morbid parasite, I find that I lack sound judgment and begin to experience homicidal thoughts.

As he places the drinks down onto the table beside Leona, he makes it a point to stand awfully close to Simone while sporting a sinister grin. Feeling confident, he takes a step forward and offers his hand.

"I'm Franco. And you must be Jovianus, Simone's newfound acquaintance."

Does this imbecile really think that I'm just going to shake his hand as if he didn't intentionally disrespect Simone with his brash behavior? He must be delusional or just plain stupid.

As he stands there with his soiled palm extended, it becomes painfully obvious that I'm clearly not on the same page as he is. Straightening my back, I cross both of my arms over my chest and clear my throat. He finally gets the message and lowers his arm to the side and continues to smirk out of amusement.

"Well, I can see that you're still troubled about my interaction with Simone. Clearly there has been a misunderstanding and I hope we can get past this."

I remain silent on the matter and refuse to be a part of whatever game he is trying to play. While both of us are sizing each other up, Ethan leisurely walks up and stands on the other side of Simone.

Sensing conflict from all three males, she cautiously departs from the brooding feud and plants herself right beside me. She then slowly slides her hand through one of my arms and positions her body closer to mine.

Franco's smirk has gone from triumph to mortified. Feeling the need to make a statement, he launches into a baseless cross examination by trying to understand our connection.

"So, it seems that I misread the signals earlier and now I understand why you are upset."

My arms remain crossed over my chest with Simone by my side while confusion crosses Ethan's face.

"And why is that?"

"Well, it appears that you have also taken an interest in Simone the same way I have and now you see me as a threat."

My lips twitch in amusement as I begin to wonder whether this poor bastard really believes that I see him as a threat or if he's attempting to gain a negative reaction from me.

What he has failed to understand is that celestials respond different to intimidation or opposition. We don't experience fear, remorse, or love the same way a human does. Audacious and vain is who we are; there isn't a weak bone in our body.

With a grin on my face, I confirm his erroneous assessment with a hint of mockery.

"You are absolutely correct."

He squares his shoulders and attempts to push his chest out to make himself appear formidable.

"Of course I am."

"Yes. It's true that I have taken an interest in Simone but not the same way you have."

"Oh, how so?" I notice that her friends have now gathered around possibly startled from our confrontation. Aemilia's eyes are up in wonder while Derek and Leona remain at a safe distance just in case things get a little out of hand.

"Because unlike you, I would never disrespect her or any female for that matter. It's obvious that you make her stomach churn every time she lays her eyes upon you. And as far as a threat goes – I'm far more menacing than a helpless tyrant whose sole target is women. I'd like to see you attempt your cowardice tactics towards a male of my stature. I can assure you that the outcome would not be the same."

This conversation takes a critical turn for the worst when the wounded animal is no longer able to contain his anger and decides to confront his fears head on.

"Are you threatening me?"

I take a step forward vaguely unaware that I have now placed Simone in the middle of our tiff. "It's a simple fact!"

But before we are able to engage in any type of physical conflict, I feel her hands tighten around my arm and Ethan steps between us to disengage the ominous feud that has spiraled out of control.

"I think it's time for the both of you to leave before someone gets hurt," his eyes shift from Franco's to mine.

The raging little bull takes this moment to display bravery by rushing towards me with his hands curled into fist knowing that Ethan would stop him. Without thinking I attempt to charge and meet my opponent head on when I'm abruptly apprehended by a delicate palm.

It's not aggressive nor strong in nature, however, her mere presence demands attention like no other. With her warm body softly pressed against mine, she lifts both of her hands to my face and pulls me in close while speaking inaudible words.

As a soothing lullaby fills my ears, I find that my mind and body have both betrayed me once more. While my anger slowly diminishes, Simone turns to face her male companions. With her back turned, she places her body directly in front of mine as if to protect me and ends our inimical dispute with a bid farewell.

"Jovianus and I were just about to leave – thank you Ethan for making him feel welcomed. I really appreciate the enthusiasm."

Her resentful remarks towards Ethan caught him by surprise as he struggles to make amends.

"Simone – I... I didn't suggest that you leave with him."

His voice is pleading and full of regret as the fact settles in that he has now upset her. And from what I've learned these past few weeks, she doesn't anger easily.

Grabbing her sweater from the back of the chair, she turns to address him before snatching her phone from the table.

"Oh, I know you didn't but if he isn't wanted here then neither am I."

She then turns to face me, "Are you ready?" With a dejected smirk I nod and we both descend through the crowd.

Ethan makes one final attempt to stop her, "Simone, please wait," however, she does nothing to acknowledge his plea as we reach the exit.

Once outside, she lets out a distressed sigh while running her fingers through her hair. It's my fault at how things turned out tonight. Had I not shown up, she would have eventually gone home and called me afterwards as usual. Or maybe Ethan would have finally come to her rescue after his rendezvous with Aemilia and the waitress.

Puzzled at how quickly she was able to mollify my seething temper without much effort, I come to terms that Simone has somehow become an important individual in my uninhibited life.

Reaching for her hand, I pull her close, "Hey, come here." She slowly comes to a complete stop and turns to face me. "You ok?" She shakes her head back and forth signaling irritation. "Want to talk about it?" Looking out towards the river, she immediately begins to express regret.

"I just want to apologize for how Ethan behaved tonight. He can be a little overprotective."

"It's not your fault. I shouldn't have come here in the first place."

"Why do you say that?"

"Well, because I might have accidently given a vibe that we are together, as in dating, and I'm not entirely sure that Ethan is ready to have that conversation." She continues to look out towards the river, possibly to avoid eye contact.

"I don't really care what everyone thinks and I'm not sorry that my friends got the impression that you are mine and that I am yours. It actually feels nice for a change."

Confused I begin to question her candid remark. "What does?" She then turns her attention back to me, causing me to become powerless once more.

"That someone like you would actually be interested in someone like me?"

I'm dumbfounded. Speechless even. How am I supposed to refute that statement? She is obviously unaware of the effects she has on me and up until I first laid my eyes on her, I was basically nonexistent. If I could change our way of thinking, then I would make her mine in an instant and let the world know that I am hers. But that isn't the case in today's climate. We have laws that must be followed whether we agree with them or not.

Closing the abandoned space between us, I cup her cheek with my palm and make a daring declaration. One that carries a hefty price should I decide to take it a step further.

"Simone, any male would be lucky to have you by their side. And as long as you'll have me, I'll continue to be there for you anyway possible."

With our eyes locked onto one another, I find myself questioning her motives and my own actions. What is she doing to me? Why me? Haven't I disappointed my parents enough? Is the goddess punishing me for my unspeakable crimes and malevolent behavior? Retracting my hand from her face, I attempt to exercise restraint by taking a step back. With her hair dancing about in the wind, she turns her attention to the empty space before us and continues to deliver her gentle persuasion of our forbidden affection.

"Can we get out of here?"

Under different circumstances this simple request would be harmless and although my body is beaming with approval, my mind isn't as willing. I cannot allow myself to be alone with her in this state.

Nothing good can come of this infatuation that I have with this mortal. This is much bigger than just me and her. I'll be placing my whole family at risk and not to mention the responsibility that continues to loom over my shoulders as future leader of my tribe. Pushing the negative thoughts aside, I decide to see where this might go.

"What did you have in mind?"

"How about your place?"

Unknown to her, humans are not welcomed in our homes. Imagine what kind of trouble I would be in if my parents or the tribe leaders found out that I have not only befriended a mortal but also extended an invitation to our family home.

Our friendship is already at risk of being exposed; there is no need to add more fuel to the fire. So instead of instilling doubt or any form of rejection, I decide to politely decline her request and propose an alternative solution.

"How about we take a walk along the Allegheny River? The moon lights it up perfectly around this time. I can take you home afterwards if that's alright."

She doesn't object and instead decides to agree, "Ok."

Reaching for her hand, I pull her close as we begin walking towards the riverfront, leaving our troubles behind.

Chapter Four

~Enforcer~

It's late fall, with only three weeks left until the official day of winter arrives. The fallen leaves will soon be covered in snow along with all the abandoned objects that have been left behind. On average the temperature at night can easily drop to the high twenties, but that can change when you're inside of an ice rink. As I finish sliding my shin pads on and ready myself for our match tonight, memories of her delicate face begin to flood my mind.

You see, today marks a turning point in my life that occurred almost four months ago. The day when my dreary and enraged world collided with a divine creature who has undeniably managed to turn my life upside down from the inside out. We have been devoted to one another since the first day we met. Our friendship has grown into admiration and I can't help but wonder if this encounter was an accident or fate. I ask myself this same question every day because it sure as hell feels like a stroke of luck.

She instills doubt, forcing me to reexamine everything that I thought I knew about mortals. As it turns out, my perception of the human race was entirely based on speculation. Everything that I've ever known to be true has been fabricated by the elders for their own selfish pursuits. If their beliefs and teachings have merit, then how is it possible for a mortal like Simone to be selfless? This attribute should only exist among our race; however, I've come to terms that no two beings are alike. Whether that being is a mortal or immortal, everyone should be held accountable for their own actions and not be condemned solely based off of one individuals mistake.

Standing from the locker room bench, I grab my helmet and descend to the ice rink with my hockey stick in tow. My nerves have got the best of me as the idea of Simone sitting in the audience becomes a reality. What if she doesn't bother to show up? Would I be ok with that? Since the season started, she has been imploring to come out and watch me play a sport that I actually respect due to its intense physicality. But I've been avoiding the subject because I don't want her to discover the assertive and aggressive side of me that I've succeeded in suppressing. She isn't aware of my cruel past nor that my temper remains in limbo which is a trait that is hard wired into our DNA.

So, without her prior knowledge I finally gave in and purchased four lower bowl sideline tickets to a mid-level professional ice hockey game; slipping them into her bag while we were eating brunch. She found them later that afternoon and called to thank me. Two days later and here we are inside a closed freezer waiting for the match to begin. I'll just act like she isn't here, watching my every move and probably regretting the day she met me.

Skating into the arena with my teammates trailing behind I suddenly find it hard to breathe as we all take our seats and wait for the announcements to commence. I'm twitchy and anxious as the dome whirrs with both laughter and startling excitement. The buzzer sounds and one by one the commentator begins the introductions over the PA starting with the player's position and their name.

Each time a member of the team is announced the ruthless fans cheer hysterically which only worsens my anxiety. With a distorted vision, I begin scanning the crowd, hoping to pinpoint her exact location when I hear my name being called.

"And playing center for the Whiskey Rebels, number 43, Jovianus Moreau!"

The chanting and howling only gets louder each time a player's name is revealed yet, I am still able to hear her voice above all as she whistles then shouts my name from the stands, "Jovianus!"

My head immediately turns to the sound of her voice causing our distressed sights to converge. Her smile is wide from ear to ear as she waves her hand in the air to capture my attention. She looks marvelous, standing there amid the fans, with a gray slouchy cable hat and a crème off the shoulder thermal. Ethan is standing next to her along with Leona and Derek.

Oh man, if I thought I was in trouble before she arrived then I'm really in trouble now. It's going to be extremely difficult to concentrate on the game tonight.

Placing my helmet on, I feel my feet begin to move from the hard-concrete floor and onto the ice. The *swooshing* sound from the skates intensifies as I speed up, eager to reach the burning light that keeps me awake at night. My blades then come to a complete stop. Feeling possessed and unable to detach my eyes from hers, I slowly lift two fingers to my lips, lightly dab them and then motion in her direction.

The crowd grows wild as she shakes her head in amusement. Meanwhile the commentator continues to narrate my pathetic attempt in wooing her.

"Sorry ladies, looks like he's taken."

I scoff at his remark because it isn't true. We're just close friends who spend every moment with each other every chance we get. The affection that I feel for her is completely innocent with no hidden agenda in mind.

Retracting my sight from hers, I begin making my way towards the center of the rink where the face off will soon begin. A surge of adrenaline spikes through me as we line up on the ice in opposition to our rivals, the Boston Shawmut's. With our skates wedged into the rink, eyes glued to the ice and backs hunched in anticipation for the drop, we can feel the tension build as the ref releases the puck and our sticks begin to wage war.

The first and second period started off pretty rough as expected given that the Shawmut's are renowned for their unscrupulous antics. Santino, who is a top defenseman in the ECHL, is not only recognized for his ability to control the puck for extended periods of time, but also for his dirty plays and ill-mannered character; from stick checking, clipping, all the way to boarding his opponents. I somehow managed to stay calm while he dominated the rink and displayed tasteless conduct towards my teammates, but by the third period I had enough.

With four minutes left in the game and a tied score, my mind is all over the place as our team moves the puck from one player to another. My teammate Viktor flies up the right wing and takes a long pass from Zach who plays forward when Santino holds him off and kicks it loose. He then shoots the biscuit across the blue line and wraps it around the boards. As Santino gains control of the puck once again, he makes a wrist shot into the goal crease only to be stopped by our goalie Lucas as he drops to his knees and covers the net. This move sets the fans into a frenzy which in turn pisses Santino off.

Upset over the outcome, Santino advances towards Lucas and delivers a tawdry shot to his face and abdomen with the knob of his stick. A line brawl quickly ensues as players from both teams drop their gloves and rush to join the scuffle. The officials struggle to end the brutal dispute while I witness mayhem unfold before me. It takes every inch of my willpower not to walk over and knock that low life to his knees. To bestow upon him the same gallantry that he has and continues to convey upon others.

But that would be far too easy because it wouldn't be a fair fight. A mortal's strength is no match for our kind. Besides, my actions would cause unwarranted interest, and no one wants that. Not me and certainly not the tribe leaders. He isn't a worthy human being. Not by a long shot.

An oppressor is what he is. A tyrant. A bully. His time will come soon enough. I'd rather concentrate on winning this game and head home than making a spectacle of myself. After a few minutes, the refs finally put a stop to the madness. Everyone scatters while Lucas is escorted off the ice rink, leaving a trail of blood behind. As a new goaltender enters the rink, I notice that Santino remains in the game while taking his position on the ice.

Are they really going to turn their heads and allow this idiot to continue playing with no penalty? Unbelievable! My fury suddenly boils over causing pressure to build in my chest. Skating to the center, preparing myself for the drop I wrestle to keep the defiant savage confined. I can feel sweat dripping down the sides of my helmet as the clock starts again with only two minutes left in the game.

Covering the ice, Riley gains control of the puck and heads for the blue line when Logan from the opposing team hip checks him and seizes it. He then drop passes it to his teammate Jack aka *the goon* who hits it into the neutral zone only to be intercepted by our forward Zach. Moving along the boards he executes a saucer pass to Viktor and loses control to the opposing team's center Alec. Viktor comes back and takes control of the puck once again. He begins making his way towards the goal crease while being surrounded by a few defense men.

Find the net. Find the net Viktor. Pick up your knees. The shot is stopped by their goalie Patrick. Damn it! We are running out of time. Santino then picks up pace, retrieves the puck while body checking Zach and knocks him to the ice.

Coming in from the right, I force my way passed their defenders in a flash and reach Santino as he crosses the blue line. Skating beside him with my stick angled ready to loosen the puck, he turns and attempts to shove me only to discover that his task will not be easily accomplished. He then stiffens his arm and aims for the net from the left side of the rink only to be blindsided by a forceful heave of my elbow. The vicious contact unexpectedly hurls his body mid-air and then crashes against the boards right before landing on the ice. The impact causes the glass to detach, flipping forward and leaving an open gap between the rink and the audience.

No longer able to focus on the game, I come to a complete stop and toss my stick onto the ground. With measured glides, I turn back around and remove my gloves then helmet allowing them to land where they see fit. As my blades begin cutting through the ice, I witness the parasite regain consciousness and then sluggishly stand.

With a haunting grin, he turns slightly to the side, spits on the ice and then wipes the remaining blood from his mouth. My rage suddenly spills over consequently inviting the ferocious beast to emerge like a disease. It comes with a hefty price. One that I know all too well and carries no remorse. I've never been verbally crafty as one might imagine; however, my actions always speak louder than words.

Just as I suspected, he attempts to lunge at me with his white knuckled fists. Without much effort on my part I halt his advances with my forearm and slam his body into the ice which causes his helmet to fly off. And no, it doesn't end there. Consumed by the violence and riveted feeling that has already altered my reasoning, I take it a step further. Bending down to his level, I clinch his jersey with extreme aggression while lifting his body off the ice and convey a graphic yet compelling message.

"You would think that someone with such skill and deceit would know when to stop wagging their tongue. Let this be a lesson for the next time you try to undermine me."

Releasing my grip from his shirt, I aim for his face and land one solid blow that knocks him out cold. Within seconds, two officials surround me and the unconscious idiot when I hear the buzzer along with cheers and angry shouts alike fill my ears.

It just so happens, while I was handling business to the left side of the rink, my malicious deed caused our team to regain control of the loose puck. Zach scored right before time ran out with a slap shot that by some miracle went into the net. There are mixed emotions from the fans who are now standing from their seats, troubled by the sight of the injured villain who remains motionless.

From here on, everything fast forwards in a blur. One minute I'm casually playing hockey in a cordial fashion and the next I'm being banished from participating in all subsequent games. Turns out, Santino's injuries were far worse than anticipated which landed me in the hot seat with the league, my parents, and the tribe leaders. Bad news sure does travel fast.

My phone has been blowing up with calls and texts from several individuals, each one having their own personal fears. Simone's texts have been mostly about my overall wellbeing while my eager parent's voicemails express their disapproval of my irresponsible behavior. And then there's the overwhelming calls from my teammates who are pestering me about my attendance for the post game celebration which usually takes place at Jack's Bar on Carson Street.

It's somewhat of a tradition that our team started three years ago although I've never made an effort to attend. I'm not much of a drinker anyway and I try my best to avoid as much human interaction as possible. Only appearing for practice, games and attending school with the end goal to graduate and head back to Canada. Besides, overcoming my anger issues hasn't exactly been easy and attending a bar full of aggressive hockey players is a headline for disaster. The only reason why I actually agreed to attend this time is because Simone confirmed that she was already there waiting for me. So, after a lengthy discussion with the coach, I shower, get dressed and head out into the cold to meet the lovely creature that I can't seem to get out of my mind.

Upon arrival I find that the bar is overly crowded as individuals wait outside to gain entry. I'm guessing the building has reached its capacity at this point. The sound of music can be heard from the sidewalk along with poised laughter that carries a welcoming tune. Approaching the door, I peer my head inside to see if I can locate Ethan and Simone when I hear my name being called.

"Jovianus...my man!"

Nestled between two blonds near a table by the bar is Zach, one of our forwards. With a beer in one hand and a half empty glass of brown liquid in the other, he quickly begins making his way to the front entrance with enhanced intensity.

"I thought you'd never show. Get your ass over here!" His boisterous tone confirms that he's probably had one to many drinks.

The brawny bouncer guarding the front door quickly turns to face me with confusion on his face.

"You're the one who knocked that guy's teeth out with one blow?"

His comment is phrased with skepticism as he lifts his eyebrows and does a swift inspection of my physique.

Now, I may not weigh 250lbs and snack on kittens in my sleep, but I'm certainly not someone whom he wants to mess with. Standing at 6' 2" with a lean build and fists curled by my side, I take two measured steps in his direction and challenge his ridicule.

"That most definitely is me."

Although the delivery of my response was somewhat composed there was an abrasive undertone that caught his attention. It's called confidence motherfucker.

He smirks while folding his sausage arms across his bulky chest and steps aside.

"Must have been a hell of a fight. They've been talking about it for the past hour."

This idiot has no idea what I'm capable of, however now is not the time to settle this pointless dispute. So rather than rearranging his face in front of these spectators, I decide to spare him humiliation and walk on through the metal door.

Zach immediately hands me a beer upon entering.

"It's time to celebrate. There's plenty of booze and females alike."

Taking a swig from the bottle, I follow him through the stuffy bar while scanning the room for Simone. Music from the jukebox continues to blare in the background as we head towards a table lined with players from my team.

"Look who I found out front," Zach bellows while placing his hand on my shoulder.

My teammates are surprised to see me and immediately begin roaring about my little dispute and our victory.

"The way you thrust his body up against the boards was truly monumental."

"No one saw that coming."

"Then he gets up and attempts to challenge you. One strike," Viktor smashes his fist against his palm, "and his teeth tumbled onto the ground."

"Went to sleep like a baby."

"Had you not stopped the dipstick, then we wouldn't have been able to score before the clock ran out."

With a satisfying grin on his face, Riley pats my back then heads over to the bar. I try my best to downplay my overly aggressive behavior and not draw anymore unnecessary attention to myself.

"Listen, I was just playing the game the way they play. Anyone of us would have done the same for the team."

Guess I didn't think this one through before reacting. But that putz Santino had it coming. Every time we play against them, he does something illegal and the ref's never call him on it. Well, he picked the wrong freaking day to try and scheme his way into winning. As the guys continue to yak about the incident, Lucas disrupts my foul thoughts by introducing the two blonds who have been following him around like lost puppies.

"Jovianus come." He places his arm around my shoulder and speaks close to my ear, "You see those two blonds over there?"

I shake my head, "What about them?"

"Well, they have been eager to meet you. And when I say eager, I really mean desperate. How about you give them the satisfaction of just saying hello."

Taking another swig from my beer, I attempt to politely decline.

"I'm not really into the whole groupie thing if you know what I mean."

"Why not? You're single, aren't you?"

"Doesn't mean that I'm interested."

"Well at the least say hi for our sake and we'll take it from there."

Lucas pats my back and then motions towards the obsessive females who have been watching me since I entered the bar. With haste they both stride over, trying their best to walk as sexy as possible while whipping their hair to the side. As they approach, he places his arms around their shoulders and escorts them into my personal space.

"Good evening ladies. This is Jovianus. He plays center for our team. Would you two beauties be so kind and introduce yourselves?"

The blonde with the shortest sweater that I've ever seen is the first to respond. With a sultry voice, she thrusts her breast forward and shoves her hand into mine.

"Hi Jovianus, my name is Pauline, but everyone calls me Paula."

Before we can even make contact, the other senseless female interrupts her friend's advances.

"And I'm Zoe, but you can call me whatever you'd like."

Wow, they sound too damn desperate and reek of alcohol mixed with cheap perfume. I make an effort to remain friendly by offering a polite smile when my sight is suddenly distracted by a moving light. As I turn to investigate this diversion, I'm greeted with pure elegance which stops me in my tracks.

There to my right, standing by a set of occupied pool tables is Simone. Ethan and Aemilia are also with her, all of which are in deep conversation that I'm currently restricted from. In that moment, everything around me disappears; the room becomes silent and still. Nothing or no one matters. I don't understand why she has this effect on me or how it's even possible, but it happens a little too often for my liking.

As I continue to stare, Simone happens to turn around and spots me ogling her. Caught off guard and not sure how to react, she smiles and graciously waves. My body automatically responds to unspoken demands as I begin to move in her direction when I hear a high and unpleasant voice shout, "Uh, heellooo!"

Blondie number two is flailing her hand in my face to capture my attention. Placing my beer bottle down at the nearest table, I tuck one of my hands in my back pocket and retrieve my wallet. Pulling out a twenty-dollar bill, I place the money in Lucas's hand and quickly dismiss them.

"Um, it's nice to meet you both. Lucas is quite a catch so don't leave him by himself. The next rounds on me."

I begin making my way towards the striking female that has caused an uproar in my life. I don't even bother to look back as I head towards my destination. My ears vaguely hear Lucas placing an order for another round of beers as I reach Simone and the pompous females become a distant memory.

Chapter Five

~Lackey~

Approaching Simone, I carefully move in for a harmless peck on the cheek all while pulling her small frame into my chest. Her hair and skin carry a sweet scent that lingers long after a shower. This delightful aroma is mindlessly appealing and intoxicating, both of which are becoming increasingly frequent. It takes all of my strength not to kiss her soft lips and by some miracle, I manage to stay composed.

I'm no longer sure that I can survive this night without incident. Probably should have went straight home instead of this place that is lurking with turmoil and unrest.

I quickly recover and explain my late arrival with an apologetic tone as I pull away, "I'm late again. Sorry. Our coach made me stay after the game."

With an alluring smile she quickly mollifies the mood.

"No need to apologize. We actually arrived like ten minutes ago."

Ethan then comes over and hands me a glass lined with clear liquid and a lime.

"Glad you made it."

Nodding, I take the glass from his hand, "Thanks," and toss back a quick drink.

A vodka tonic on the rocks – nice! Things have changed for the better since our last disagreement given that we both share a common interest – Simone.

Turns out, it was a simple misunderstanding and after several weeks of tension, we finally confronted the inevitable and settled our differences in a cordial fashion. He made it clear that if I were to hurt her in any way shape or form, then I would have to answer to him. And I made it known that we were just friends; my sole interest is her overall wellbeing. It took time, but we eventually overcame our male arrogance, formed an alliance to protect her and now we have the upmost respect for one another.

Aemilia then comes over and greets me with a friendly kiss on the cheek.

"Where is Leona and Derek?" I ask out of curiosity given that they made an appearance at the game.

"Oh, they caught a movie afterwards and mentioned something about meeting up later."

Ethan shrugs his shoulders out of indifference and continues whispering into her ear. As I begin to inspect the place for any signs of trouble, Aemilia interrupts my perplexed thoughts.

"So, I heard you guys won. Looks like I missed a good game huh?"

Here we go again. The same tune but from a different spectator. I clear my throat before responding and try my best not to sound annoyed by the constant reminders of the unfortunate events that unfolded earlier.

"Yes, you are correct on both accounts."

"You really nailed that guy on the ice today. Is he ok?" I sense a bit of concern in Ethan's tone however, I'm less inclined to disclose all of Santino's misfortunes that he brought upon himself.

Placing my glass down onto the table, I look him directly in the eye and provide a dry, less humorless response which only prompts more questions, "He'll live."

"Is it always that intense?"

"It's all part of the sport. This team is known to play dirty, that's how they win. Guess they met their match tonight."

With his eyebrows cast down and a smirk on his face he scoffs, "You think?"

But before I can rebuke his judgment, Aemilia's fascination with male arrogance and egotism unpredictably captures her interest.

"Did you really slam him on the ground and knock his teeth out?"

Neither confirming nor denying her question about the irrefutable incident that everyone happened to witness, I decide to focus on the *why* rather than the *how*.

"My sole interest was to make sure that we scored before time ran out, and we accomplished that."

All three individuals turn their attention to me in disbelief like I'm some kind of sadistic enthusiast who revels in violent behavior. Well, this is who I am but it's not how I want them to perceive me to be and today does nothing to prove otherwise. Feeling the need to defend my actions, I begin to explain the logistics of the sport.

"Look, hockey is about exercising possession and control. It's both mentally and physically intense. Fighting is expected and everyone who plays the sport knows this. You have to anticipate the hits and either go with it or get knocked out. It's that simple."

"I heard that guy went to the hospital for a concussion."

Picking up my glass from the table, I down a mouth full of whiskey to distract myself from the oncoming annoyance that is beginning to fester. With the glass still in my hand, I focus on the swooshing brown liquid as I speak.

"Yeah, well don't believe everything you hear. When I left the locker room earlier, I was assured that he would be alright."

I don't understand why everyone is making such a big deal out of this. Was I the only one on the ice that noticed his lewd behavior? They're making me feel like some kind of villain when I should be thought of as someone who executed a virtuous deed for the common good.

As everyone gets settled and overcomes the fact that hockey is a contact sport, Simone and I get a few minutes to catch up while Ethan and Aemilia head back to the bar. Placing my callous hand over hers, I lean in and murmur into her ear.

"I want to apologize for tonight."

Confusion crosses her innocent face as she contemplates my revelation. "What for?"

"There was a reason why I didn't want you to see me play tonight or any night for that matter. It's undeniably an aggressive sport and I don't want your perception of me to change because of it."

She immediately counters my statement. "Jovi, I would never think that way about you."

Looking away, I can't help but wonder what she really thinks of me after everything she has witnessed. This violent and assertive immortal is who I really am. Not this patient, respectable being that I've fabricated to win her over. And for what? It's not like we can actually be together. I'm ashamed that it felt good to inflict pain on a human who was no match for me. He had no idea that I had the upper hand by default.

Feeling distraught and conflicted, I'm easily swayed when her warm palm cradles my chin, "Hey, look at me. Look at me Jovi please."

Leaning into the table I find her soft eyes and instantly become powerless when she speaks.

"I want you to know that the bond we have goes beyond friendship. I have so much respect for you and nothing or no one can ever change that. Do you understand what I am saying?"

Her voice is both calm and soothing. I'm lost for words as our faces remain inches apart and I'm unexpectedly captivated by her mere existence. Without thinking, I lift my hand to her face and place it underneath her right cheek.

My thumb slowly begins to graze her lower lip as I lean closer and utter her name, "Simone..."

She quickly responds as does her body with a simple, "Yes."

That guileless act awakens a part of me that I had thought to be nonexistent. I don't know nor understand what is happening to me but what I do know is that I've stumbled onto a place of no return. Not wanting to lead her on, I quickly drop my hand and break eye contact while changing the subject.

"What were you... drinking?"

"Oh, uh...water. No underage drinking here, but... if you have something else in mind then I'm all in." She begins to laugh which changes my mood as I offer to buy us some drinks.

"Come, let's go fill our liver with some alcohol then."

Taking a hold of her hand, I intertwine my fingers with hers and begin making our way to the bar. While waiting to place our order, I faintly hear a disagreement of sorts coming from outside.

Weirdos come in all shapes and forms especially when alcohol is involved so it's no surprise that disputes erupt in establishments as such. Looking around in search of Ethan and Aemilia I quickly realize that they are nowhere to be seen. Those two are impossible. A few moments later, players from the opposing team enter the bar which causes a bit of chaos from my teammates and fans alike.

The brawny bouncer promptly interjects, and the Shawmut's confirm that they are just here to have a few beers and want no trouble. The crowd then scatters, and everything turns back to normal as I grab our drinks and head back to the table.

"Who are those guys?"

I take a swig of my beer before answering, "Members from the opposing team that we played today."

"What are they doing here?"

I can see concern on her face as she conveys the question that I'm sure everyone is asking themselves at this very moment.

"Well, it's a public bar so I imagine that they are here to have a few drinks like the rest of us."

Lies. All lies. It's the exact opposite. Everything Ethan said earlier is true; I did give their teammate a concussion. I also managed to knock three of his teeth out in the process and sadly enough, I enjoyed every minute of it! They are here with one mission in mind. To confront the player that knocked their best defenseman out cold.

My mood suddenly turns serious as I come to terms that it has become unsafe for her to remain in my presence. She then begins speaking to me casually, unaware that a plot is being devised by a bunch of angry males who have no idea that I'm far more powerful than the four of them combined. I have to figure out a way to get her out of here. "Did you hear what I said?" She takes another drink from her beer while focusing on my reaction.

"Yes." I shake the troubling thoughts from my mind and force a smile as I continue speaking. "I was thinking about Clodia. She wanted me to pick up dinner on my way home and I'm afraid it's getting late."

Simone begins to fidget as her gaze scans the area by the bar.

"Where's Aemilia and Ethan? I came with them here and I don't have a way of getting home."

"I'm sure they wanted to be alone but don't worry, I can take you and we can call them on our way out."

"Ok." She is unphased by my emotionless reaction.

Placing our drinks down onto the table, I slowly position my hand to her lower back and usher her out the side door in hopes that we aren't being followed. However, my assurance is short lived when I hear several feet hitting the pavement behind us shortly after our departure.

My vehicle is parked along the street some blocks down and there is no way that I'm going to be able to get her to safety before they reach us. Under different circumstances, I would have turned around and met my adversary, ending the fight with one swift move. But underneath this fearless warrior is a more compassionate being who only has one thought above all. Simone. She is precious cargo and her worth is immeasurable in every way. I can't just place her life at risk for my own personal vendetta. Not while she's in my care.

Frantically digging in the pocket of my jacket, I locate the keys to my vehicle and reach for her hand. Gently pulling her towards me, I halt our advances and move my mouth close to her ear without ever turning around. Swiftly speaking urgent words that only she can understand.

"I want you to keep walking straight ahead and don't look back. My car is just two blocks down, lock the doors and turn the engine on. Do not under any circumstances stop until you have reached my vehicle."

The euphoric bliss in her eyes quickly disappears and is replaced with apprehension as she pulls away to look at my face.

"What are you talking about?"

At that precise moment, the belligerent males begin their ridicule while shouting my name. "Jovianus. Is that you?"

Fully aware that I'm running out of time, I flip her hand over, slide the keys into her palm and close her fingers. Placing my hand on the side of her neck, I pull her face close to mine and look directly into her eyes. "Do you trust me?"

She hesitates at first, confused at the request but quickly responds, "Yes... Yes of course I do."

"Then do as I say and don't ask any more questions."

"But..."

"Please Simone. Go.... Now!"

The last word unexpectedly came out with a growl which causes her to instinctively recoil, almost tripping along the way as she begins to jog towards the end of the street.

"Of course that's you; I recognize that cowardice retreat anywhere."

Ignoring their malice insults, I keep my eyes glued on her until she reaches the edge of my vehicle. Pushing the unlock button on the remote, she turns and takes a quick glimpse in my direction before opening the door.

Closing my eyes, I exhale sharply and mentally prepare myself for the altercation when a sudden surge of possession takes over. My temper spills without warning as I turn to face the raging mortal and his lackey's who might not recuperate from their impeding injuries.

There in front of me are four males, each one frayed in their own way. The tall dingy guy, the ringleader with the cigarette in his mouth is the first one to speak.

"Now why did you have to go and tell her to leave. This reunion would have been more exciting if she was around."

His comment about Simone flips a switch in my brain that I haven't experienced in ages. Back to the days when I was out of control and couldn't turn it off. Curling my fingers into my palms, I lift my head and square my shoulders as I take a step forward and meet him head on. Two of his comrades' step closer in my direction as if to intimidate me. Their advance only infuriates me further as I chuckle from disbelief while keeping my sight affixed to the ringleader's face.

"I was hoping to resolve our differences amicably, but now you've made it personal and it seems we are past that part, wouldn't you agree?"

My voice is low and menacing, gearing towards an ultimatum that he so willingly accepts. Taking a long drag from his cigarette and discarding the bud, he then takes a defensive stance with his fist paired in front of his face, ready to strike. They've got me surrounded at all angles in the middle of the street, as if I would even attempt to escape.

The funny thing is that I have no intentions of leaving this fight, not until I've had my fill of retribution. From my peripheral I can see that the mortal to my left is still holding a beer bottle while the male to my right begins cracking his knuckles. I'm unable to see the asshat that has positioned himself behind me, however, I can feel his presence and have every intention of introducing myself.

I slowly begin removing my jacket and throw it onto the ground as I confirm our plans for the night.

"Alright then. Let's get on with it."

What these idiots failed to understand is that I've already thought this whole ordeal through. While I was walking out of the bar and up until I turned to face the arrogant males, I was playing out every move in my head. My mind is running at a hundred miles per hour, examining every detail of my opponents as I wait for the quarrel to commence.

The dingy male attempts to make the first move by throwing a punch in my direction, eager to make contact with my face, but fails as I sidestep his advance. Spinning my body to the left, I curl my fingers over the neck of the beer bottle that dummy number two is holding and smash it across his buddies' face to my right. This sends him flying into the unforgiving asphalt but not before colliding with the halfwit that was standing behind me.

The dingy male and dummy number two both lunge at me when I thrust a hard kick straight into the ringleader's chest, knocking him hard against a light post.

Dummy number two already has his arms locked around my chest from behind as he tries to lift my body, yet he can't seem to find his strength. Bending my body forward and reaching over my shoulder, I grip one of his arms and flip his weak frame straight into the pavement. The violent impact ends his tattered pursuit, knocking him out cold like his other two comrades.

As I turn around to inspect the area, I take notice that halfwit is the only one standing. He slowly begins to move forward in a crouched position while waving a sharp blade. I quickly raise my hands with my palms outward in a surrendering manner hoping to diffuse the already hazardous situation.

"Do us both a favor and put the knife down before you hurt yourself."

"Oh yeah? Well, how about I walk over to your whore and gut her like a fish while you watch?"

I begin to laugh hysterically, mostly out of anger because he so unwisely threatened someone who has become an important and permanent resident in my life. With my lips curled back, I hiss taunting words that will surely provoke him further.

"I'd like to see you try."

He immediately becomes irrational and begins to shout in a heated manner while blinking his eyes erratically.

"Who do you think you are?"

I can see his lips quiver out of fright and anger as he pushes the blade forward in my direction. Slowly inching closer to him without his knowledge, I proceed to distract him with more direful statements.

"Someone you shouldn't have fucked with."

"I think it's the other way around. You have no idea what we are capable...." His words are promptly cut off as I land an effective blow to his jugular sending him to his knees and ending this grueling encounter.

I can hear the blade involuntarily drop to the ground as his hands wrap around his throat while he struggles to breathe.

Walking over to his limp form, I bend down close to his body and deliver the final words that will certainly have him startled for months to come.

"The next time you or your friends feel the need to torment or disrespect another human being, just remember how easy it was for me to disband your gang of misfits, only next time none of you will be lucky enough to walk away with your life."

Within a matter of seconds, he falls backwards and continues gasping for air. All four men remain secluded to the concrete floor like wounded animals, three of which are unconscious.

Retrieving my jacket from the ground, I dust it off and begin making my way down the street to my vehicle where Simone is impatiently waiting.

As I approach the door to my sedan, I notice that her hands are clasped tightly around the steering wheel. Lifting my fist to the glass window, I lightly knock to capture her attention which causes her to jump from the seat.

Startled and nervous, tears begin to stream down her cheeks as she struggles to open the door and leaps into my arms while sobbing uncontrollably. Pulling her close to my chest, I try my best to soothe any doubts that may have settled.

"Hey. Hey don't cry. It's just me."

She continues sobbing into my shirt, "I thought you were hurt, and I didn't know what to do. I didn't know what to do."

She repeats this over and over unable to control her anguish. I pull her back slightly so that she can examine me for herself. "Look at me. I'm fine. I'm not hurt. Nothing happened to me."

Slowly wiping the tears from her cheeks, she begins to inspect my face and body, puzzled that she is unable to locate a single injury. She then grabs my hands and flips them over, carefully studying them and eager to confirm if what I'm saying is true.

"You see, I'm fine. Everything's fine." She shakes her head in agreement and calms down a bit while wiping her nose with the back of her hand. We both remain quiet for a few moments as I give her time to digest the fact that no one was hurt. Or at least no one that she cares about was hurt. Unsure if the culprits will be coming back for more, I decide to break our silence so that we may leave this ghastly memory behind us.

"I'm sorry that I made you cry."

"You didn't make me cry." Her hoarse voice is weak from weeping.

"Yes, I did. You're crying because of me. It's the same difference."

She tries her best to change the subject about her wellbeing and dives into the offender's whereabouts.

"Where are they? What did they want?"

With a smile on my face, I dodge her question and distract her from the upsetting reality about my true nature and the fitting deceptions that I continue to feed her.

"It doesn't matter now. What matters is that you're safe. Scoot over and let's get you home."

Slowly sliding into the passenger seat, she buckles her seatbelt and leans back while closing her eyes. I shift the gear to drive and descend towards the highway lost in thought, wondering what my life would have been if we'd never met.

Chapter Six

~Funus~

Today the sun is blue when it should be cornflower yellow. Some would even go as far and say that the capricious sun is colorblind with its depressing hues and weary spirit. Its energy has been wasted beyond grief like those who have lost a loved one, emanating pain and despair. Dullness is all we see. Opaque to be exact.

The sky is a bruised canvas painted by an artist who's brush strokes resemble rough waves crashing against the ocean's surface. The possibility of the sun shedding even a fraction of its gleaming light has diminished with every passing minute while it takes refuge behind wounded clouds like a fugitive.

The atmosphere remains lifeless and still. Unmoving even. A low rumble sounds every so often, sending woeful reminders of the impending reality that another life has been lost, but in this case its two. White stargazer lilies and several gladioli arrangements that vary in colors flank both caskets. Crammed bodies dressed in black attire over crowd the damp soil of Union Dale Cemetery. Close friends and coworkers alike have gathered here today to pay their respects and grieve with their loved ones. Umbrellas of numerous sizes hover from above while the relentless downpour continues to soak the ground beneath our feet, releasing a fresh earthy scent from the plants and spores.

The front row that is reserved for family members remains rather empty. Occupied by their only child, Simone, and a few of her close friends; Ethan, Aemilia, Leona, Derek, and myself. She has no immediate living relatives in the United States. Both of her parents were also the only child in their family. They are survived by Simone and an estranged aunt that lives on a distant island whom she has never met.

The worst part of this tragedy is that blame's herself for their deaths. She somehow feels responsible because she was the one who was supposed to be driving her parent's vehicle and not them. In her mind, it should have been her who met death and not the other way around. How is she supposed to move forward in life if she refuses to absolve this self-inflicted torment? What I would give to turn back time and change the events that brought us all here today. The dense air has me anxiously tugging at my necktie while I shift in my seat as the catholic priest begins the rite of committal service. With the church bell tolling in the background, I begin to look back to a week ago when Simone received the devastating call that would change her life forever.

We were all on our third day of spring break, celebrating the much-needed time off from an overbearing education system. Instead of running off on some wild vacation with the possibility of getting into unnecessary trouble, we all decided to stay here in Pittsburgh. It was Monday night and Simone was going to borrow her parent's station wagon and drive to Aemilia's house where we would all meet up, but at the last minute our plans changed. Her father decided to surprise his wife with a dinner date and requested that we provide transportation for Simone instead.

So, after picking her up, we headed to the south side of town that is home to more bars and pubs that anyone could care for. Being that Simone, Aemilia and Leona are all under the age of drinking, we set our eyes on eating dinner first and a little window shopping afterwards. This entailed playful banter on the sidewalks of the city along with good humored waltzing as we swap partners to an imaginary tune.

Derek and Aemilia abandoned their post and decided to walk the remainder of the way, passing a newly lit cigarette while engaging in casual conversation as Ethan and Simone tango beside Leona and myself. I'm not much of a dancer but that doesn't stop me from swinging Leona to a soundless jingle that only we can hear. They continue to laugh about their newfound talent as Ethan twirls Simone causing the hem of her dress to hike up a bit from the light breeze. It's hard not to notice her even when she isn't purposely distracting me. Those soft eyes and carefree laughter only hypnotize me further and does nothing to stop me from tripping on my own two feet. Damn it. Get it together Jovi. It's impolite to stare.

The loud music in the background echoing from various bars is totally off beat for our highly skilled leaps and prances. As I spin Leona onto the sidewalk one last time, Ethan quickly interjects and whirls her straight into my arms without warning. The exchange was so sudden that neither of us was ready for it causing her to bump into my chest with her lips almost glued to mine. Quickly recovering, I clear my throat and look away while placing one of my hands on her waist and the other interlaced between her fingers. I can feel her velvet skin melt into mine as we slowly begin to waltz. And although I try hard not to make eye contact, my sight betrays me when her spellbinding voice utters, "Jovianus."

In that instant I become immobilized and I'm no longer in command of my own ship. Our laughter is quickly replaced with a serious glare that intensifies causing me to pull her body closer to mine, solidifying the chemistry that I continue to repudiate. No longer able to formulate thoughts or words, we become lost and unaware of our surroundings. We slow danced longer than expected while our friends carried on with their free-spirited nature as if they didn't notice our connection. Knowing that I had to let her go at some point, I end our union by twirling her into the empty space before me. She ends our waltz with a curtsy, and I return her gesture with a bow. Her gaze lingers as does mine and it becomes evident that our feelings for each other has grown immensely over the course of seven months.

The celebration carried on throughout the night with Ethan, Derek and I wetting our whistles at several pubs while the girls indulged on some nightlife at a local club. We all were scheduled to meet up before midnight where the festivities would continue at Ethan's house. Our evening was going as planned with me being the designated driver and the responsible one who only had two alcoholic beverages. Needless to say, alcohol doesn't affect our brain's communication as it does with mortals. It would take a substantial amount of alcohol consumption over the course of several days in order to have any type of negative effect on our mood or behavior.

I witness my other two comrades have their fill of endless beers while we bar hopped continuously, never staying in one place for more than thirty minutes. It was getting close to midnight and we hadn't received a call from either of the girls. Thinking that they possibly lost track of time, I decide to call Simone to confirm their location. Her phone rang several times and finally went to voicemail. I called again, over and over with the same outcome. My calls never went to voicemail before, so I instantly panicked and made my way through the bar, pushing aside anyone who stood in my path. Ethan and Derek must have noticed my unusual behavior because they were on my heels the moment my feet landed onto the sidewalk.

"What's wrong Jovi?" Ethan's intense stare grabs me by surprise as he scans the area for any signs of trouble.

"Ah...," I begin fidgeting with my phone as I look up, "It's close to midnight and the girls haven't called. I tried Simone's phone, but it keeps going to voicemail."

"Maybe they lost track of time or decided to go home early and caught a cab."

Derek tries to calm my nerves with endless possibilities that are not logical because one of us should have gotten a call by now if that were the case.

"That's what I was thinking but wouldn't they have told us? We had plans to meet up later, they wouldn't just bail without calling first."

"I'll try Leona and see where they're at."

Derek immediately retrieves his phone from his back pocket and begins dialing as he holds the device to his ear.

"Apologies if I'm overreacting, but it's unlike her not to answer my calls. If they did decide on going elsewhere, she would have told me. Something is off, and I don't like it."

The trepidation in my voice does nothing to hide my feelings for her, but that is the least of my worries. All I can think about is her safety as I struggle to keep my anger in check.

"Don't worry. We'll figure this out. I'm sure it was an oversight." Ethan pats my back and provides a reassuring smile.

Looking down into my phone, I begin checking my call history when my phone abruptly rings and vibrates simultaneously. I quickly answer it before the screen can register the caller.

"Simone!"

"No Jovi, its Aemilia." Her voice is urgent and apprehensive as she speaks my name.

"Aemilia, is everything ok? Where are you?"

"It's Simone. We are on our way to the hospital right now."

My heart drops to my stomach while I digest the fact that something has happened to her. How could I have been so stupid and allow them to roam the town by themselves knowingly putting them at risk for the unthinkable? I slowly begin to fall apart, and silently pledge to hurt anyone who has dared to cause harm to her. Swallowing hard and focusing on Aemilia's words, I gather the courage to ask the one question that looms above all.

"Is she hurt?"

"No. It's her parent's. They were in a horrible accident and the hospital will not release further details until they speak to her in person. We are on our way now."

This is as bad as if she were the one physically hurt. This can't be happening, not to her.

"Tell me what hospital and we will meet you there."

She provides the name of the hospital as I begin jogging towards the end of the street with the phone glued to my ear. Ethan quickly follows suit with fear marred on his face as Derek trails behind.

"And Jovi."

"Yeah."

"Please hurry. It doesn't sound good and she is on the verge of losing it."

On that note, I hit the end button to my cell and rush to my vehicle that was parked a few blocks away. I fill Ethan and Derek in on the news as we hit the pavement running like our lives depended on it.

The guys sobered up pretty fast given the circumstances while our minds drifted into every possible outcome. By the time we made it to the hospital, which took roughly twenty minutes, we were informed that the girls had recently arrived. The nurse quickly escorted us to a private waiting area located on the second floor where we met up with Aemilia and Leona. Simone was nowhere in sight.

Walking into the room, I begin biting my bottom lip while running my fingers through my hair as I pace back and forth from impatience. Derek and Leona both take a seat in the far corner of the room while Ethan remained standing near the entrance. I'm on the edge and feeling like a mad man because I'm itching to be reunited with her. I want to be able to whisper words of comfort. I want to tell her that everything is going to be ok. That her parents are going to pull through and that there is nothing to worry about. But that's not going to happen any time soon. No. Because at this very moment, she is alone. Secluded to some part of the hospital with a stranger while they convey uncertainty about her parent's future. Not only will they place unnecessary doubt but will also witness as she slowly falls apart with no one to console her.

The world around me begins to crumble as seconds turn to minutes and time slowly passes us by. I find myself wandering into the hallway as my eyes start searching for answers. Where is this moronic doctor?

This anger that has always troubled me like a disease suddenly resurfaces and takes over my mind. My mood suddenly changes, and I can feel my temper spike as I struggle with my evil twin. Breathe Jovi. Just freaking breathe before you fly off the handle. You can't afford to unleash havoc right now. It doesn't suit you and will only make matters worse. Simone needs the reasonable and caring being who is logical, not some pompous ass whose idea of resolving conflict involves imposing physical pain onto others. This type of behavior will not solve anything.

Closing my eyes for a brief moment, I inhale and take a few minutes to collect myself and calm my nerves before I do something really stupid. When I blink them open again, I notice Aemilia exit the room and roam past the nurse's station probably in search of some coffee given that it's a little after 1:00am. Leaning my back against the wall, hands in my pockets with my head tilted back, I remain *hopeful that maybe her parents were going to pull through when a woman appears in my peripheral vision. She is wobbly and unbalanced as she sluggishly makes her way down the hall. Quickly shifting my body away from the yellow wallpaper, I take notice that the female is Simone.*

Her eyes are swollen, lips plump and dull with her hands to the side as she continues to walk in my direction. I witness as tears overflow onto her cheeks and down her chin. She is hanging on by a thread and at that moment our worst fears are confirmed. Cautious not to overreact, I slowly take a few steps when her eyes unexpectedly roll back, and she collapses. I somehow managed to reach her in time before her head hit the floor. As it turns out, her parent's car wreck was fatal, and they died on contact. For unknown reasons, the vehicle they were driving veered off course and into incoming traffic, causing a collision with an eighteen-wheeler and burst into flames. The doctors wanted to inform her in person as there was no hope in saving them.

Shaking myself out of the reverie, I hear the catholic priest complete his sermon and launch into a silent prayer while sobs and muffled cries continue in the background. Everyone then stands from their white resin folding chairs as the priest utters the final words, "Amen," concluding the service.

Simone remains seated with abandoned tears streaming down her cheeks as she tightly clasps my right hand that is settled on her lap. Each attendee, one by one, begins making their way to the front and places single white daffodils on the top of each casket, bidding their farewells. Several individuals have assembled directly in front of us, waiting to convey their condolences by a way of physical contact. She doesn't even notice them; she remains seated with a dejected stare unaware of her audience.

Placing my arm around her shoulder and balancing the umbrella, I gently lift her body to a standing position while she leans against my chest for support. She does her best to acknowledge each attendee as they approach and whisper words of encouragement into her ear. I become aware that her innocence is incapable of being restored while in this tattered state.

All too soon the cemetery site becomes empty and distant. Leona and Derek both hug her and descend to their vehicle that is parked some rows down. I hand Simone the umbrella and give her some personal space to speak with her dear friend Aemilia as she approaches. Careful not to steer to far, I stay within arm's reach while briefly speaking with Ethan. I overhear Simone inform Aemilia that she is not ready to leave, and I quickly interject.

"I can stay with her until she is ready. I'll call you both when we leave."

Aemilia confirms our plans with a gentle smile and informs her that she will be over later in the evening to keep her company. They both engage in a lengthy hug before she too begins making her way to her vehicle. Clodia then comes over with a cheerless smile and wraps her arms around Simone. After a few moments, she politely excuses herself and departs. She then walks over to the caskets that remain above ground and shares one final moment with her parents before they are laid to rest.

Ethan walks over, plants a kiss on her cheek then makes his way across the pebbled path, towards his car with his head hanging low. I stay behind with the rain hitting my face, allowing her to grieve in silence. Within a matter of minutes, four funeral workers approach and begin clearing the area while prepping the caskets to be lowered. With puffy eyes and a runny nose, she heads straight into my arms.

I am all too eager to oblige as I pull her body into my chest and gently wipe away her tears with my thumb. She is filled with pain and uncertainty. Hopeful but not yet confident. Her world came crashing down from one minute to the next without notice. It's hardly fair. Not for her anyway. I don't say a word and allow her to mourn peacefully in the arms of someone who understands her loss. Because we have all been here at one point in time. Just when you feel like everything is going your way you get knocked down from your skyscraper. It feels like you're falling into an endless pit. Surrounded by darkness with no light. But I will be her calm after the storm. Her personal serene when everything seems out of place. She is the only being that matters. No one, and I do mean no one comes before her.

Unknown to me, my priorities shift and tips the scale in her favor. The winds of time suddenly transform, and I can feel a change on the horizon. Things will be different from now on. I don't know when or how but they will be different.

As the funeral workers begin lowering both caskets into the burial vaults, the rainfall lightens with the sun peering from behind the once gloom clouds. No more low rumbles nor the sound of hard rain hitting the soil. It's quiet, with complete stillness. Carefully squirming out of my arms, she takes a few steps back then turns to face the caskets that are being covered by dirt and speaks for the first time since her parent's accident. She is hesitant at first, almost like she isn't sure what to say but slowly eases into the conversation.

"In the weeks leading up to the accident, I had a dream." Her voice is low and flat with no emotion whatsoever while she fidgets with the umbrella and her eyes are glued to the caskets.

I want to ask her what her dream was about and why she feels that it's important to mention this, but I know that I must be patient. I have to allow her to clear her conscious of any misgivings. So instead of asking her questions, I stand back and wait for her to continue.

"I don't know why I remember this dream specifically, but even after my parent's death I have continued to have this same dream, except it is more frequent and vivid."

She then lowers the umbrella and proceeds to close it while keeping the same momentum about this vision. Her voice remains low and controlled as she continues speaking.

"A beautiful woman in a colorless robe appears from afar. She speaks to me in a foreign language that I do not understand. Strangely enough, she seems familiar, but I've never met her before. I don't feel scared or threaten by her presence. She has quite the opposite effect on me."

I'm not sure how to feel about this. She must be as confused as I am and is looking for answers that I'm unable to provide. For now, I'll remain quiet and reserved.

"Only one thing is certain from this dream and I understood this part loud and clear. She told me that *it was time.*"

Coming up from behind her, I slowly slide my fingers into her left hand as she turns around to face me. I then press my lips on her forehead and plant a delicate kiss that is filled with promise. She closes her eyes as I move my mouth to her ear and vow to never leave her side. Assuring her that everything is going to be ok. She then lifts her head and blinks away a few more tears with those hazel eyes as our gaze's lock. Our mouths are mere inches apart, but I won't make any advances.

Not today. Today, I will be whatever she needs me to be. And today, she needs a friend. So instead of closing the distance between us, I settle on caressing her face with the palm of my rough hand. I can feel our warm breath skim the surface of our parted lips. And in that instant, everything fades. It's instantaneous. We are in our own world. Nothing and no one can reach us as we stare into each other's eyes, in search of something more.

It is evident that we belong together as our mere existence radiates purpose and burns with desire. Our bond only strengthens and is solidified by our undeniable devotion. She is the missing puzzle in my life. The embers to my heart that longs to be ignited. Simone has somehow managed to quell my rage and steady my hand. Something that I never thought to be possible.

Pulling away with our fingers intertwined, we both descend towards my vehicle hand in hand as the funeral workers continue to shovel dirt into the burial vaults.

Chapter Seven

~Derelict~

Graduation **took place** over two months ago, and against my parent's wishes I remain in the States. The arrangement was carefully mapped out; get a degree and move back to Canada where I would be groomed to become the leader that I have inherited against my wishes. Sure, there have been numerous obstacles along the way, ranging from my unapproved standards of behavior all the way to being labeled as volatile and unstable. Still, no one was prepared for the illicit proclamation that would soon be unraveled. Not even me.

It was a dark secret. One that was effortlessly tucked away, out of reach from everyone including myself. This untold enigma carried a resilient message, yet it was so fragile, more than life itself. Only one word could describe such skillful deceit.

Denial. And indeed, I was in denial.

I was in denial because I knew that this type of emotion did not come without consequence, especially if it involved a foe or adversary. But in my heart Simone was neither of those. She has been my savior; liberating me from this torment that has not only damaged my reputation but also my soul.

For the past year, I've spent every free moment of my life with this mortal and we have been inseparable. It was a surprise to me at first because I couldn't comprehend my own feelings towards her. But as time passed, I let my guard down and became fully aware that there was more to life than the one I had been living. Our feelings quickly turned into something more. Much more than anticipated or that I cared to admit.

What I felt for her ran deep within me, something that I didn't and couldn't understand. She had come into my life like a hurricane, uninvited and unleashed chaos. She became my paradise, so pure and exquisite. Being pulled into a world of unknown and guided only by her soothing voice. Placing all my trust in her and not caring what loomed ahead of us.

She was the air in my lungs that I couldn't live without; the light to my darkness that allowed me to see when I was lost. She brought me back to life, made me feel free and sure of myself again.

But as this love blossomed, our friends quickly took notice and so did my parents. They demanded that I return at once, but not without objection. The accusations of falling in love with a mortal began to fall on deaf ears and soon I was confronted with an ultimatum. This set me on fire, causing rebellion followed by a confession that silenced even the mute.

Falling in love with a mortal was not exactly a goal or ambition that I strived to achieve, nonetheless I somehow managed to succeed in that department. It was a contradiction, like walking pneumonia. It had become *too dangerous* and *irresponsible* on my part. And they were right – I was stupid and cavalier but never regretted one minute that I spent with her.

I had no choice in the matter – my father is the chief to all five clans. His word is law and to defy him would mean that I would be turning my back on our beliefs and the citizens of our tribe.

"Pack your bags immediately and return to La Malbaie." Were the exact words my parents spoke to Clodia and I at three a.m. this morning when my heart was ripped out of my chest.

I wasn't surprised at the request and knew that it was inevitable because this had been the plan from the start, but it still hurt. Knowing that I had to leave half of myself behind wasn't making it any easier on me or anyone else for that matter.

The only available airfare at such late notice was scheduled to leave tomorrow at 6:00am, so I had roughly 24 hours to pack and hopefully see her one last time. The problem was that I didn't know what I was going to say to her. She was fully aware that I would eventually leave Pittsburgh and head back to Quebec to continue my education, but with the intent that we would remain friends and in constant communication.

This too was a lie. It was untrue for many reasons starting with the fact that she is my mortal enemy and we could never have any type of relationship. Not in this life or the next. I can't continue leading her in believing that. It's not fair to either of us therefore it must come to an end. I need to focus on my future for my tribe's sake.

Unable to sleep or concentrate on anything else, I immediately make plans to contact her at first light. But making the actual call proved to be the most difficult task yet as I'm hanging on by a thread over the receiver waiting for her to pick up. After four rings, she finally answers relieving me of my anxiety.

"Hello." A mellow tone greets me followed by a yawn.

"Hey, sleepy."

"Jovi." Her throaty voice sounds uneasy as she speaks my name. I hear shuffling on the other end of the receiver followed by a thud while I patiently wait for her to come around. "Are you ok?" She is suddenly alert and apprehensive.

"Yes, everything is fine." Delighted to hear her voice I stifle a smile that is forlorn.

"It's 6 o'clock in the morning."

"I know...I just...," I trail off for a few seconds and shake off any regrets that may have settled, "I'm sorry to wake you but I really needed to hear your voice."

"Do you want to come over?"

"No. No. That won't be necessary." I pause for a few additional seconds unsure how to broach the subject about ditching her friend for me. "Listen, I know that you have plans with Aemilia later this evening, but I wanted to know if there was any way you could cancel? I really need to speak with you about something rather important that cannot wait."

"Yes of course. What time did you want to meet?" Her concerned voice echoes into my throbbing ear.

"Around 7 this evening."

"Where?"

"Anywhere you'd like so long as we are together." The break in my voice makes me sound weary and desolate which was unexpected on my part.

"Are you sure everything is ok? You don't seem to be yourself."

"I just really need to see you that's all." I sigh with a hint of longing.

"Ok. How about we meet at Jack's Bar on Carson Street?"

"That sounds perfect."

"See you tonight then?"

"Yes."

The line goes dead as I hit the end button on the cell and swiftly throw it onto my bed. Pacing around the room like a mad man I begin to wonder how I got myself in this situation to begin with. It's amusing how I actually think that I have a choice in the matter.

I remember a time when I would have jumped at the idea of leaving this dreadful place. But now, after meeting her I can honestly say that I don't want to leave because if I do then I will be forced to face my worst fear. The fear that I am too weak to continue this perilous journey without her. I have somehow managed to keep a platonic relationship with Simone although I've always wanted more.

Quickly jumping into survivor mode, I attempt to justify my heartless actions that will soon follow. Who am I fooling here? Open your eyes. This idea of us being together is not logical because we currently live in a world full of hatred and deceit. Mortals have no respect for one another let alone for a different species that they don't understand. Their hearts are full of greed. They are only concerned with their own wellbeing therefore our species cannot coexist as we do not share the same values.

Detaching the adverse judgments from my thoughts I begin packing my clothes for our departure and allow my mind to wander into unknown territory as I dwell on tonight.

*****

Its twenty minutes after seven and Simone has not made an appearance. I've been sitting at the bar with an empty glass of water waiting for her arrival. Several regulars have started to pour in, filling the place with laughter while alternative rock gushes from the jukebox. Two unoccupied pool tables are located to the far left of the room surrounded by backless bar stools.

The mahogany countertop behind the bar is filled with countless rows of clear and dark liquor bottles that are waiting to be used. A string of colorful heart shaped sticky notes with handwritten compliments dangle just above the cash register. Several advertisements and drink specials are plastered on the wall, radiating a welcoming atmosphere.

The bartender comes over again, checking to see if I'm ready to order, but I quickly dismissed him with a friendly nod and hand jester. I'm starting to get nervous as I wipe my clammy palms on my blue jeans. My mind begins to speculate whether I've made the right decision to see her one last time. And I haven't decided whether I'm going to be honest or deceptive.

Taking in measured breaths I feel my heartbeat slow down to a normal rhythm when I suddenly hear the door open from behind me. A sweet lovely aroma instantly fills my nostrils and blinds me to the core.

The once strong and courageous male is suddenly the pawn piece in her chess game. Weak. Restricted. And at her disposal. This body is no longer my own as it eagerly obeys unspoken demands and effortlessly makes its way over to her. She catches sight of me, and I watch as her eyes light up with joy causing her lips to curve into that beautiful smile. My mind is suddenly clear with determination as I open my arms, welcoming her touch. Within seconds she is encased in my embrace. I can feel the warmth of her breath on my neck as she whispers into my ear causing the hairs on my arms to elevate.

"I'm sorry, I lost track of time."

Her elegant soft-spoken words are delivered with such persuasion that even an immortal wouldn't be able to escape her hypnotic commands. Carefully pulling her away from my chest, I look into her eyes and caress her cheeks with both of my hands, comforting any doubts that may have settled.

"It's ok, just glad you made it. Come."

Grabbing her hand and entwining her fingers with mine we begin to make our way to the bar where I was previously settled. I encourage her to take a seat as I motion towards the vacant barstool beside me.

"What would you like to drink?" She removes her dark green sweater and drapes it over the backrest of the barstool then moves over to sit on the seat.

"What were you drinking?"

"Something very boring that I'm sure you want no part of."

I quickly lift the half empty glass to her nose and allow the bland scent to overpower her sense of smell. She smiles and shakes her head while swatting away the glass.

"Uh, just a coke please." Flagging down the bartender I quickly place an order for a soft drink and a bud light.

"So, tell me. Why were you late?"

I turn my attention to her as we begin to engage in casual conversation hoping to distract my mind from the impending news that I'm forced to deliver.

"I have an exam tomorrow, so I got caught up studying when I finally noticed the time and got here as fast as I could."

She then reaches for her hair with both hands and moves it to the side of her face. I find myself distracted and unable to concentrate as my eyes begin to wonder onto her lips. Within a matter of seconds, she waves her hand in front of me and interrupts my daze.

"Hey, you ok?"

"Yes of course. So, was Aemilia upset that you cancelled your plans with her?"

"Surprisingly, no. I told her that I had to study for an exam tomorrow, which was not exactly a lie." She giggles with enthusiasm.

The bartender arrives with our drinks and hands them to us with a napkin wrapped around the beer bottle. I acknowledge his presence with a friendly grin and turn my attention back to her.

"What exam were you studying for?"

"Calculus."

"Think you'll pass?" My huge grin and wrinkled nose are hard to conceal. She quickly takes notice of my humorous banter and decides to play along.

"Definitely pass." She shoves my arms with her hands and begins to laugh. "Shouldn't you be conveying words of encouragement and not uncertainty?"

"You see, that's where you're wrong. I never doubted you for a second." Her dimples are briefly revealed as she breaks away from our contact and takes a drink of her coke. "What can I say, you're a special girl." I shrug both of my shoulders while taking a swig of my drink.

"Oh yeah? How so?" She carefully narrows her eyes at me and crosses her arms around her chest.

"You're intelligent, witty and beautiful. I could go on and on but there aren't enough hours in the day."

"Wow." Shaking her head out of amusement and disapproval, she rests one of her arms on the bar and the other balled up against her cheek. "Is that how you sweep women off their feet?"

"Are you telling me that it didn't work?"

"You weren't even close. Besides, I'm too smart for that." Her eyebrows arch upward, signaling that she isn't impressed with my advances.

Laughing and taking another drink of my beer I respond with sarcasm.

"Well then, I shall work to improve my skills and win you over."

"Jovi, you don't have to try hard with me."

"I strongly disagree. I have quite the competition with all the gentlemen lined up waiting to whisk you away."

"Yeah, right! Where are these so-called *gentlemen* and why haven't I seen them?" She air quotes the word gentlemen and rolls her eyes.

"You really are oblivious, aren't you?"

"Oblivious to what?"

"To your charm and... all the males throwing themselves at you." I utter the last part of that statement with a mild undertone because it hurts to admit that I'm not the only one that has fallen head over heels for her.

"Name one."

"Franco."

"Franco hardly counts. He is Ethan's friend and knows that I don't feel that way about him."

"Trust me, Franco wishes he was in my shoes right now. What he would do to have a fraction of your attention."

"Sounds like someone is jeal-ous!" She singsongs the last word and begins to laugh.

"Of course I am. Do you know how hard I've worked to try and capture his attention and all along he has been chasing you."

Swiping at my teasing hand she chuckles, "Stop it," and then bursts into laughter as I join in. After a few moments, her mood changes and becomes somber. It catches me by surprise because I wasn't expecting the conversation to take such a critical turn in a short period of time.

"Well, it doesn't make a difference."

"And why is that?"

"Because I hardly notice him or anyone for that matter." She starts to fidget with the seam of her gray t-shirt while looking down at the floor. "I only have eyes for one and he isn't captivated by my charm as you would think."

Suddenly I find myself in a grim state because I know that she is referring to me. Unsure how to refute her candid words, I quickly turn the tables and counter her statement.

"How do you know? You've never taken the time to put yourself out there."

"What does that mean?"

"It means that your head is either buried in books or you're too busy spending time with me. I'm sure whomever this lucky gentleman is, he's probably under the impression that you are not interested."

Her head slowly rises as she meets my gaze. She remains silent for a few moments as our eyes stay locked onto one another.

My breathing becomes urgent as I silently beg for her to tame the beast inside of me. The connection is mutual and undeniable. Our minds are fused into one and I know that this can go whichever way I'd like. In an instant, she could be mine and I hers without a doubt. Should I confess my love, give in to her demands and leave it up to fate or should I do what is expected of me for my tribe's sake? Funny thing is that I already know the answer to my own question.

Without hesitation, a measured and striking smile forms on her lips as she chooses her words carefully.

"You know what?"

"What?"

"For once I think you're right."

My voice is hoarse as I begin to stammer and find myself lost for words. "I ...I am?"

"Yes, you are. I haven't been attentive or available as I should be. The next time I see him I will be sure to show him just how much he means to me."

And on that declaration, I swallow. Hard. My desire to be with her is so overbearing that I'm unable to conceal it. Keep it together Jovianus. Don't cave. You know what you must do.

Breaking eye contact I swiftly turn my body towards the bartender and order another beer. As we are waiting, I stay silent, lost in thought and torn between what decision I should make. Her stare is burning a hole right through my left arm and I cannot find the courage nor strength to break her heart because it will also break mine.

As the bartender brings my drink, I decide that I must end this playful mood of ours no matter the price. I can tell that this abrupt request is eating at her curiosity and that I won't be able to prolong the news forever. It's settled then – it's now or never.

"Jovi, are you sure everything is ok?" She places one of her hands on my shoulders, sending shivers down my spine. I carefully move my beer bottle to the side as I turn my body to face her and clasp her hands in between mine.

"Simone." My voice is a dejected murmur that I hardly recognize.

"Yes." She responds almost instantly.

As I try to open my mouth and launch into a prepared speech about how much I love her and that we should run away together, my words fail at the attempt. I feel defeated as my head hangs low from both guilt and sorrow. Sensing that I have a troubled mind she removes one of her hands from my grasp and sets it on my face, cradling my cheek with her palm. This is something we did often to each other; providing comfort and ease whenever requested.

Slowly lifting my head, I place my free hand over hers, close my eyes and cherish our final moments together. After a few seconds, I open my eyes and slowly move our hands down onto my lap as I attempt to explain.

"I requested that we meet today because I have something important to tell you."

Our eyes are locked on one another with such intensity that I can sense the anxiety radiating from her form.

"Ok." Her voice is but a mutter as she speaks this word with caution.

The space between us is filled with silence while I compete with my former self, the good and the bad, between light and darkness.

I knew that this would be the hardest decision that I ever had to make and was sure to regret. Loving her recklessly hasn't exactly had a positive impact in my life. I had finally found what everyone spends their entire life searching for and now I am forced to set it free, removing that blindfold of ecstasy. Whatever this is, it felt real and I didn't want it to end but I've learned that sometimes love isn't enough... even if that love is reciprocated. There is no happy ending to this, no matter which way I try to turn it.

"Jovi, there isn't anything you can say that will change the way I feel about you." Her expression is hopeless as she squeezes my hand, attempting to boost my confidence.

My happiness is quickly replaced with anger followed by annoyance. I'm angry because I can't have her. Irritated for allowing myself to fall for a mortal. Enraged because despite everything that I've done, I will never be able to live my life the way I intended as my future has already been dictated by my tribe.

The darkness slowly begins to creep its way up and rises above the inner battle as the light starts to fade. It is diverting me towards the path that will least likely exploit my vulnerabilities which is a sign of weakness that a future leader cannot afford. Feeble and defenseless. That is exactly what I am when I'm in her presence and I must put an end to it. Love is a deception of the mind, nothing more. I repeat this mantra to myself over and over until it is embedded into my brain.

My mood suddenly shifts course and too soon I am confronted with the fury that continues to loom inside me. Heat begins to course through my veins as I become aware that I've lost control of my own emotions. I'm furious for more reasons that I can count as I begin to question the true meaning of love.

Why are we allowed to long for something that was never meant to be ours? At this point I don't even fight it, instead I welcome it and allow the darkness to consume me.

"Jovi?" She shakes my knee, bringing me back to reality. Dropping her hands from my lap I try my best to sound convincing as possible and avoid eye contact as I turn my head to the side.

"Simone, I'm not who you think I am."

"What?" Her eyebrows immediately crease downward and hover just above her eyelids.

"I've been lying to you since the first day we met."

"What are you talking about?" She shakes her head out of confusion.

"I'm talking about..."

My words trail off as I briefly close my eyes and try to regain control of my emotions but fail at the attempt when I realize that the light is no longer within reach.

Seconds later I open them and meet her gaze with full force, unable to make this any less painful.

"You have no idea what I am or have become!" I blurt the words out faster than the wind can carry them.

My anger is armed, ready to unleash its wrath and destroy anything in its path.

"Jovi, I know you better than anyone." She attempts to reach for my hands but stops when I flinch at her touch.

"No, you don't! You only know what I chose to tell you." My voice is full of emotion mixed with fury and deceit.

"I don't understand where this is coming from. Did I do something wrong?" She becomes frantic as doubt settles in. Quickly avoiding eye contact I focus on a picture behind her on the far wall.

"I have certain obligations that I've been running away from my whole life of which I must now face. I've been distracted for the past year and now... now it's time for me to fulfill these responsibilities." My voice is harsh and emotionless but straight to the point.

"Are you saying, that, that I've been a distraction to you?"

Uncertainty has crossed her mind as she moves further back into her seat, shocked at my outburst.

"Yes." The word leaves my lips before I even had a chance to retract it.

Tears begin to form in her eyes as the poisonous statement sinks in. I quickly become aware that her wounded heart is not the only injury I've caused tonight but that doesn't stop me from asserting the devastating confession.

"You've been weighing me down this whole time. I've...I've been blind to the fact that I'm selfish and I don't have room for anyone else in my life. I can't do this anymore and I'm here to tell you just that."

Malevolence radiates from this declaration with no remorse whatsoever as rage begins to bolster my self-confidence. My chest is frantically moving up and down from the adrenaline that is pumping through my veins.

"What has gotten into you? Is this some kind of sick joke?"

She attempts one final plea as scathing tears stream down her cheeks and onto her lips. I return my gaze back to her face and deliver the damaging statement that will free us both from this haunting encounter.

"Let's face it, we have both been holding onto something that never was, nor could be. This," I motion between us, "Whatever we thought we had, it isn't real. It's time that we both accept the truth and move on with our lives."

Silence fills the air as I continue to deliver this ill-fated curse. "I'm leaving tomorrow morning and I will not be returning so its best if we just part ways forever."

The heartless Jovianus has resurfaced; I have transformed into the mighty spiteful warrior once again. A lost soul that has no regard for anyone other than himself. I've reached the point of no return and the feeling is vigorous! My odium is impenetrable like a bullet proof vest. Power and dominance feeds' my ego while I revel in the aftermath. I feel like the worst part is over, however, I am vaguely unaware that it has just begun when her tears are replaced with resentment. She quickly transforms into someone I no longer recognize and catches me by surprise when her menacing tone snaps me back to reality.

"Oh really! So, that fatuous speech about putting myself out there was a lie?" She straightens up in her seat and slowly begins to inch closer to me without ever breaking eye contact. "You sit here and tell me that I'm oblivious to my charm but the only ignorant one here is you. Don't you see it?"

Her haunting stare and gravely tone are full of fury as she continues to deliver blow after blow. I feel stupefied and puzzled, unaware that she is slowly breaching the barriers to my heart that I have carefully built to protect myself from feeling any emotions.

"I'm not interested in anyone else because I only have eyes for you. You're the one who I've been longing for this whole time. I've been patiently waiting for you to notice me but now I see that this wasn't the case after all!"

I'm not even sure she is aware of her sudden mood change as she unleashes her own personal mayhem. In the twelve months that I've known her, she has never shown any signs of aggression or anger. My foul mood begins to diminish, and it is somehow replaced with regret.

I don't understand what is happening to me as I begin to plead, "Simone, please hear me out."

She quickly shuts me down by lifting the palm of her hand to my face.

"Don't. You've said enough, and I heard you loud and clear. You want nothing more to do with me, so I'll make this as simple as possible and relieve you of your distraction."

Without another word, she gets up, grabs her sweater and storms out of the bar.

I helplessly watch as she disappears through the exit door and out of my life. To distract myself, I turn my attention back to the bartender, who is filling a glass with bourbon and coke for the drunk male that is sitting next to me. Grabbing the half empty bottle, I take a long drink and slam it onto the counter. Breathing heavily through my nose I attempt to justify my brute actions but the images of Simone in tears somehow overcome my senses and I quickly begin to struggle with my alternative personality once more.

I cannot allow my vulnerabilities to consume me if I am to become the ruler of our people. I try chanting the words that previously freed me from this unnecessary agony. Love is a deception of the mind, nothing more. Love is a deception of the mind, nothing more.

But to my dismay it doesn't work. I make one final attempt to erase this self-reproach that has started to build, but the pain is far too great. Pain that will not go away in a matter of days, months, or years because this pain originates from something beyond measure. Love. Love that I've been deprived of my entire life because the world cannot accept us as we are.

I've lost my inner battle and the light has won over darkness once more. At last, my true nature has revealed itself. Finally accepting the fact that I am madly in love with Simone, I come to terms that these feelings can no longer be suppressed.

Not accepting the fact that I've messed things up for us, I gather my wits and muster the courage to confront my fears head on. Grabbing cash from my wallet I rush to pay our tab and dash outside. As I begin scanning the street for any signs of her, I soon come to realize that she is really gone. This is what I wanted, isn't it?

Chapter Eight

~Conception~

I'm not giving up! This isn't over, not like this. Jogging to my car that is parked across the street I swiftly retrieve the keys from the pocket of my jeans and crank it to life. Reversing out of the parking space with urgency and into the main road, I head towards Bloomfield hoping that she went straight home and not to Aemilia's.

Every passing minute seems like an hour as I become overly anxious to see her again. I don't even bother turning on the radio as I welcome the silence trusting that it will clear my mind. The only sound piercing my ears are the occasional buzzing of the traffic lights that I continue to run into.

Regret suddenly settles into my mind and too soon I am confronted with bitterness. This rage is geared more towards myself. How do I always manage to screw things up? I should have gone with my instincts and comforted any qualms she had the moment they left her lips. It pains me to know that I am responsible for making her cry, something I promised her and myself that I would never do.

After about fifteen minutes of driving I arrive at Simone's home. My heart is rapidly palpitating as my vehicle pulls into the gravel driveway right behind her 4-runner. I notice a dim candle burning on a window seal from the side of the house. The kitchen lights are on and I can sense movement, confirming that the house is occupied. This is definitely good news, but now I must face a new challenge. The challenge of getting her to open the door and allowing me to explain.

Impatiently yanking on the handle, I rush out of the vehicle and don't bother to close the door. A sense of urgency guides my feet over the spiral stone path and lands me at the entrance within a millisecond.

With one mission in mind, I lift my fist to the door, knock three times and take a few steps back. I wait a few moments for the door to open but quickly become anxious and decide to use the doorbell, just in case.

To my right I see white sheer curtains sway behind the huge square window. Feather like footsteps approach and the door slightly creaks open with Simone's body blocking the entry.

"What do you want?" She blurts out with a stern and bleak tone. Her eyes are puffy from weeping, but it doesn't stop her from delivering the ill-mannered question.

"Can I please come in for a second?" My request is nothing short of a depressing plead.

"No!" She exclaims and attempts to close the door, but I swiftly place my hand in the way and halt the humiliation.

"Please Simone." I begin to beg because I have nothing left and I wouldn't know what to do with myself if she doesn't forgive me.

"Haven't you tortured me enough today?" Her nose is runny as she attempts to swipe it with the back of her hand.

"I didn't mean to hurt you. Please let me in so that I can explain. I promise it will be brief and then you never have to see me again."

She doesn't seem convinced, but she also hasn't tried to close the door in my face again. I attempt one final plea before giving up. "I only have a few hours before my flight departs and I won't be able to rest knowing that we left things unsettled. I'll beg if that's what it takes."

My voice breaks on the last sentence while I struggle to keep my emotions together and avoid further heartache. No words escape her lips as her gaze slowly leaves mine and my face is greeted with a wooden door.

This time I don't fight it, instead I just stand there on the entryway, sulking. It's all my fault and I have no one to blame but myself. I continue to stand in front of the entrance, just staring at the carved wood door for who knows how long. Finally, just as I am about to turn around and walk down the sidewalk, I hear the door creak open and she reappears wearing the green sweater from earlier.

A relief of stillness washes over me as she steps aside, and I carefully walk through the entrance and into the foyer. I hear the door close and lock behind me while I skim my surroundings.

Slowly turning around, I find her standing to the far right of the wall with her arms crossed over her chest. Once again, I find myself misplaced as I begin to fumble with the seam of my own shirt. After a few moments, she is the first one to speak and break our stroppy silence.

"Why are you here Jovianus?" My name rolls off her tongue like it's a curse while she emphasizes every letter. She remains cautious and watchful while trying to maintain a calm and collected tone.

"I… I came to apologize." My gaze is locked onto hers, observing her every move hoping she doesn't ask me to leave.

"For what? For being honest? Apology accepted. You can be on your way now."

Shifting her body away from the wall she begins making her way towards the front door. I'm speechless and begin questioning her motives as well as my own. So, instead of cowering and giving in to her demands, I take a stand and go with my instincts.

"No!" I shout with just enough authority that will cause her to hesitate and buy me more time. Time that I don't have as it continues to trickle by like the sand of an hourglass.

"No?" She phrases this one word with such sarcasm that it wounds me more than

I knew it could. I know she is beyond upset and she has every right to be, so I try my best to remain controlled as she continues to lash out.

"That's the problem, I wasn't being honest."

"And you're going to be honest with me now?"

"Yes."

"Why? Because you saw me cry and feel remorseful?"

"That's not why I am here?"

"Then why are you here?"

"Can you please stop and let me speak!" My voice is loud with a shrill edge to it that stops her in her tracks as I finally had enough of her ridicule.

I know it's my fault, but I'll be damned if she doesn't hear what I have to say. Giving myself a few moments to calm down, I proceed to concentrate on her reaction and make sure that I'm safe to continue while choosing my words carefully.

She just stands there, a few feet from the front door shocked at my outburst. Simone has never witnessed this side of me and as much as I despise my second half, I know that he will be the only one who can restore my confidence at this very moment. I begin to slowly pace back and forth in the foyer while I summon the courage to speak. She just stands there, good natured, and willing, probably out of curiosity.

After confirming that I have no idea what I am doing, I decide to leave this moment to fate. The only way to get through this is to speak from the heart. No more prepared speeches or useless ideas that will jeopardize my relationship with her again. Screw it. Here it goes. I stop pacing and warily turn around to face the mortal that has brought me to my knees.

"I want you to know that you are wrong."

Her voice is soft and calm as she studies my face in search of sincerity. "About what?"

I place all my cards on the table and slowly advance, making every step count as I pronounce each delicate word clearly.

"I'm not only captivated by your charm, but I am also taken aback by your worthiness."

As I speak the last word, I have somehow managed to close the distance that has kept us apart since my arrival. My heart begins to race as wild thoughts inhibit my mind and I silently vow not to hold back any emotional or physical contact. I'm all in, and there's no turning back.

"What?" A whisper of misperception escapes her lips. Puzzled and intrigued at my statement she remains absorbed by my words.

"I wasn't lying when I said that I thought you were intelligent, witty and beautiful. And yes, we have both been oblivious to what others perceive us to be, including each other's perception, however, I will no longer shy away from my feelings towards you."

She remains silent and focused as shock settles in from my confession. Her light breathing causes her mouth to slightly part, pushing me over the edge. Now that I have her attention, I continue to pour my heart out and profess my love to her.

"You have made me question everything that I've ever known to be true. Things that I never thought possible and out of reach have resurfaced from underneath the rubble of my own ruin. From the first time that our eyes met in Benedum Hall up until this very moment, it has been an exciting journey. One that I will treasure forever and will truly miss."

"What are you saying?" Her voice is but a murmur, a mild breeze in the wind.

"I'm saying that since the first time I laid my eyes on you, I knew that you were the one for me. I don't know how or why, but I knew that I wanted you to be mine. I have tried to fight it every day since, but I found that the more I fought these feelings the more I wanted them to be true. I was instantly drawn to you for reasons unknown and that cannot be explained, and I haven't been able to stop thinking about you."

Taking a final step forward, I carefully reach out and place the palm of my hand at the base of her throat while pulling her face inches from mine. "The truth is, I don't think I ever will." Pausing for a few moments I allow my words to sink into her thoughts before I reveal the final phrase that will free us both. "Simone, I am in love with you."

Her breathing becomes urgent as does my own. She slowly begins to shake her head and takes a step back in denial.

"Why have you decided to tell me this now?"

"Because I finally chose to listen to my heart instead of my head. I thought that by hurting you it would be easier for me to leave, but it turned out to be hazardous for us both."

I reach for her hand and to my surprise she willingly surrenders her grip. With our eyes affixed onto one another, I intertwine my fingers with hers and slowly raise my free hand to her face. I then begin tracing her lower mouth with my fingertips. She gently closes her eyes as her lips part and welcomes my touch. Our breathing quickens, and I soon realize that I am reluctant and unable to stop my advances.

"You see, I only have eyes for you too and have also been longing for your touch. It's been you all along. I've been a fool this whole time but refuse to continue being one."

Releasing our grip, my hand gently wraps around her lower waist as I pull her body into my chest. Her eyes remain closed and I find myself eager to taste what she so willingly offers. Carefully pulling her face towards mine, I kiss her gently at first and then feverishly. With each passing second, our demand increases, taking us to a place of ecstasy. Our mouths are relentless and unwavering as they nibble and pull. My mouth suddenly breaks contact and moves to her neck, kissing her ear lobe to her throat.

A low tantalizing moan escapes from her mouth as my hands slides underneath her sweater and they begin to explore her back. I then move my mouth back to hers and allow her lips to possess mine once more.

Without thinking, I reach for the zipper to her sweater and gently pull it downwards revealing her gray t-shirt. Unsure if I've gone too far, I don't remove it from her shoulders as I continue to kiss her, unable to stop myself. The desire to be with her has become extremely agonizing. Unable to hold back I swiftly lift her off the floor and cradle her small frame into my arms. Our mouths never break apart as the amplified kiss deepens.

Without my knowledge, we have somehow ended up in her bedroom. The room is dark and quiet with only the sounds of our heavy breathing to fill the silence. Placing her down, she slowly slides out of my grip and attempts to remove her sweater when I halt her advances. She seems a bit confused but before any suspicions could settle, I clarify my intentions.

"I want you to know that I am leaving in a few hours, and I'm not sure if or when I will return."

"Are you having second thoughts?"

"Never. Not with you. I just want you to be sure, that's all."

"Jovi, I've never been more certain about anything in my life than this moment right now."

As I retract my hand, I witness her sweater slowly slide off her shoulders and land onto the floor. Several weightless thuds begin to sound and before I know it, we are both bare. The light from outside bounces off her bronze skin causing her outer core to shine bright like that of a star. Unlike humans our vision is sharper at night, allowing me to observe every feature of her body.

I'm completely captivated by her beauty as those striking hazel eyes bore directly into mine. Her stare is full of ache and yearning which mirrors my own. No longer able to contain the helpless beast inside of me, I cautiously move forward and place my rough hands on her waist.

As our bodies become one, we quickly become lost in this moment that is burning with desire. Our breathing only intensifies, and it becomes evident that our love is perpetual.

It's 2:00am, and Simone's head remains resting on my chest. I know that I will have to leave soon and that I'm unable to escape it. My phone has not stopped buzzing since my arrival as it continues to vibrate on the floor. I don't bother to answer it because I already know who it is. As I attempt to move, I am instantly immobilized by her lips and become lost in the moment.

Another thirty minutes' pass when I finally muster the courage to speak.

"My flight leaves in about three hours and I have to be at the airport in two."

With her eyes still closed she mumbles, "Mmmm, I know. I just want to feel the warmth of your body for a few more minutes."

Slowly turning my frame towards her, I kiss her mouth tenderly and snuggle my face into her hair while drawing light circles on her back with my fingertips.

Her arms instantly wrap around my torso when I whisper, "Me too."

After a few minutes, I hesitantly pull away while she settles on the pillow beside me. Walking over to the restroom, I proceed to take a quick shower and change. Approaching the bed, I find her fast asleep. As I'm sitting there admiring her solace, I come to realization that I have not only jeopardized and possibly forfeited my life, but hers as well.

What have I done? How could I have been so selfish and irresponsible? I can't risk this tattered secret with anyone, not even Simone. Knowing what I must do I tenderly caress her cheek with my index finger, stirring her from a peaceful dream.

"Hey beautiful."

She begins to stretch and murmurs, "Jovi," while attempting to get out of bed.

"No, don't get up. I just wanted to inform you that I have to leave now."

Her groggy voice is barely audible as she shifts about under the sheets. "I will miss you more than you will ever know."

Moving a lost strand of hair from her face, I touch my forehead to hers and utter, "I will always be with you." I then place my hand on her chest right above her heart. "In here."

She then smiles, closes her eyes, and whispers the most bizarre thing.

"I don't know how or when, but you will come back to me."

I'm surprised by her statement as she calmly goes back to sleep. Gently placing my hand over her head, I summon the words that will liberate her mind from tonight's event, erasing all traces of our encounter.

In that moment, I realize that I've lost a part of my soul, and I'll never be whole again.

Chapter Nine

~Incubus~
Four Years Later............

For as long as I can remember, I've continuously struggled to identify who I am as an individual. I've always felt like I didn't belong, as if a part of me was missing and with each passing minute I was slowly fading away. Losing a piece of myself until the day would come when I would finally cease to exist as I helplessly watched from afar.

My mind feels distant and misplaced; unable to distinguish the difference between fact and fiction. It didn't help that I had no resemblance to either of my parents. I'm sure I looked awkward to outsiders as they stared at a dark-haired girl with hazel eyes and freckles that stood out against a bronze complexion, whereas my parents were both blondes, blue eyed with olive skin.

My mother always told me that I looked a lot like my aunt, whom I've never met for reasons unknown.

When I would ask questions that were probably a bit pressing, my parents would change the subject to avoid answering them. But I never lacked affection by either of them. No. It was the exact opposite.

They loved me unconditionally and supported every decision I made no matter how crazy they thought it was, but something still felt off. Like everyone around me was in on a dirty little secret that I wasn't privileged to.

And then came the dreams, strange and enigmatic, like flightless animals falling from the sky or an upward lightning strike. Most of the time I couldn't even recall what the dream was about, however, I do remember that they felt real.

As time passed, I learned to cope and deal with the snippets that my imagination created from these dreams. But after my parents passing, they became more intense and puzzling. A constant reminder that I wasn't alone and that maybe, just maybe there was more to my life than the one I had been living.

Is it possible for an individual to have been reincarnated from a past life with no recollection of their former self? Or could these visions be a figment of my own imagination? Yes, I absolutely think that either of these concepts are a possibility.

But the dreams never stopped, and today only proves that my subconscious remains at odds with its own thoughts. Because as I lay consciously asleep, my mind continues with its wicked torment that seeks no end to this incubus. I have not discovered how to awaken from this brute nightmare as my skin crawls with this infectious plague that is eating me from the inside out. I'm slowly being buried alive while my former self witnesses as I submerge beneath the shame.

Blinded by my core existence, I'm fully aware that darkness is about to take over again. Renounce and surrender consumes' my thoughts as I have become dependent to this despair. My mind and body are both drained from this unspoken battle and I no longer have the strength to continue fighting. Focusing my thoughts on my son, I push every other quarrel aside and seek for tranquility. Within an instant I'm surrounded by total darkness and everything has finally gone silent.

Not sure how long I lay frozen in silence when a small gust of light appears from afar and jolts me back to life. Small specks bursting with blue flames fill the empty space of my confinement. A dim light, pale as the moon appears from a distance as a humid breeze slowly passes over my skin.

Without warning I vaguely hear a faint voice whisper my name, "Simone."

I turn to face the dull light and a woman clothed in a colorless robe appears. She continues to walk in my direction and the beam gets brighter and brighter as she approaches. I feel safe and protected for reasons unknown; puzzled that she seems all too familiar.

A measured smile forms on her lips as she places her hand on my chest and speaks.

"Remember. It is time. You must save him," she commands with clarity.

I don't know how, but I understood what she instructed me to do.

Then out of nowhere my whole frame starts to shake uncontrollably causing my head to tilt backwards. My eyes roll behind their sockets as an electric current begins coursing throughout my body, paving a path to restoration. Tiny flecks of blue lights are flowing all around us, lifting me into midair. My head, limbs and torso continue to convulse over and over while I'm suspended above the ground. Shaken, trampled and lifeless I lay, waiting for this torment to end.

A depleted voice then murmurs into my ear with forced pronunciation, "Embrace it."

Concentrate I think to myself. It will all be over soon so stop fighting it. As I relinquish my conflicts with this encounter and close my weary eyes, peace begins to consume me. My breathing slows down as I steady my heart to measured beats. I'm suddenly filled with strength and purpose as a power far greater than any form I've ever felt blossoms within me.

The convulsions quickly end, and I'm lowered back onto the ground. The woman in the colorless robe retrieves her hand from my chest, smiles and swiftly disappears. Bright lights beam from where she once stood, like a dying star, imploding its gravitational collapse. I'm suddenly brought back from the darkness that once swallowed my existence and emerge from my state of sleep.

Sensing a presence of some sort, I manage to open my eyes when my skin is greeted with a light chilly breeze. I can feel someone or something staring in my direction which is difficult to ignore. Distraught by this notion, I turn my head towards the gaze that has all the tiny hairs on my arms sticking up.

Focusing my vision, I see a tall dark silhouette hovering just a few feet from my son's sleeping body, watching, waiting, with one arm extended as if to touch him.

I blink my eyes several times to clear the haze that clouds my sight. Then I realize that there is an intruder in my bedroom, in the middle of the night within a few feet from my child. Frightened, my first reaction is to scream at the top of my lungs in hopes that the earsplitting sound will scare whatever is here. I'm expecting a thunderous and menacing tone; but instead I'm greeted with more silence. Feeling confused I make another attempt to shout, my lips struggling to form words that are not there, but quickly confirm that I have no voice.

I attempt to sit up, but my arms are limp, being held down by some invisible restrains as I strive to yank free. Panic settles in when I try kicking my feet and the blanket doesn't move an inch. It feels as if I've been purposely paralyzed. And to make matters worse, the dark shadow cannot hear or see me. Its gaze is solely focused on my helpless little boy and it appears to be getting closer and closer by the minute.

What is happening to me? Why can't I move and what is holding me down? I immediately start to freak out and begin to feel heat consume my body once more. My stomach aches of fear as I watch this horrific scene play before me. This shadow grows closer by the second. It is practically in my sons face now, studying his traits while swaying its head from side to side.

I move my gaze from the spectator and settle my eyes on my son. He is resting, mouth still open and eyes shut, fluttering from a beautiful dream. Then out of nowhere, Mateo smiles tentatively as if someone has made a vow that will be fulfilled sooner rather than later.

There are no voices coming from this stranger that now stands one foot from the bed. The only sound I can hear is a loud ringing noise beaming through my ears as if a bomb exploded and damaged my eardrums. As my eyes proceed to roll towards the back of my head, the room begins to spin uncontrollably. Maybe I should close my eyes in hopes that this is a delusion, a ruse that my mind is playing on me. But then I come to realization that this, whatever *this is*, is possibly not a dream but perhaps real, horror quickly settles in.

Too many questions are running through my mind that I cannot think or focus on the task at hand. How do I capture the attention of this intruder and get him away from my baby boy? What does it want from us? And why can it not hear nor see me?

Then all of a sudden, a surge of adrenaline kicks in as I gather all my strength and fears and place them deep in the pit of my stomach, hoping to gain will power. It all happened so fast that I didn't know what I was doing. Biting down hard, I start yelling at the top of my lungs while tugging against the invisible restrains and finally manage to free myself.

Liberated, I immediately shove the covers from my chest and anxiously claw my way to my son. Without thinking, I growl at the figure before me and bellow,

"Get the fuck away from him!"

The dark shadow swiftly turns in my direction and takes one step back, startled at my outburst. My next move is critical; unsure if it is here to harm us, I know that I cannot take any chances and must appear fearless in order to ensure our safety. So, as I stare at the empty space between us, I begin to wonder what *it* is going to do next and notice that its features are masked by the night, no details to give away its identity. There is no face as my vision remains clouded by a veil of some sort. This presence radiates evil and its body language is shouting *danger,* but my anger does not allow me to become threaten by this prowler. It does the exact opposite.

Taking a deep breath and balling my hands into fist, I slowly move closer to Mateo all while never taking my gaze away from the intruder's form. It doesn't move an inch and instead continues lurking as if waiting for an opportunity to seize him. I slowly place one of my fists over my son's body while leaving the other hand free, ready to attack if needed.

Hovering over his sleeping silhouette, I expose my teeth and snarl as if I were a lioness protecting its cub, "I said get the fuck away from him!"

Alarmed, the imposter takes a few steps back and it stumbles on something which almost causes it to trip. Meanwhile, it inadvertently placed its figure in front of the beam shining through my blinds. I'm now able to see features of a male as his eyebrows are creased downward from either anger or uncertainty. His lips are tight and set in a brim line with high cheekbones and eyes as light as the ocean sand which seems distant and cold.

Not taking any more chances, I instantly start swinging my fist into midair hoping to land a punch while displaying dominance. With my lips curled back and my teeth clenched together, I claim my position in a low and patronizing voice.

"He is mine, not yours, mine! Do you hear me?"

In an instant, the male figure realizes that I have caught a glimpse of his face and then everything vanishes. Gone, just like that and I find myself surrounded by darkness once again.

Abruptly stirring from my state of sleep, I open my eyes to a quiet room with beads of sweat on my forehead. My body automatically sits up and my eyes start to wonder off into the night. The air feels awfully warm in my room although its 52 degrees outside. My throat begins to feel strained, like I had been screaming or yelling as I reach for my neck.

I'm no longer covered by my quilt as I sit motionless on top of my covers wondering why I am awake at this hour. That's odd, I'm almost certain that I covered myself when I went to bed. Within seconds, the haunting details from my nightmare begin to replay over and over in my head. While my body is trying to catch up with what my brain is still sharing, I look over to see my son in the identical pajamas and in the same position as my traumatic dream. I start to freak out and scramble over to Mateo, placing my shaky hand on his chest to confirm that he is still breathing.

His heart is pounding rapidly, like the wings of a hummingbird. I just sit there, staring at his face and trace his perfect features with my eyes. Feeling content that his lungs are still pumping air through his body, I hastily move to the right of the bed and turn on the table lamp.

The bedroom is now illuminated by a dim light as my eyes begin to adjust to the faint brightness. I immediately begin to explore my surroundings, searching for anything that might be out of place. My sight only reaches so far, therefore I'm not able to thoroughly inspect the entire room from my current position and decide to investigate further.

Jumping off my bed, I slowly walk over to the spot where I dreamt of the prowler. Not sure what I expected to find and what to search for, but I don't see anything out of the ordinary. I then move my gaze towards the two large window panels and verify that they both remain locked with screens intact. No forced entry there, huh that's weird, but then something on the floor catches my eye to the far left.

My house slippers and sweatpants are now sprawled in different directions leading towards the window by Mateo. My adrenaline spikes two notches as I continue to stare at the motionless articles on the floor.

Why are my belongings out of place? I notice that the lock on my door remains fastened. Confused and flustered I quickly return to my bed and place myself at Mateo's side, hugging him so tightly that I can feel his chest contract.

Indecision quickly follows suit as I begin to question my logic. Was someone really in my bedroom, or was I sleepwalking again? I decide to settle for *crazy* because I must be delusional since I have not been sleeping well these pasts few months.

Realizing that it's 3am, I attempt to erase these illogical thoughts as I close my eyes in hopes of sanctuary.

Chapter Ten

~Manifest~

The sudden buzzing of an annoying alarm clock begins to sound uncontrollably which jolts me from my slumber. After a few seconds, it becomes difficult to ignore and I find myself blindly reaching over the nightstand in search of an off switch and end up knocking over a glass of water instead. A light thud echoes from the carpet as I locate my phone and hit the *end* button, then collapse my head back onto the feathered pillows.

The sun's rays slowly begin to peer through the sheer curtains, casting a shade of warm heat on my eyelids. It doesn't take long before I open my eyes and I'm greeted with crème colored walls. Two huge paintings hang in the center of the room that resemble the work of Eugène Delacroix, reminding me that I'm not in the confinements of my own home.

As my sight begins to focus, I feel a body move underneath the silk sheets beside me. Slowly sitting up with the soft fabric wrinkled around my waist, I look at my watch and confirm that it's a little after 10am. I have less than 45 minutes to get ready.

Removing the covers from my lap, I attempt to quietly escape but fail when a blonde beauty reaches over and places her arms around my abdomen.

She whispers into my ear, "Come back to bed for a little while longer," and then kisses my neck causing her hair to tickle my shoulder blade.

A soft smile forms on my lips while I consider the possibilities. Turning my head, I meet her lips with a gentle kiss as my hands caress her upper arm.

"I'd love to, but I can't today. We can meet later this afternoon."

"But it's Sunday. What's more important than spending some quality time with your girlfriend?"

Standing up from the bed and walking over to the closet, I pause before opening the door.

"Trust me, if I didn't have to leave I wouldn't, but I'm meeting my parents for brunch today in La Malbaie. And this time Clodia will be there. I haven't seen her in over a month."

Her lips are quickly transformed into a pouting sulk, "Ok."

She then lays back down onto the bed and purposely leaves her naked body exposed. Shaking my head, I continue my quest of gathering fresh clothes and pursue a cold shower.

The forty-minute drive from Baie-Saint-Paul to La Malbaie unexpectedly becomes grim causing my mind to drift. All too soon the fresh memories of where my life was four years ago and where I'm at now begins to consume my thoughts. My brain unexpectedly shifts and before I know it, my past resurfaces from thin air. I suppose that these suppressed feelings continue to reemerge because somewhere deep within my pneuma I regret my abrupt departure and now wish to redeem myself.

Turns out, eluding the polite *farewells* and *goodbyes* in order to spare any convoluted explanations can really take its toll on a friendship. I'm not entirely sure that they would even consider me their *friend* anymore. Who am I kidding here? They tolerated me because of her, and now that I've gone and ruined this *among other things*, they will never trust me again.

The problem is that I thought by leaving *her* behind, in the past then I wouldn't have to think about her, every second of every day. Oh, how wrong was I. Because

169

no matter how many distractions crossed my path or the countless females that warmed my bed, nothing or no one was ever good enough. Sure, it was pleasurable and stimulating but it only filled the empty void for that moment, temporarily satisfying a need that would soon be vacant once more. The images of her lovely face remained wedged in my head and I would find myself calling her at all hours of the day from private numbers just to hear her voice.

Sulking over a broken heart that was never meant to be loved. The light that once shined was taken away and I was possessed by darkness once more. The more I fought to justify my actions the harder it was to forget and let go. Because in my mind, I had lost a part of me that was irreplaceable. And here I was, trying to move on with my life without the one individual who mattered the most - Simone.

Feeling betrayed by my parents I turned rebellious and refused to take my rightful place as leader of our tribe. Finding anyway to exert my anger I began to experience reckless behavior and ended up into brawls with other members of our community for no reason. Partaking in endless alcohol consumption just to drown my sorrows with hopes of easing the pain that remained a constant reminder.

I felt suffocated and imprisoned. No matter what I did or who I hurt, the pain of her loss remained. I was numb and cold. An empty soul per se.

Instead of being respected by the elders and amid our race I was feared and loath. The tribe's council members soon labeled me as *destructive and toxic* yet again.

This is not the image or leader that I planned on being if I were to accept my fate. I knew that I had to shape up, but how? How am I expected to become the chief destined to lead the five tribes if I didn't even know how to control my anger? I am young, and one of the most powerful beings among our species. They needed me and here I was, acting like a child by throwing a fit over losing someone that was never mine to begin with.

Trying hard to erase the last few years of my life proved to be the most difficult task yet. It took a few years but I somehow managed to move forward. The anger was very much still there so I decided to divert that rage. I trained daily with our private and eventually buried those feelings for her deep within my consciousness. Telling myself every day that it was a mistake and my fault for allowing myself to love a human, a mortal that has no respect for our kind.

I eventually went back to school and continued my education in mining engineering at the Université Laval in

Quebec City and accepted a position at my parents mining company as their senior mining engineer. Always staying occupied, burying my head with work and women. Occasionally answering emails *mostly from Ethan*, just to acknowledge that I was doing fine. A quick explanation that I had to leave to take care of family affairs with promises of returning soon but never giving too much away.

My life had finally felt as if it was coming back together – but unknown to me, that was about to change.

*****

Arriving at Groesbeck Manor was something that I was definitely looking forward to. Clodia, my younger sibling had finally returned from her trip abroad to Brazil and I was anxious to hear all about it. As we sit at the breakfast table on the terrace with a pot of tea and endless laughter, my mum interrupts Clodia mid-sentence to ask about the one individual who matters the least to me.

"Darling, how is Varinia doing? Why didn't she accompany you here today?" Squirming in my seat, I force a smile and clear my throat before answering.

"Oh…. she uh... had a prior engagement to attend but is otherwise doing great." I take a sip from my black tea expecting her to drop the subject as my anxiety slowly creeps its way up to my chest. I hate talking about *Varinia*;

ever since we started dating my mum has been pressing the *marriage* issue. What she doesn't understand is that our relationship is a sham. She is just an idea to keep my mind occupied from the upsetting reality that I've lost a part of my soul some years ago.

Varinia is beautiful and extremely attractive but she's also high handed, vain, and part of a social class whose sole concern is to deceive those around her by using them for her own benefit. She isn't a contributing member to our society. So, do I care for her? Sure, I do. Do I like spending time with her? As much as I enjoy spending time with my co-workers. Let's just say that she has been a much-needed diversion from my corrupted disposition that continues to emerge like dark clouds on a sunny day.

"You two seem quite captivated with each other."

Damn it. Here we go again. My forged smiled doesn't reach my eyes as I set my drink down.

"Yeah, she's quite the catch." I'm not sure if she believes me because I don't believe it myself.

"Well, I hope she's the one. You're not getting any younger you know!" She states as a matter of fact while taking a bite of her scone.

Ignoring the pressure that has suddenly began to mount, I try my best to remain appeased when a sharp elbow to my ribs disrupts my concentration. As I turn to face the little firecracker to my right, it becomes abundantly clear that Clodia remains at odds with Varinia but as usual fails to mention why. To my surprise, this doesn't bother me as much as it should, given that she has remained a constant in my humdrum life for the past year.

Changing the subject, I engage in casual conversation about our week and Clodia's trip when my brother Titus mentions that a post card from Ethan arrived yesterday. How was Ethan able to track down my parent's address is a mystery, however, that's the least of my worries. My brother Titus is the one I should be focused on as he proceeds with his never-ending charade of discrediting my allegiance.

"The post card had a return address from a hotel in Montreal with a message that he was in Canada for a few weeks."

Our mum didn't pry for information nor did she wait for me to react because in her mind she knew that I had moved on and that my past was exactly that, in the past.

"Hmm," was all I managed to say while taking another sip from my tea, attempting to elude his vile stare.

The treacherous question dawdled, leaving a bad taste in my mouth. Why would Titus lay emphasis on this occurrence in particular? Ethan had previously made several attempts to reach me and this was never highlighted before.

With a sarcastic tone, he continues to press the matter, hoping to gain a reaction.

"I hope you don't plan on reaching out to him and go back to your old irresponsible ways."

Still no response from me as I remain lost in thought. I find myself struggling to suppress the anger that is slowly starting to build.

"I mean, it has been four years. It's time that you let go of the past and accept your place as the leader of our tribe, wouldn't you agree?"

His dreadful voice is laced with malice and greed as he continues with his quest of disparagement, but he had no idea what was in store for him. "Are you worried about failing brother? Is that it?"

How could he possibly know what I was feeling or what I went through to get my life back together?

"Because if you are, then I don't mind taking the responsibility for you, just say the word."

No longer able to hide or control my emotions I immediately become defensive and act on impulse to defend something that no longer exists. Standing to my full height and pushing my seat back, I slam both of my hands on the table which causes the plates to clatter and roar, "Enough!"

My voice is loud and thunderous causing Clodia and our mum to jump back, frighten from my outburst. But that doesn't stop me. No, I'm just getting started.

Inching close to his face, I look directly into his eyes and rebuke his baseless accusation with a less than friendly tone.

"How dare you bring up the past as if it were yesterday! Would it kill you if you had a little faith in me? Evoking what once was only reminds me of what I no longer am. Believe me when I say that I regret every minute of defiance that I put our parents through. Have I not proved to everyone that I moved on? I've done everything asked of me, everything and this is what I get, interrogation over a fucking post card?"

Titus knew that this topic was a sensitive subject and that I would react this way. He didn't seem bothered by my violent behavior and appeared satisfied with himself; content that I displayed any type of negative reaction to his mockery. With the biggest grin on his face he leans back into his chair, arms crossed over his chest and watches chaos unfold. Upset that my loyalty is being probed I hastily question my parent's position on the matter.

"If anyone feels that I lack conviction then allow Titus to rule in my place and spare everyone the heartache."

At this point I become aware that the past can never be erased. It has been a thorn in my side that continues to prick and stab its way back into my life for reasons unknown.

My father immediately interjects to avoid a full out argument while trying to defuse my sudden outrage.

"Son, you know better than anyone that neither the council nor our citizens have the power or influence to dictate who becomes the next ruler of our tribes. The goddess has already presented her divination and declared you as our future leader. And now it's time for you to take your rightful place at the head of the table. We only have your best interest at heart. No one is attacking you. You have done everything we've asked, and we couldn't be prouder. Have a seat and let us all conduct ourselves in a respectful manner. Am I right Titus?"

He glares at my despicable brother for a hint of a second before turning his gaze back to me. Titus has victory written all over his face; mission accomplished for proving his point that I was not ready to lead and that my emotions were still unstable.

Power is all he seeks, and he doesn't care at what price. He must have forgotten the seer's prophecy conveyed unto all; that I was to reign, but not before loss and great sorrow. I presume the *loss* part is referring to me losing *her,* and the *great sorrow* pertains to the enormous disappointment that I've been to my parents, our tribe, and the high council. Truth be told, I wasn't ready, not yet anyway. However, I couldn't let my family down again. I must place all differences aside and lay claim to this ominous responsibility.

My brother's eyes never leave mine when he finally speaks.

"Yes, of course father," validating his position on the matter while readjusting himself in his seat. "You've done a great job and we are more than pleased to have you back. My intentions were not to anger you. I was simply stating the obvious." He smirks with a hint of wickedness as he raises his eyebrows.

I turn my attention to our mum and sister who have remained quiet and collected throughout my outburst. Clodia's thoughts are somewhere on a distant island as she displays no emotion towards the ordeal. She doesn't seem influenced by my declaration because she knows me better than anyone and understands the pressure that I will soon face.

My mum on the other hand is directly affected as uncertainty beams from her eyes. She has stood by me throughout my many phases of arrogance. The last thing I want to do is upset her.

Freyja the seer has warned me about the dangers and how quickly it can subdue our consciousness; inflicting havoc and turmoil unto whomever crosses our path. Darkness looms over us all, waiting for an opportunity to cease the light and corrupt our innocence. It is up to us to overcome this temptation and prevail, otherwise we will continue to dance with evil and become part of *the shadows* who are cast away in the reformatory forever.

Titus continues to struggle with this darkness and soon his greed and hunger for power will push him over the edge. Freyja has foreseen his future plagued with hatred and anguish. But I will not allow his destiny to become my own. I will continue to fight in hopes that I become a true leader whose fate will liberate us all from segregation.

I immediately turn my attention to our mum to apologize for my abrupt behavior.

"I'm sorry, I don't know what came over me. The past is in the past and I have no intentions on going back."

Sitting down next to her, I instantly clasp her hands while giving her that heartwarming smile that she loves.

She returns the same sentiment and tries hard to hide her concerns while staying silent on the matter.

With a composed and gentle demeanor, my father concludes our heated dispute. "Well then, glad that's all sorted out. Now, time to discuss more pressing matters."

He takes another drink from his tea then launches into the *business* aspects of our conversation.

"We have a council meeting tomorrow in preparation for our future visitors that is scheduled to take place in the coming weeks, and we would like for you to attend."

Looking up, surprised that my presence has been requested, I find myself eager to uncover what issue has caused the council members from different parts of the world to gather under one roof in such short notice. Then I quickly remember that I have an important meeting in the morning that cannot wait, thus I have no choice but to reject their request.

"As much as I want to attend, I'm afraid that I am unable. There is an important meeting with one of the head engineer's that requires my presence."

Both of my parent's nod in agreement.

"Not to worry son, we understand and will attend on your behalf. Should we require your assistance, we'll reach out to you after the meeting."

That concluded our *business* discussion which I was happy to avoid. I had other things in mind and couldn't think straight after Titus reopen old wounds. I've worked so hard to avoid this part of my life, but it seems as though I am constantly reminded of it every day no matter what I do.

Later that night I put more thought into the post card that Ethan sent. I weight my options on whether I should respond or just continue to ignore unnecessary human interaction. I can't ignore the fact that my past continues to resurface like a constant reminder that I have unfinished business back in the States. Maybe I need closure that's all. And I have been working more than usual so taking a little time to catchup would do me some good. Feeling that it was time to stop evading my friend, I settle on reaching out to him. What could go wrong?

Bringing my laptop to life I start typing the email:

"Hey Ethan,
Received your postcard, and glad you reached out. I was planning on hiking in Grands Jardins National Park located in Charlevoix this coming weekend. Let me know if you're free. You can stay in the guest house at my place in Baie-Saint-Paul. Will you be coming alone?"

I pray to the goddess that he isn't with anyone we know so that I'm not confronted with inquiries about my departure four years ago. Ethan isn't one for back paddling; he doesn't ask too many questions and is indifferent about personal details. He's too wrapped up in his own world to care two cents about someone's private life.

Ethan is the kind of friend that you call when you want to go out and paint the town red, never courting one woman at a time and almost always host the best social gatherings. This is the only reason I decide to respond because the fact of the matter is that I do miss his companionship. And having contact with someone from my past shouldn't be too bad.

Ethan replied almost instantly:

"I thought you'd never agree. I'm available this weekend and will catch a flight to Charlevoix Saturday morning. Will need you to pick me up at the airport since I don't know where you're staying. This time around I'm traveling alone, partially for business and the other for pleasure. My number remains the same. Talk to you soon."

When the weekend finally arrives, I pick him up from the airport and we drive back to my place. He gets settled in and we both pack for our hiking trip that will take place in a few hours. During our hike, we catch up on what we missed out on and chat mostly about work and women, typical guy stuff. Ethan begins to gloat about his new love interest (the new flavor of the month) he has back in the States and how he thinks she is *the one*.

He mentioned that while he was out and about with his new eye candy Nicole, doing some window shopping he ran into Simone at Van Gogh's Art Supply on Market Square.

This isn't news as we all used to run with the same crowd in the same town, so I had no reason to feel awkward when I hear her name after all these years *even though it did strike a chord*. The conversation was casual until he mentioned something about her son and paint. I almost choked while drinking water out of my insulated polar bottle, spitting out whatever I did not get to gulp down. This newfound information immediately stopped me in my tracks and had me pause momentarily.

"Did you just say that Nicole has a son?" I asked, searching for confirmation that I misunderstood what he said.

Ethan starts to chuckle, "Ha, Ha. You are funny man. No. I said that Simone's son opened a paint tube and splattered acrylic paint all over Nicole's jeans while I was commencing the introductions. It was funny because he started laughing and then we all burst into laughter."

A puzzled expression crosses my face as I begin to wipe the remaining water from my mouth with the back of my hand. I see that Ethan is staring at me in confusion, probably wondering why I have a crazed look like I didn't speak his language.

"Are you ok? You look like you just saw a mountain lion." He turns around to look behind him as I regain my posture and straighten up.

"Nah, I'm good. I think I got a cramp from all the walking. Don't think I drank enough water before we started our hike," was all I could manage.

He grins and continues to power walk towards the end of our hike as if nothing he said has just affected me in the most painful way possible. After all this time, she still affects me in a way that no one else could. Momentarily confused at my sudden mood change I can't seem to focus on anything else Ethan is talking about.

"Well, this was some much-needed exercise. The view is beautiful; I can see why you haven't come back to the States. It's incredibly quiet and peaceful out here."

I sigh because that is not the reason why I unexpectedly left Pittsburgh and moved back to Quebec.

"Yeah, the view is astonishing, especially this time of year."

I seal the cap to my water bottle and follow suit, closing the gap to the end of our trail. Feeling a little anxious because I'm unsure if what I am about to say will reveal my true emotions.

"So, I know it's not news to you, but it certainly is to me. How old is her son?" Ethan looks up and starts laughing, picking up his water and taking a quick swig.

"That bad huh?"

He chuckles again and notices that I am not laughing; instead, I have a solemn look on my face. He then lifts both of his hands in defense while still holding his bottle in one hand. "Look, I know you two had a thing for each other but come on, it's been a few years since you left. Nothing ever came of it, playing hooky with each other's feelings and never acting on them. It was time for her to move on and sometimes things do not work out the way we intend. Besides, you seem happy here, left Highland Park and everyone else behind without looking back. No one could get a hold of you until now. You disappeared and the most updates we ever got were elusive like – I'm good, rehabilitating – whatever that meant. Not trying to give you a hard time just had to say what everyone else has been thinking." Ethan explains with a bit of agitation.

I give him a smirk while creasing my eyebrows downward as if I haven't taken offense to his comment. Squatting at the end of our trail and leaning beside a tree to tie my shoe, I hide any reaction that may appear on my face. I cannot deny what he just said because it is true to some extent, but I'm shocked to learn that she moved on with someone else. Curiosity gets the best of me as I find myself asking intrusive questions about her personal life.

"Who's the chap; the father of her son I mean?"

He shrugs his shoulders and looks down to face me.

"Not sure, she doesn't like to talk about it. We've never seen her with anyone other than the same crowd as before."

I stand up and we start to walk towards my vehicle in silence. Still dazed about Simone having a child has me feeling some kind of way. Could it be jealousy? Damn, I don't know. I can't trust my erratic feelings anymore because they are defective and unreliable.

"How is she? Is she doing ok?"

"She's actually doing well. Shortly after her parent's death, she sold the house in Bloomfield and moved to Regent Square. Then about a year ago we became business partners. Actually, I'm a silent partner. Well, more of an investor. Anyway, we opened a sculpture gallery and she currently sell's her sculptures and other artists work there as well. It's also a supply store so it keeps her pretty busy."

I'm not surprised to hear that she has somehow managed to succeed amid all the madness that she was forced to face. She has a strong personality and a great support system that includes friends who love her.

Stopping in front of my vehicle, with one hand on the door handle I look up at Ethan to capture his attention before he passes me.

"Listen," I begin to clear my throat, "I would like to keep this reunion amongst ourselves. You're right, I have moved on and don't want anyone to make me feel guilty for not looking back. I had my reasons and don't feel that I owe an explanation as it was personal and an extremely hard decision for me. I hope you can understand."

Ethan walks over and responds the best way a friend knows how.

"Sure man, no hard feelings. Only a few of the gang knew I was here on business so don't worry; I understand. You're right; your business is no one else's but your own. Anyway, I'm glad you agreed to hang out. It has been really good to see you again old friend."

Looking down, I smile but mostly to myself because he is right. It feels good to spend time with a friend that I once trusted.

"Thanks Eth," is all I could manage and nod to conclude our conversation as we both get into the vehicle and head back to my place.

*****

The next day I drop Ethan off at the airport and bid my farewells. Assuring him that I would visit the U.S. as soon as work permits.

"It was great seeing you Ethan. I will definitely make arrangements to travel to Pittsburgh soon. Work has kept me busy now that I am helping my parents with their mining company. It's industrious but I like it because I stay focused and out of trouble."

"I know how it is and staying out of trouble is good. Hopefully, you don't wait too long before you visit. Your family still own that place in Highland Park?" Ethan asks out of curiosity.

Walking to the rear of my vehicle I open the cargo compartment, pull out his luggage and hand it to him.

"Yeah, we never sold it. Some of our family members currently maintain the property but no one's really lived there since we left."

"Gotcha — well, now that I know you do have somewhere to stay, I wanted to invite you to a bash that I will be hosting. It's a small event for Nicole in a few weeks at my place. Nothing big, more of an intimate crowd with a couple of her close friends and some of mine. It's her birthday so I wanted to do something extra special for her, if you know what I mean," he grins and raises an eyebrow waiting for my response.

I frown at his request because I'm not sure how I'm just supposed to resurface as if nothing happened? Like I didn't just leave and turn my back on my friends and all the important people that mattered. Would they even accept me after all this time? Not to mention that I would be reopening old wounds and defy my parent's wishes to leave well enough alone. They would definitely be disappointed to learn that I was in the U.S. without a probable cause.

Ethan sensed that I didn't have an answer for him, so he departs, leaving me to think about it.

"Alright then, I gotta go before I miss my flight. Keep in touch and stop being a stranger. I would like to introduce you to Nicole before we get engaged." He winks his eye, alerting me that he is joking.

"Ha, sure. Have a safe flight and take care. We'll be in touch soon."

He nods and disappears through the glass doors and into the busy crowd. I jump back into my SUV and start to head home.

While driving, I immediately start thinking about Simone again and can't seem to shake her from my mind. It's clear that I am still in trance about the conversation I had with Ethan yesterday. Any feelings that I thought were suppressed have obviously resurfaced, slowly tip toeing their way back into my subconscious and consuming my every thought. It's hard for me to believe that she was romantically involved with another male.

Did she not love me as much as I loved her? Who is this mysterious male that she has failed to mention? Its jealousy. I'm jealous. That's what I'm feeling. Jealous that she moved on and although I've tried, it's all been a lie.

These new findings are quite unsettling; feeling indomitable I resolve on accepting Ethan's invitation and resurface in the states.

Maybe this is what I need; to see that she is happy so that I can finally close that door and hopefully open a new one. Just a few days. After all, it's been quite some time since I've had any interactions with my past. I'll be sure to make it quick, keeping conversations to a minimal then head back.

Surely no harm could come of it.

Chapter Eleven

~Chivalrous~

It's the end of a work week and the beginning of a new day as I struggle to open the back door to S&E Sculpture and Ceramics Art Gallery. After fidgeting with the keyhole for like five minutes, it finally unlocks. I swiftly rush Mateo inside and turn off the alarm while flipping the main light switch on.

Checking the time, I confirm that I only have ten minutes to open the store. Placing Mateo's belongings on my desk, I work on getting him settled, grab my denim apron and dash out to the front to unlock the main entrance.

I complete a few more task then flip the on switch to the *open* neon sign that is located at the top of the glass door. Once everything is in place, I walk over to the sound system and set the station to *gentle piano concertos*. Kismet by

Alexis Ffrench gently plays in the background and sets the mood for a lighthearted day.

Deciding to start on some much-needed paperwork and left-over inventory from the night before, I settle on a seat behind the counter and begin my morning. The day passes by sluggishly and business has been rather stagnant than usual. It's midday as I settle on grabbing a couple of new art pieces from the back that recently arrived from a few local artists and some limited items from my own collection.

Carefully placing all twenty-four statutes on a cart, I slowly wheel them to the front of the gallery where the sculptures are displayed for purchase. Today's pieces are a bit different than the usual inventory. Lately I've been intrigued by rare trees from around the world, so I decided to create a few of my own from clay and wire.

First up a Baobab Tree that is native to Madagascar, Africa, and Australia. These trees can reach heights up to ninety-eight feet and have a wide trunk that stores water in order to endure the harsh drought conditions.

Next, we have the exquisite Socotra Dragon Tree which can only be found in Socotra Archipelago in the Arabian Sea. This evergreen is my favorite because of its unique appearance that resembles an umbrella that has been turned inside out.

And finally, two more models of the Methuselah Tree that grows in eastern California, high in the white mountains and remains one of the oldest living trees in the world. There are also a few funky models designed by local artists which are made from various elements that include but are not limited to glass, wire, bottle caps and metals. I start off by rearranging the ancient castles from the medieval era and place them to the far right of the room. I then tackle the small floral sculptures and relocate them towards the opposite wall, clearing the middle section for the new arrivals.

One by one, I cautiously begin placing each statute onto the glass shelf inside the lighted display cabinet and position them at just the right angle to make them more appealing upon entering.

Grouping them by theme and limiting three pieces per sill, I am finally able to complete the hour-long task and tend to other matters. After pushing the empty cart back to the storage room, I decide on replenishing the supply section that is located towards the back of the store. As I begin loading my cart with sculpting materials, I hear a few beeps, alerting me that customers have entered the gallery. Before rushing to the front, I give Mateo a kiss on his forehead right before wheeling the cart through the open storage door.

Making myself visible for the two potential clients that just arrived, I make sure to wear a polite and welcoming smile as I approach two females dressed in business like attire.

"Welcome to S&E Gallery. My name is Simone. How can I be of service?"

The woman in a light purple pencil skirt is the first to turn around and greet me while her friend's eyes are affixed on a newly displayed guitar sculpture made from discarded parts of old antique clocks.

"Hello."

"What brings you two in today?"

"We're just browsing at the moment," she pauses for a few seconds before continuing, "I actually heard about this place so decided to stop by for a bit. Will it be alright if we just look around?"

"Absolutely. Take your time. I'll be over by the paint brushes should you two require my assistance."

Her friend responds without ever breaking eye contact from the display cabinet, "Thank you."

With a cheerful grin I pivot and set off on restocking the hand brushes. I can hear light whispering as I squat and begin sliding the plastic packages onto the metal tube hooks. Peering from behind the cart, I witness them pointing to several other figures, intrigued with the various shapes and colors. After a few minutes of making my rounds to each station, my ears are suddenly filled with three more beeps. I quickly stand to investigate and confirm that the two women have left, and a lone male has entered the store.

With his back turned and hands stuffed in his pockets he remains motionless. Something must have caught his eye, causing him to enter my gallery. I silently proceed to approach the newcomer, curious to see what has piqued his interest and hopefully make a sale. Careful not to startle his concentration, I decide to align my body with his and speak with a gentle tone.

"Welcome to S&E Gallery. How can I be of assistance?"

He instantly turns his body in my direction and returns the same polite jester.

"Hi," is all he can muster and smiles longer than necessary while staring directly at my lips then quickly turns away. "Yes. Um... I would like to know a little more about this piece," he points to the goddess sculpture. "Who is she and what does she represent?"

Walking closer to the dark blonde stranger, I clear my throat, place my hands behind my back and launch into a brief narration of her fable.

"This is the Celestial Goddess Gaia, the ancestral mother of all life. A primordial deity, she is the first goddess to be born into the cosmos and attributes to our mere existence today."

Stepping closer to him, I continue the conversation with a description of her purpose.

"It is said that she has the power to manipulate all plant life and inanimate things such as minerals. She is the divine embodiment of life itself, the creative force of all living beings and the soul of mother nature."

With both of his hands gently tucked away into his pockets, he remains focused. Captivated by her beauty, his silent voice barely reaches my ears as he becomes lost in her violet-blue eyes.

"Powerful and yet so beautiful."

"She is beautiful." I mirror his emotion because that is exactly how she made me feel when I first set my eyes on her.

He then reaches for the sculpture and gently touches the emerald scales on her arms while taking in every detail of her figure. Her long fish tail braid drapes over her left shoulder, partially covering her bare breast and hangs just below her knees. There are various vines sprouting from her feet that intertwine with her toes and climb up towards her calves. A single white stephanotis is covering her sexual organ which represents reproduction in nature. She radiates dominance and beauty while offering life and nourishment to all.

"Are there any other pieces like this one?" He finally turns to face me and provides his undivided attention while I quietly fidget with my denim apron.

"I'm afraid not. Each art piece is unique. These artists spend a tremendous amount of time focusing on every detail of their sculpture therefore it makes it hard to replicate."

"Do you know the artist who created this particular piece?"

I smile politely but secretly took offense to his comment for reasons unknown. Before I could understand my snide response to his innocent inquiry, I vow to be unpleasant instead of introducing myself as the artist who delicately crafted this masterpiece.

"Actually, I do. Would you like to meet her?"

"I would be honored to meet her. This is an extraordinary piece and I've never seen anything like it."

Politely nodding and excusing myself, "Great. Stay here and I'll go get her."

I begin making my way towards the back of the store. Quickly removing my clay stained apron, I suspend it over the rustic coat hanger, close the door and walk back out into the gallery.

As I approach the gentleman who is so intrigued with my statute, I can't help but wonder why he would automatically assume that I wasn't the sculptor or an artist for that matter. Do I know the artist? Really? I am the freaking artist! Who does this guy think he is? Walking up to him, he turns his attention to me and half smiles with confusion on his face. "Hi."

"Um...hi." I offer my right hand to him, "my name is Simone and I am the artist who created that extraordinary piece of the Celestial Goddess of Life."

His face immediately turns apologetic while reaching for my hand, "And I'm Santino who is clearly an idiot."

Removing my palm from his I quickly accept his apology.

"No, it's ok. Not only do I sell other artist work here at my gallery, but I also sell my own." I emphasized the word *my* to let him know that yes, I do own this store and no I'm not just a stock clerk.

"So, not only are you the actual sculptor but you also own this gallery?"

"Yup." I nod my head in agreement while providing a sardonic smile with my hands in my back pockets.

"Great. I'm going to go and crawl into a dark hole now."

As he turns to exit, I quickly stop him by reaching for his arm. Guilt has finally got the best of me while I struggle with my emotions. This is truly out of character for me as I'm not usually this hostile.

"Really, it's ok. There was no way you would have known."

As he turns around, my hand accidentally slides down his arm and he capture's it with his right palm. I notice that I have dried clay stuck underneath my fingernails and quickly remove my hand from his hold. Looking up and smiling, he continues to interact with me as if I haven't been rude enough already.

"I really am sorry. I wasn't insinuating that you weren't an artist or that you didn't have talent because clearly you do."

And there goes his eyes, straight to my lips again. Oh, why does he have to be so handsome? And not to mention that he also smells painfully delectable.

"Well, thank you. I accept your apology." I take a few steps back to give us some space because it suddenly feels rather warm.

"So, tell me. How did you hear about the Celestial Goddess of Life? I'm eager to know more."

"Um, let me think." I place my index finger on my lips, lost in thought wondering where I've heard her story from. "I'm not sure actually. Her story is a fable. Over the years I've come to admire her beauty, courage and strength which is everything that she stands for. Sometimes I even wish I was more like her. Couldn't get her out of my head so I decided to create this sculpture that mirrored how I perceive her to be."

"And why do you think that you are not like her?"

Oh boy, this little chat of ours has suddenly turned awkward and I'm starting to feel a little uneasy while stating the obvious.

"Because she is a deity and I am not."

"You don't have to be a goddess to have those qualities; beauty, courage and strength."

He formulates these last three words carefully with measured pronunciation. I was so wrapped up in our conversation that I didn't notice when he stepped closer to me. As I look around, I take notice that we are surrounded by several clay sculptures of Greek Gods and Goddesses.

Knowing that I must change the subject, I swiftly try to squirm myself out of this tortuous discussion.

"So, did you see anything else that you might be interested in other than my masterpiece?"

Damnit Simone! I want to kick myself for that one. I'm positively sure that my comment came out wrong and he might misinterpret it for flirting.

Clearing his throat, he chuckles and stuff's his hands back into his pockets before answering my question.

"Well, I'm definitely captivated by this sculpture and its artist but unfortunately for me, I'm only going to woo the Celestial Goddess from my mantle back home."

Normally I'm shy around males but for some reason I don't feel threaten by his candid remarks; if anything, he makes me feel squirmy. I'll just brush them off. A man like that would never set eyes on a female like me. He is only making advances because I inaccurately set off a vibe that I was interested, which I am not. Deciding to ignore the second part of his comment I confirm the transaction with a forced smile.

"Great choice. I'll box it up so that you can be on your way."

Without further delay, I pivot and grab the goddess sculpture from the glass stand then make my way towards the storage area in search of a container.

After I finish wrapping up the art piece that took me six months to carve from clay, I head straight for the checkout table where the mysterious stranger is already patiently waiting for me. I try my best to focus on the register as I ring him up.

"That will be $487.12 please."

He pulls his wallet out of his back pocket and produces a credit card while casually handing it over. Just as I slide the card through the machine, he decides to break our awkward silence.

"Have I offended you in anyway?"

Tearing the receipt, I hand it over to him and respond with a less than friendly tone, "Not at all." I then reach for the package and place it onto the counter for him to retrieve.

"Then why are you deliberately avoiding me?"

I look up and for the first time I notice that his irises are hazel like mine. His broad shoulders and lean stature stand out against his crisp white long sleeve shirt. Any woman would love to be flattered by a male as such but not me. I don't have the luxury nor time to entertain silly ideas of such.

"Santino… I want to thank you for purchasing my most prized possession and I am extremely grateful that you were interested in the background of her origin, but I believe we both know that the only reason you are being overly friendly is because you're feeling guilty about our misunderstanding earlier. I get it and it's ok."

He pauses for a few moments stunned at my word choice no doubt when suddenly his voice appears to be full of remorse.

"Well then, I want to apologize for the second time because that was not the impression that I intended to give off. I honestly think that you are the most beautiful woman that I've ever set my sight on and it's been extremely difficult to keep my eyes off of you."

"Excuse me?"

I'm flabbergasted at his constant honesty because it's not what I expected. I'm not angry that he thinks I'm beautiful. I'm just shocked that he actually has the guts to say what's on his mind with such boldness.

"Do you have any idea how attractive you are? I noticed you through the window while I was walking down the sidewalk and I just knew that I had to meet you. Then you approach me, and a sweet melody of words leave your lips."

I don't respond and instead resolve on staying silent because I cannot muster the courage to refute his seducing tactics. I'm honestly lost for words.

"Can we start over please? I just feel like we might have gotten off on the wrong foot." His eyes are pleading and full of regret.

I find myself in a resentful state because I've been rude to him from the moment he walked through the doors and I cannot understand why. Am I upset because I feel some type of personal attachment to this sculpture and he is now breaking that invisible bond with his purchase or is it that he assumed I wasn't such a great artist? Regardless, he doesn't deserve this ill-mannered treatment, especially not from me. Finally snapping out of my daze, I tuck a lost strand of hair behind my ear and smile.

"No, you don't need to apologize. I'm the one who should be apologizing for my rude behavior. It's just that I don't know how to react to your comments."

"Then join me for dinner. Tomorrow night. We can talk about whatever you want and get to know one another."

"I'm terribly sorry but I can't."

"Can't or won't?"

I shrug my shoulders, "A little of both maybe." I feel a bit ashamed for not lying to him.

"You have a special someone, is that it?"

"No!" I immediately scoff. "It's just that I don't have the time. I'm busy with this store and I've got a lot on my plate right now." Walking from behind the counter, I carefully approach him and attempt to justify the reasoning behind my rejection.

"Look, you seem like a wonderful person, but I don't do dates nor boyfriends. All I can offer at the moment is my friendship."

"Then you're in luck because friendship is all I am seeking."

I don't say anything because at this rate, how can I turn him down? His good-natured attitude remains hopeful as he continues to implore his virtuous cause.

"Listen, I really feel terrible for making an assumption that set us off on the wrong foot and would love nothing more than to take you to dinner. I promise that my intentions are honorable and guarantee that I will have you smiling the entire evening. Please say yes."

I immediately place my hand over my mouth to stifle a laugh because he has somehow managed to subdue my foul mood and convince me to agree to dinner all at once without his prior knowledge. Geez! If he only knew that a night out is exactly what I need after... No! Don't go there. Don't you dare think about him and ruin any possible chance of happiness after all this time. Quickly compartmentalizing that thought, I remove my hand from my mouth and accept his proposal out of guilt, and because I just want to.

"I just want to make a few things clear first."

"Shoot." He is definitely enjoying this for his own personal amusement and can't seem to stop smiling because I've been defeated.

"I am only agreeing to this dinner for two reasons: one, because I feel guilty about my despicable behavior towards you as a human being and you have somehow managed to remain a gentleman throughout this ordeal. And two, because I honestly haven't been to dinner with the opposite sex in over four years."

"I'll take it. No complaints here."

"Ok then."

"Alright, it's settled. Tomorrow night at 7?" His smile touches his eyes as he swiftly flips the receipt over, grabs a loose pen from the counter and begins to jot down his name and number.

"I'll leave you with my cell. Call or text me the address where I should pick you up. Or you can call me to just talk or…anytime." He continues to trail off and seems awfully nervous while fidgeting with the receipt.

"Ok."

I'm unable to contain my smile as I watch him fiddle with the pen. His sudden edginess makes me feel a little better that I am not the only one with confidence issues. He then hands me the piece of paper.

"It's been an absolute pleasure meeting you Simone and I look forward to dinner tomorrow night."

Carefully taking his package from the counter, he fidgets with his purchase while we exchange glances and then proceeds towards the front of the store.

"Likewise," is all I manage to say while holding the receipt in one hand and my pride in the other.

He stops at the foot of the entrance, turns to give me one final glare and continues to exit when Ethan emerges at that exact moment. With one hand on the door, they exchange a sociable glance as Santino departs and Ethan's watchful eye sizes him up. A curious smirk instantly forms on his lips warning me that he has gone into full detective mode. Folding the receipt in half, I swiftly shove it into my back pocket before Ethan can reach me and begin a dreadful interrogation. Shaking away the fuzzy feeling, I immediately start to organize the counter as he approaches.

"How's it going beautiful?" He leans on the counter with one elbow propped up against his cheek and provides his undivided attention.

Walking behind the counter in search of notepads, I busy myself with unnecessary work as I tidy up the workspace.

"Aw you know. Same old story. Manning the counter, inventory, sales. The usual."

"Are you telling me that nothing interesting has happened since my departure?" He raises both of his eyebrows and motions towards the exit where Santino just disappeared through.

Oh boy, here we go. Ignoring his sarcasm and giving away no indication that I've got a date tomorrow night, I interject his debriefing and turn the tables on him.

"So, what brings you to this side of town so early in the afternoon?"

"Oh, I just happen to be in the neighborhood and thought, what the heck, why not stop by and visit this joint."

"Uh huh, so how was your trip to...where was it that you went to this time and for what reason?"

"Well, as you're fully aware, I occasionally dabble in other business ventures that often requires travel outside of the U.S. So, that's what I've been doing for the past two weeks. Just got back yesterday and wanted to see you."

"Right. So why don't you tell me the *real* reason you're here?"

"Always so eager for information."

With a huge grin on his face, he reaches into his jacket and takes out a small square envelope. He then begins to toy with the four-sided packet between his fingers while giving me a questioning glare. I continue to ignore his probing glances and set off on sorting the pile of mail that has gradually grown over the past couple of days.

"I wasn't lying about wanting to see you. Are you doing ok? How's Mateo?"

His mood has gone from playful to serious in a matter of seconds. He worries too much about me and Mateo. Our love for each other is mutual but sometimes he can be overprotective.

"I'm fine, really. It's been quiet around here. Mateo is in the office, coloring and eating oranges."

He then stands and leans in closer as another customer walks in and goes straight to the supply section.

"Glad to hear. So....," he continues to twirl the small white packet in his hand, "I've got something for you."

"What is it?"

"This my most esteemed friend is an invitation to Nicole's birthday party which I am personally delivering to you." He then hands me the envelope as he continues to speak, "It's scheduled to take place next Saturday at my house of course."

"Of course." I mirror his obvious response.

"And both Nicole and I really want you to come."

Taking the invitation from his hand, I flip it over and pull out a light pink card stock that's imprinted with fancy calligraphy.

"Well, since you went out of your way to personally deliver this announcement then I guess I'm kind of required to attend."

"And you're absolutely correct. So, please clear your busy schedule and be sure to arrive on time otherwise I will send someone to get you."

"Always so bossy."

"I'd like to call it *decisive* thank you."

"Call it whatever you'd like, it doesn't change the fact that you're bossy." Smirking in a playful manner, he turns and makes his way towards the back.

"I'll let you tend to your customers while I keep Mateo busy for a while. I brought him a present from my trip abroad that I'm sure he will enjoy."

His voice trails off as he disappears out of sight and I head towards the new customers.

Chapter Twelve

~Prophecy~

The sun's warm glow is beaming through the stained-glass windows and bounces off the tall creme pillars, casting rays of white lights into the dark room. Tiny specks of gray dust can be seen underneath the hand carved baroque chairs that align the walls. The boardroom is crammed with leaders from each tribe including the chief, high council members and their most trusted advisors. Each attendee is dressed in their tribe's customary clothing, providing a colorful array in this dreary chamber.

It's been over two decades since all five leaders have assembled under the same location to discuss politics. After learning that an urgent council meeting was about to take place, I knew that I had to be a part of it, even if it meant as a prowler.

I'm curious to discover what could be so significant that caused many to travel across the world to La Malbaie? Well, that's what I'm about to find out.

The chief, Atilius Cato Moreau, stands at 6 "4" with his lean built and dark brown wavy hair as he clears his throat to capture the audience's attention. I however remain silent and heedful as I bury myself deeper into the shadows of the manor's hidden passage. As it turns out, trying to remain undetected has been much more difficult than I could have imagined.

"I want to thank everyone for coming out on such short notice." His half smile slightly reveals a small lined dent on his left cheek as he glances around the room and takes in the spectators.

"Everyone, please take your seats and let us begin as there is much to discuss." He motions towards the chairs and dark wood benches in front of him. Hushed murmurs resonate throughout the congregation's chambers as everyone gathers to be seated.

Leaders are positioned at the front of the room while the council members are positioned beside the chief and along the walls and their advisors are settled in the center of the room. The whispers finally come to a complete halt while everyone begins to settle into their places. No one else is allowed in the chambers unless they are part of the high council. His wife and council member, Naevius Petronia Moreau, gently glides her hand over the blue silk gown that hugs her body before taking the seat next to him. They both represent the Nahanni tribe which is located here in Canada.

"It has been a long time since we have all gathered as such, and unfortunately it isn't for a matter of celebration. Some of you have traveled from across the ocean just to be here today and I want you all to know that it is for a very good cause. As we commence, I ask that everyone please keep an open mind and focus on the matter at hand."

He narrows his blue-green eyes and lightly tugs at the collar of his white button-down shirt. Just about everyone in the room has provided their undivided attention while they take in the words that Atilius is conveying. I take notice that the guards to my left have closed the wrought iron doors indicating that this conversation may be troubling, thus must be restricted.

Clearing his throat, he continues, "As everyone is aware, our former leader Renan Kricati was accused and found guilty of treason for committing adultery with a mortal and was sentenced to death many moons ago. His actions and punishment marked history for our species and will forever be remembered as an unspeakable act on his part."

The boardroom is no longer quiet as everyone embarks on unsettled discourse about the subject; mostly out of disagreement and confusion that a celestial would even consider such a revolting seduction towards a human.

Not only did Renan violate one of our most sacred principles, but he also sent a message that his actions were justified, and he was above the law due to his position. Because of this, the council and leaders had no choice but to make an example that this type of defiance would not be tolerated no matter your status or title. His punishment has never been heard of, not for a chief anyway.

Renan was revered, well respected, and feared at the same time so one can imagine the revolt that occurred when his punishment was carried out. Many didn't believe that he was capable of such accusations and others just didn't care what he did because in their eyes he was a deity, chosen by the goddess and destined to unite both worlds – mortal and immortal.

No one really understood what *united* meant, however, it seems as though Renan took it upon himself to fulfill that destiny and shared his bed with a human wench who was no one of importance. The mortal in question also shared his fate.

Renan was kept alive until she was found, which took several months as he refused to give away her location. He maintained his innocence claiming that the seer revealed a vision of what was to come.

Noita, the seer with this *so-called prophecy* refused to speak, vowed silence and was condemned to the reformatory to live out the remainder of her life. Since then there have been numerous tales of a potential offspring from Renan, yet there has been no physical proof of such existence.

"I know what most of you must be thinking," he begins to raise his tone, attempting to silence the panic that has gradually progressed. "Why is Renan of any importance after all this time? Well, prior to his sentencing there were rumors that his mortal was with child and this was his sole reason for prolonging her whereabouts. It is said that he finally decided to reveal her location only after she gave birth, thus eliminating any tangible evidence. Renan never refuted these allegations, nor did he own up to them. We have searched high and low till the ends of the earth and found no such being. And although we have not been able to validate whether there was any truth to these accusations, they have continued to haunt our fretted minds long after his demise. To even consider that this is a possibility truly jeopardizes our mere existence on this planet that we share with the humans. It would be a disgrace to our species and everything that we stand for."

Concern has now turned to anger which is radiated throughout the dim room. Their voices are no longer hushed as the observers continue to express disapproval of such actions. Watchmen from every tribe are standing at each pillar, serving as bodyguards to their leaders. Their appearances are fierce; from their combat boots and muscular built all the way to their black attire.

They illustrate no emotion or expression as the discussion continues. "I come before all of you today to report that this rumor is no longer considered speculation but possibly holds some truth."

And just like that, his true purpose for this gathering is revealed. Their impatience is quickly replaced with fury. Many begin to voice their frustration faster than a response can be formulated.

"How is this even possible if celestials are unable to procreate with mortals?"

"What does this mean?"

I am more concerned on the timing of it all and wonder how long Atilius has known about this *possibility* and what finally changed his mind to share this vital information with the tribe leaders. Oh, this is better than I thought!

"Everyone, please remain calm and allow me to explain." His voice is both commanding and unyielding as he allows everyone a few moments to settle down and really digest his statement while delivering this troubling news.

"A few weeks ago, Freyja had a vision of a powerful creature emerge from the depths of a clandestine hibernation. I'm not sure what this means or if there's any immediate danger, nonetheless, it would not be in our best interest to intimidate nor to antagonize this outsider. Our sole priority should be the safety of our civilization and maintaining the peace with the humans. For this reason alone, I come before you to seek guidance on how to approach this rather delicate situation."

Full on chaos has now erupted inside the chamber with so many voices speaking at once. Many are scared, and others are in denial that this creature could really exist. I don't believe it myself because it can't be true. Renan's fate was carried out over twenty-three years ago; there is no freaking way that his spawn has been able to maintain a low profile and now suddenly decides to reveal itself. I call bullshit; something else is going on here.

Pétur Skári Haugen, leader of the Nökkvi tribe from Iceland is the first one to speak as he slowly stands from his chair. His pale skin is accompanied by small wrinkles as he squints his frail eyes into focus. Salt and pepper hair drapes from his head, partially covering the left side of his face.

"I summon your seer Freyja to come forward and provide her testimony to this new revelation. Only then will I entertain the possibility of a half breed living among us. Bring her forward and let us hear what she has to say on the matter."

At that exact moment, the remaining leaders stand one by one to share Pétur's sentiment.

"Freyja should come forward." Ibrahim Malik Totah, leader of the Nusuk tribe from Socotra Island confirms the same.

The remaining two leaders, Effiom Moswen Iwu from the Nilotic tribe in Africa and Sávio Guga Ruebe from the Nadöb tribe of Brazil nod in agreement and stand with the other tribe leaders. Seer's are only called upon for guidance or sought out for healing but never has a seer been summoned to speak or validate their prophecy. Atilius has no other choice than to fulfill their request. He brought them here to seek their guidance so he must comply and summon the witch.

"Very well then." He nods in agreement and motions for one of his watchmen to come forward. Swiftly whispering into his guards' ear, the burly male nods and quickly departs from the board room.

Everyone remains anxious as silent dialogue continues in the background while the chief tries to appear composed. Moments later the doors creak open, and Freyja emerges with two of her maidservants as she slowly begins making her way down the aisle.

The chambers have gone completely silent as she continues her measured strides with only the sounds of her steps stinging our ears. She is a sight to see, with her long blonde locks hanging down her back and Persian blue eyes that stand out against her olive complexion. Her slender figure is covered by a yellow silk wrap that plunges at the neck, showing off her divine assets and striking curves.

Everyone is taken aback by the beauty radiating from her form including the female council members. It's too bad seers vow celibacy, otherwise I would have added her to my collection of mistresses.

As Freyja approaches the flight of steps, she slowly lowers her head and torso with one hand behind her back while murmuring, "Atilius."

Her two maidens remain a few steps further behind while performing the same gesture. Without further ado, the chief swiftly walks down the steps, one at a time and places himself in front of the witch as he speaks, "Freyja, please come forward."

He politely offers his hand and that's when I vaguely become aware of their instant connection. Gently lifting her head while avoiding direct eye contact, she places her delicate palm in his as they both begin to make their way up the steps and settle in the center of the chambers.

From their feather like touch, all the way to how their bodies respond to one another, it's hard not to notice the chemistry. He has not been able to take his eyes off of her since she entered the chambers and I don't blame him. She is by far the most attractive being I've set my eyes on. Freyja has everyone's full attention as Atilius cautiously proceeds to explain the current dilemma.

"The council, leaders and advisors would like to hear for themselves what you saw in your vision. We understand that you are under no obligation to neither justify nor validate what you foresaw, and you may speak freely if you wish." He clarifies his intentions while being conscientious not to displease her.

"Will our future leader be joining us? His advice is instrumental to our discussion."

"I am afraid that he is unavailable at the moment, but rest assured that he will be briefed on all matters discussed here today."

Her smile reaches her soft eyes as she nods in agreement and turns to face the spectators. When her sight reaches Ipra and Gersemi, she pauses for a brief second then proceeds to speak in a boisterous tone.

"First and foremost, I want to clarify that my loyalty belongs to the goddess and I only answer to her exclusively." Her voice remains steady and controlled mixed with dominance and anger as she continues to relay her influential message. "The goddess is the *only* divine creature who has the authority to question my motives and the last time I checked, no one in this chamber was a deity!" She exclaims to the prying eyes that are staring at her with dishonesty.

I take notice that Gersemi has managed to slip away as the doors soundlessly swing closed. What did Freyja command her to do? Damn it, I can't leave now, not unnoticed anyway.

"Just this one time will I allow to be summoned and treated with such unworthiness. For those of you who do not agree or question my judgment know that you will have to answer to the goddess just as I do."

She begins to leisurely walk back and forth between the leaders and council members. The room remains soundless, yet our minds are hexed with the echoes of her deafening voice.

"I want to expound my true purpose and reasons for my sole existence in this one life that has been granted to me. Like my ancestors, I have been appointed as seer of our race which is necessary for our survival. Some may refer to us as oracles or even a witch, but the term used to describe what we do is not of any importance."

Her eyes briefly land on Atilius as she continues to speak. "The goddess has gifted me with special powers that will enable our species to thrive in this world that we share with the mortals. I can control some of these special gifts which have been bestowed upon me but not all." She pauses for a brief moment as she looks around the room, taking in her audience.

"A few weeks ago, I saw a prophecy of a potent creature awaken from its slumber. In this vision, this being shared our strengths but none of our weaknesses. Its inner core emanated with such massive energy that it caused me to become visually impaired for the duration of the premonition. Someone with that much power did not evolve from our species alone and validating whether this creature is a direct descendant from Renan Kricati has yet to be confirmed. At this point, the divination only illustrated that this being does exist and whether it knows what they are is unknown."

Everyone remains quiet as they consider the possibility that a creature of such status could be actuality. Sávio is the first one to break the silence which captures everyone's undivided attention.

"What is the purpose of this vision? Should we be worried for our safety or were we just summoned here on an impulsive theory? How do we know that this *so-called* prophecy delivered onto you wasn't merely a dream?" He chuckles out of ignorance and idiocy like a nervous tick which was not well received.

"Why does the sun rise in the east and set on the west? Because some things just are! The goddess presented this prophecy unto me for a reason, and I'm not entirely sure that we'll be ready for what is about to come. We all know that Renan was the most powerful being among our species and that the goddess chose him to lead all five tribes which only occurs once every one-hundred years. What I am saying is that if Renan did procreate with a mortal, then the human in question was not just an ordinary being. There was more to her than she led on. This is a fair warning to all, that the world we live in is about to change."

I'm starting to think that Sávio misunderstood her purpose for even being here. I heard her loud and clear; she doesn't owe an explanation to this lot and she surely doesn't answer to any of them.

"I've heard that attacks on the humans have been on the rise recently. Perhaps it's this creature, this being that has been preying on the weak, lurking in the shadows undetected because we have been kept in the dark about its existence. Tell me seer of the Nahanni tribe, what do you make of these findings? Is there truth to this rumor?"

Ibrahim seems apprehensive on the matter, but he does make an appeasing argument. These tales have always engulfed our ears and to this day have become more frequent.

Turning to face Ibrahim she provides her undivided attention and begins to address his concerns.

"You have brought up some valid points that our community is currently facing, and I'm afraid that these rumors do hold some truth. But it is difficult to corroborate whether these attacks originated from this creature given that it has been dormant until recently. And although I share your trepidation, I cannot help but wonder whether the culprit is one of our own. Let us not forget that the political human faction previously attempted to denounce our armistice which led to an uprising that subsequently segregated our species to different parts of the world. They continue to covet that which cannot be gifted, our powers. Mortals tend to fear what they do not understand, and in their minds, we are still considered a *liability*. If given an opportunity, they would cleanse the world of our kind. And it will only be a matter of time before this violence reaches their doorstep. These allegations will certainly tarnish the treaty with long term effects that could potentially push us to the brink of war. We cannot continue to turn a blind eye while the offender soils our integrity. This matter must be addressed regardless of the offender's status. Wouldn't you agree?"

Ibrahim clasps his hands together and lowers his head out of respect. Unfortunately, not everyone shares his understanding as light murmurs and side conversations continue in the background, hesitant to accept the reality that an organism as such is even a possibility.

"If these things that you are speaking of hold merit, then I have no doubt in my mind that this vile creature has been conspiring against us all along."

Effiom's apprehension is resonated throughout the chamber while my instincts are telling me that Freyja knows more than she is willing to share. Ignoring the uneasy clamor from his audience, Atilius proceeds to seek guidance from this deceitful witch he so blindly considers an ally.

"Freyja, what do you propose we do?" His question is more of a plea than an inquiry.

Focusing her attention on the noble leader, the slow smile that forms on her lips offers no absolute as Atilius approaches her. Staring into each other's eyes with blatant influence, it becomes evident that admiration is not the only emotion being exchanged between the two. Her silvery tongue is quick to oblige with keen words portraying a guileless act.

"It is important for everyone to understand that the goddess does not provide guidance on what we should do. She only provides a prophecy of what is to come. It is up to us to decide the course of action that we should take in order for our species to continue to thrive on this planet as we have since the beginning of time. The facts from our past surely affects our future, therefore I will need more information on Renan's background, the woman who was persecuted and the seer who provided this prophecy twenty-three years ago. It is impossible to formulate a decision on a matter that we do not understand. We must approach this delicate situation with caution and not speculate nor be alarmed just yet."

The witch slightly bends her knees, lowers her head, and politely excuses herself. "If you are done with me then I will be on my way."

Taking a step forward, the chief offers his hand to the merciless sibyl, "Yes of course."

Lifting her head, she places her palm into his once more as they both begin to descend one step at a time. He walks her all the way to the double iron doors with Irpa trailing behind like a lost child.

Before exiting, she swiftly turns around and comes face to face with Atilius. They both exchange glances for a few seconds before she disappears into the dark vestibule.

The chief then joins the other leaders who remain standing and lends them his undivided attention. Their advisors and the rest of the council members have embarked in individual discussions while everyone else remains troubled with the information presented to them.

This whole situation doesn't seem right. Something is off and I can't put my finger on it. What the heck is Atilius up to? I also noticed that Gersemi never returned from her early departure. Feeling the need to investigate further I decide on following Irpa and Freyja while everyone is still distracted.

Slowly crawling out from underneath the shadows, I stay veiled behind the forest green curtains and patiently make my way to the hidden passage that remains slightly opened.

Quickly shutting the brick door behind me, I hurriedly sprint towards the solar room. Stepping through the concealed entry I shut the passage and search my surroundings. Validating that I'm not being followed, I quickly begin making my way to the foyer that leads to the witch's living quarters.

The hallways are currently empty as the estate's staff is occupied with the recent arrival of our guest. After about five minutes of darting through several corridors, I finally reach the seer's chambers. Neither of them are present so I do what I know best – break in and remain surreptitious, however my quest is short lived when I reach for the door handle and I'm instantly thrown onto my back.

The impact was sudden and unexpected; therefore, I was not able to break my fall which caused my head to hit the concrete floor. A stinging pain immediately takes up residence at the back of my skull while a sharp sting shoots through my upper body.

Squinting my eyes, I attempt to focus my blurred vision while mouthing an assortment of profanity just to avoid making a spectacle out of myself. That diabolical sorceress put a spell on her door; how did I not foresee this?

As I remain on the ground mostly out of shock and not agony, I hear light footsteps approaching from afar. With my brain lacking oxygen and my lungs about to collapse I somehow manage to pick myself up from the floor and trot my limping ass to another hidden passage. A few seconds later, two feminine voices over power my heavy breathing.

"Do you think it's safe for her to travel by herself at this hour?" A few pauses....

"The real question is whether she can complete the task that has been entrusted upon her. We all have a purpose for our existence in this life or the next. We must remain positive and pray that the goddess will be with her until she has fulfilled her duty."

"What about Atilius? What will he think when she isn't present for the evening meal?"

"Remove these doubts from your mind sister. Atilius is not the enemy. There are others who conspire against our common goal. Come now and let us restore our energy as there is still much work to be done."

I sensed hesitation in her response. Hmm...if Gersemi has just left the grounds of the manor then maybe it's not too late to find out what she is up to.

Chapter Thirteen

~Envenom~

It's Saturday evening and I'm sitting on my bed, reading the invitation that Ethan personally dropped off over a week ago. The invite is for a small party at his place on behalf of his *now* girlfriend Nicole. As it turns out, it's her birthday and Ethan thought it would be nice to show her some gratitude. Hmm...sounds to me like someone is going to great lengths to receive approval from her family and friends.

At first, I wondered what he was up to as Ethan is not someone who can be taken seriously when it comes to women. But after seeing the effort he has placed in making this relationship work, I can't help but wonder if he is finally thinking about settling down. Good for him, if Nicole is the one to calm his storm then I am happy for them both.

Now I must face a more problematic issue, like finding something to wear and a sitter for Mateo. The party starts at 7pm and I still haven't got a plan in place. Sighing, I stand from the edge of my bed and walk over to the closet.

As I begin to rummage through graphic tees and worn jeans, I faintly hear my doorbell chime. A few seconds later, an echo of little thumping feet can be heard from the hallway. Mateo's brown wavy hair appears at my door as he points towards the family room alerting me that we have a visitor.

Bending down, I take him into my arms and tow us both to the front door. I decide to peek through the faux wood blinds and confirm my suspicion – of course it's Aemilia. I wouldn't be surprised if Ethan put her up to the task of ensuring that I actually make an appearance and not cancel as usual. Darn, how am I going to get out of this one? I mentally prepare myself for the wrath that will soon follow before opening the door to greet my best friend.

"Hey you. What brings you to my neck of the woods? And dressed so sexy may I add." I smile teasingly while placing my hand on the side of the door, attempting to block the entry.

Aemilia rolls her eyes and pushes the door open, letting herself in. She strolls past me and saunters straight to the couch, placing her bag on my coffee table.

"Yeah right, like I would let you bail on me. I know what game you're running and I'm not about to buy it. Where is Mateo's sitter and why haven't you showered? Do you know what time it is? We are going to be late!" She exclaims with one eyebrow raised and her legs crossed.

I close the front door and march towards the living area to face her with Mateo's hands clasped around my neck.

"I can't go Em," I begin to whine like a child. "You know that I don't have a reliable sitter and I can't find anything to wear. It's a sign that I should stay home as tonight has *disaster* spelled all over it."

With a pouty frown, I try to weasel my way out and hope that she doesn't press my real motives for why I intend to abandon our plans for the evening.

"You are so predictable; I knew this would happen. But not to worry because I decided that this time, I would help absolve your problems."

"What did you do?" I ask suspiciously because I know that this can't be good.

"Well, I took it upon myself and asked Ethan if Mateo could be your date in the event that you didn't have a backup plan and guess what, he was actually delighted. This is not like a huge party with fancy cocktails or anything. He assured me that it's a small…."

I cut her off before she could continue her long winded explanation while motioning my hand to stop.

"Yeah, yeah, it's a small intimate gathering, blah blah I know. I got the invitation too. So, tell me, if it's nothing fancy then why are you dressed like a minx?"

I begin to eye her outfit because she is dressed to the nines for it being such an *intimate* party. She looks incredible with her pink cocktail dress which is heart shaped around the chest and embedded in a floral bead pattern at the top and along the edges. The top layer of her dress has lace and the bottom floats right above her knees followed by white heels. The only piece of jewelry on her body is a white diamond bracelet and dark pink egg drop earrings which completes her getup. Her dark blonde straight hair is tied to the back with a beaded hair tie which highlights her light brown eyes. Aemilia proceeds with her grueling persuasion as she narrows her eyes.

"So dramatic today, are we? Well, for your information, I'm dressed like a vixen because I intend on being one tonight. We both know what kind of successful and exuberant men Ethan is acquainted with. I'm single so

I figure why not!" She exclaims while crossing her arms over her chest in defense.

Now that she is here, what am I going to do to get myself out of this one? Exhausted I continue to make excuses, stammering along the way.

"Well, I uh, I don't think it's a good idea for Mateo to be around drunk adults and half naked women like yourself. You really should change you know. What if you show up looking all sexy and everyone there is dressed down, then you're really going to feel like a fool." I tsk and shake my head while placing Mateo back down.

"No, I won't. I will feel like the most confident and empowered woman in the room. You should try it sometime. Now let's stop focusing on my attire and redirect our energy back to you. We have the sitter thing checked so now the final issue, your wardrobe."

She stands from the sofa and begins to eye me up and down while looking disgusted with my choice of style.

"What? I just got home from grocery shopping. I am not about to wear heels to the store as if it were a catwalk."

I begin to look myself over as well and wonder what the heck is wrong with my clothes. Aemilia has been single for as long as I can remember; not because she can't find a man who will not commit but because she chooses to remain a free spirit. She feels that with a commitment comes drama and she isn't ready for that just yet. She's the kind of girl who flies by the seat of her pants; someone you call when you want to have an eventful evening. And I am the complete opposite, yet we still have so much in common.

Aemilia takes notice that I have not changed my mind and leaps in for the kill.

"Uh huh, right. So, I brought a couple of decent matching garments that will accent your curves." She begins to circle me with a finger on her lip while studying my form. "I've got it! The perfect dress has come to mind. You're damn lucky that I'm a fashionista otherwise you'd be wearing pajamas to a cocktail party."

I provide her with my *I don't think so* expression because I am not about to wear whatever she has in mind. Our fashion choices are totally in reverse like day and night, so whatever she has in store for me cannot be good. Sensing that I'm about to protest she starts to walk towards the front door.

"We are going to this party so stop looking at me like that Simone De Luca."

"Em…" I attempt to object yet again but before I know it, she walks past me and out the front door. Reappearing a few moments later she has several bags hanging from her arms that not only contain clothes but shoes and makeup too.

What have I gotten myself into? I open my mouth then immediately close it because I know that I'm already on the losing end of this discussion. It's Ethan we are talking about here. He would be disappointed if I didn't show up. I have a bad feeling about this but what's a girl to do?

"Alright then, let's get this over with already." I whisper in defeat.

Aemilia jumps with excitement and clasp my hand, dragging me to my bedroom where the torture will soon follow.

About an hour and a half later I have been transformed from a mother to a seductress. She has curled my dark brown hair into large wavy locks with my hair tossed to one side. My makeup is done to accent my hazel eyes with my lips covered in light pink lipstick and thick long lashes that finally serve a purpose.

My lean body is covered in a sheer knee length cream sleeveless dress with a floral lace pattern that hugs my body in all the right places. The color stands out against my bronze skin and a crystal heart shaped necklace with matching earrings. I must admit that I do feel sexy and beautiful. I just hope we are not overdressed because if we are, then I am going to kill Aemilia.

Mateo is looking sharp as well, dressed in dark khaki pants, light blue polo shirt and his brown loafers. Brushing his wavy hair to the side, I managed to groom his locks with a couple of rogue strands going the opposite direction. I feel nervous and I don't know why as I do a look over in the mirror once more while turning sideways to make sure that I'm not showing too much.

"You're most welcome!" Aemilia gawks at me while clapping her hands together in excitement. Giving her the side eye, I quickly interject and set some ground rules.

"Just for the record, we are only going for a few hours and then I'm leaving with or without you; no matter who or what you're doing." There, I told her.

"Damn, that was rude, but I get your point. Understood, a few hours and we are off, I promise."

She confirms before we walk out of the house and head off to a party surrounded by friends and strangers alike. For reasons unknown, I can't shake this terrible feeling that has stirred my conscience. I will ignore it for now and hope that it's just me overreacting to how I am dressed tonight.

We arrive in Highland Park an hour late and the event has started without us; *that's unfortunate*. Ethan wasn't telling the whole truth when he mentioned that it was a private event because the street is lined with vehicles on both sides. I'm suddenly nervous and feel my heart beating erratically. Aemilia notices me fidgeting and gives me a heartfelt smile to calm my nerves.

"Well, at least we don't have to park our own car." She motions towards the valet parking where three males dressed in dark blue attire are patiently waiting for guest to arrive.

Ethan always did know how to host the best parties and usually goes all out, no matter the occasion. His fortune was inherited through generations of wealth. But he has remained humble despite his upbringing which is a miracle because when it comes to women, he remains clueless.

Aemilia drives her Lexus towards the three young gentlemen, and I start to feel anxious. We get out of her vehicle, hand the keys to a handsome fella, and start to make our way towards the back of the home with Mateo in tow. The three-story brick Victorian style home is lined with colorful poppies and green shrubbery all around. There is a wide U-shaped driveway that curves from the street to the house and back.

We turn the corner towards the side of the house and end up in the backyard which is decorated in café string lights that are hooded by woven shades. Fresh picasso calla lilies and baby's breath are also hanging on a twine above the patio and around the luscious green yard.

There are several people outside and Reverie by Debussy is playing in the background. Three attendants dressed in black with white bow ties and light gray vest are walking around with trays of hors d'oeuvres and flutes of pink champagne. A dance floor has been placed in the middle of the courtyard which is aligned by numerous decorated tables and more floral arrangements as center pieces. There is a large pool to the far right of the yard and an outdoor stainless-steel kitchen that is occupied by additional waiters. I notice that both Aemilia and I are taken aback by the view.

We enter the home through the double glass doors and take in the crowd, which is mixed with familiar and unknown faces, possibly from Nicole's side. The same music that is playing outside is also present indoors.

There are two built in bars on each side of the living area which are currently occupied by bartenders and newly arrived guest. The interior of the home is also covered with additional floral arrangements that vary from blush peonies to white sweet peas. There is a grand spiral staircase present to the far left that leads to a private living area upstairs.

I instantly spot Leona Clark, my other bestie who is here with her now fiancé Derek Posey sitting down on a lovely divan enjoying champagne. I quickly waive at them before making my rounds when we run into Ethan and Nicole.

"Hey beautiful!" Ethan reaches over, embraces me in a brotherly hug and kisses me on the forehead. "You look stunning as always!"

"Thanks Ethan. You don't look so bad yourself." I wink at him and take in his remarkable appearance.

The gray trousers hug his waistline which reveals his strapping built. A mat of hair is visible from his white-collar shirt that is slightly unbuttoned, showing off his masculine chest. His gray suit jacket has no bow tie but the olive tone to his skin still brings out the blue hues in his eyes. With dark blond hair and a close clean shave, there's no doubt in my mind that he will remain flirtatious throughout the evening.

"Why thank you but I am almost certain that you will be the one stealing the show tonight."

He gives me a quick look over and begins to laugh while taking a swig of the light brown liquid in his hand. Ok. Not sure what he means by that but whatever.

"Well I won't take all the credit; it was Aemilia who transformed me into this." With a sheepish grin I motion over my body with my hand.

"Nonsense, you have natural beauty so don't sell yourself short." He smiles at me then finally turns his gaze to Mateo and Aemilia.

"Well, glad you all made it. Hey little man, give me a high five." He squats and lowers his palm to Mateo who is more than pleased to smack it then throws his little arms around his neck.

Ethan hugs him tightly and quickly places him back onto the ground but not before tousling his wavy hair. He then stands and clears his throat while suddenly turning serious.

"Em." Is all he could muster while immediately lowering his head to avoid eye contact.

Aemilia then mirrors his half ass greeting with a simple, "Eth," seeming bored with the exchange while playing with her bracelet.

Since we approached the duo, Aemilia hasn't been able to break eye contact from Ethan. It's unnerving but funny at the same time. I don't understand why Ethan even bothered to invite her if all they ever do is act weird around each other. I attempt to break the silence in order to avoid speculation from Nicole.

"Thanks Ethan for allowing Mateo to come as my date. I'm not sure that I would have made it if you wouldn't have agreed."

I feel awkward that I'm the only adult here with a child. Damn you Aemilia!

"You don't have to thank me. We all adore him. Who wouldn't want him around?" He assures me and winks at Mateo while snaking his arm around Nicole's waist and pulls her closer to his body.

I quickly turn my attention to Nicole who is hanging on his arm, taking in every word he speaks. Her platinum blond hair hangs straight down her backside covering the exposed skin from the open back dress. She is wearing a black sheer see through gown with sequence that screams *look at me*. Any sudden moves and the material on her body will rip to shreds.

The expensive three inch heals on her feet seem awfully painful to walk in. Her soft brown eyes and bright red lipstick stand out against her pale white skin. Nicole is perky and attractive in her own way with that frisky smile and girlie laugh all the way to her teasing touches that linger a bit too long. She is a young free-spirited sorority girl who spends her father's money as if it grew on trees. I'd bet her definition of a romantic evening includes frat parties and

243

skinny dipping so I can see why Ethan is so intrigued by her wildness as he was once in her shoes.

We both reach for each other and engage in a kindhearted embrace.

"Happy Birthday Nicole. This is an exciting celebration and you look incredible."

I try my best to remain neutral and pleasant, meanwhile Aemilia and Nicole are now busy throwing daggers at each other. I guess Nicole caught on that those two had, or should I say, have chemistry.

Aemilia manages to sneak in a snide comment hoping to galvanize a reaction.

"Oh yeah, it's your birthday huh? I guess a Happy Birthday is in order."

She has a grin playing on her face while toying with the flute of champagne close to her mouth and her eyes lowered as if to antagonize them both. When I turn to look at Ethan, I notice that he is staring at Aemilia. I'm surprised that Nicole completely ignores her criticism but not before elbowing Ethan in the ribs. He certainly has a soft spot when it comes to Aemilia and I'm not entirely sure if he was gawking in awe, or because she was finally getting under his skin.

This is nothing new, most of their interactions always start and end in the same exact manner. They play coy, exchange smug insults, make up as if it never happened and then the cycle repeats. I however keep a smile on my face and give Aemilia the *cool your jets* look before turning my attention back to Nicole.

"Thanks Simone. I'm really glad you made it but sadly don't share the same sentiment for all of our guest." She manages to emphasize the word *all* while eyeing Aemilia.

Wow – this is too much drama for us only being here a mere ten minutes. I see that my crazy friend Aemilia tastes victory because she begins to laugh hysterically at Nicole's statement, and out loud may I add. We all turn to look at her with eyes wide in surprise while Nicole's anger only doubles given that Ethan's gaze has continued to linger on Aemilia longer than necessary.

What is it with these two? I try my best to ignore my best friend's sudden moment of psychosis but then she does the unexpected. Almost instantly she ceases laughing, polishes off her drink, struts over to Ethan and leans over to his right. Her light pink lips are mere inches from his ear when she hastily whispers a few words, turns back to smile at Nicole and then disappears into the crowd.

That. Just. Happened.

We watch in horror as she fades, and I somehow summon the courage to turn my attention back to the chaos that was playing right before my eyes. It seems Nicole had enough because she brashly squirms out of Ethan's arm and storms off in the opposite direction. I turn to face my friend who now looks more confused than ever. My smile fades quickly and turns apologetic on behalf of Aemilia when Ethan abruptly burst into laughter himself. Now I'm the one confused because he is as crazy as she is.

He announces, "This is definitely going to be an interesting night," and swiftly guzzles his glass of brown liquid.

I raise my eyebrows in surprise, "Ok. I'm going to pretend that didn't just happen and try to enjoy whatever is left of the evening."

"As you should, now I need some more scotch before I do something that I will surely regret in the morning."

With a big grin on his face, he walks away pleased with his current situation. Oh my goodness. We might need to leave sooner than I thought. What in the world is going on here? I'm going to find my lunatic friend before she gets herself escorted out of this shindig.

As I proceed to find Aemilia, I feel someone's gaze on me that seems all too familiar. I quickly turn to face the gawker, but to my surprise I don't find anyone that I recognize. Hmm… must be my nerves. Relax, I tell myself as I make my way to Leona and Derek who are both in deep conversation.

"Hey Simone. Is everything ok? You seem worried?" Leona stands up and greets me with a smooch on both sides of my face while narrowing her brown eyes.

Her short blonde curls are weaved into an intricate braid that loosens at the end. She is wearing an off-white pant suit that is open in the neckline with no jewels around her neck or wrist. The only piece of jewelry on her body is a pair of diamond studs. Her tan stands out perfectly against her choice of attire which is completed with open toe heels. She always looks stunning, even without makeup.

"No, I'm fine. Just the same old story with Aemilia. By the way, have you seen her?"

"Not since you two walked in. Hey Mateo, come with Auntie Lee." She crouches down and places Mateo in her arms. He twists in her grasp to get comfortable but quickly settles into her embrace.

"Hey Derek. How are you?" I pull him into my arms and wrap one arm around his shoulder. He returns the polite gesture with his eyebrows cast downward like he's confused or something.

"I'm good. Glad to see that you decided to come, considering that ..." And he is swiftly cut off by Leona as she interrupts him mid-sentence.

"Honey, why don't you go and grab us some drinks." She then turns to face me, "What would you like to drink; Champagne or a soda pop?"

"Champagne will do for now. I don't want to drink too much since I have this little guy with me." I tickle Mateo under his chin, causing him to giggle at my light touch.

"Absolutely. I'll be right back."

I watch as Derek strolls through the crowd and towards the bar. He is a highly energetic guy with a very humorous attitude. In college he played a variety of sports, ranging from football to Lacrosse which explains his athletic built. I'm sure whatever he was about to say had to do with Aemilia and her senseless antics. Leona disrupts my pensive state when she reaches for my hand.

"Well, look at you. Oh Simone, you look stunning. Let me guess, you finally let Aemilia have her fix and play dress up. Am I right?" She confirms the obvious because everyone knows that I'm an artist. Someone who wears paint splattered clothes with endless wrinkles and doesn't have time to doll herself up.

I motion towards my attire, "Yes. Aemilia is behind all of this. Thanks for the compliment." I then proceed to roll my eyes in a mocking manner which causes us to burst into laughter.

"I really mean it though, you look beautiful. I'm sure every man in here is finding it difficult to peel their eyes from you."

I smile shyly as we both engage in a casual conversation when Derek returns from the bar and is now accompanied by a familiar face that I was not expecting to see. Franco Alves.

This neurotic male has been pursuing my affection since college and I have never given him the time of day. He eventually ceased all efforts and moved to another state. I thought I was in the clear until handwritten letters began to arrive at my home and place of employment. At first, they were geared more towards a friendship but as the communication increased so did his obsessive tendencies. All too soon we were back where it all started, however this time it came with a marriage proposal.

Who in their right mind would ever think that a proposal over certified mail would lead to a positive outcome? Not that it would have mattered in our situation; needless to say, his method of persuasion did not work in his favor. And, I haven't seen or heard from him since, that is until this very moment. Talk about awkward!

My blood swiftly rushes to my cheeks and I feel my stomach churn. Maybe this is what Derek was about to spill before Leona stopped him.

"Ladies, look who I ran into at the bar."

He hands us our glasses and Leona places Mateo down to take a sip of her cocktail. I grab Mateo's tiny hand and pull him close. Trying my best to not look at the man before me, I quickly learn that he is unavoidable.

"Hello again Leona." Franco places his hands around her arms and lands a friendly peck on her cheek.

She accepts his generosity and returns his smile. He then turns to me and against my will our eyes meet like magnets. With a lean built and great sense of style, he is every woman's dream. Unfortunately, he is not my type. Besides, my mother always told me to follow my first instinct and my intuition is telling me to stay away.

Reaching for my free hand he gently moves it towards his mouth and grazes my knuckles with his lips. "Hello Simone. Beautiful as ever." Damn it, where's Aemilia? She would know exactly what to say to get me out of this ghastly situation.

"Thank you Franco. You're too kind." I manage to remain polite after clearing my throat several times. My fingers remain trapped within his grip when I feel Mateo tug on my arm and yelp, "Mommy."

Oh, how grateful am I that he is here with me because now I have an excuse to run off somewhere that doesn't include the one person whom I've been trying to avoid. Quickly breaking eye contact I remove my hand from his and squat down to acknowledge my son.

"What's wrong honey?" I gently rub his cheek with the back of my hand. Knowing exactly what he needs I quickly gather my wits and turn to excuse myself.

"My apologies but I have to step away for a moment and attend to Mateo. It was great seeing you Franco."

"It's always a pleasure." His smile is a bit unsettling as his greedy sight lands on my chest. I'm sure those foul gray eyes have now moved onto my other assets as I turn my attention to Leona and Derek but I'm too busy to care at the moment.

"If you happen to see Aemilia before I return, please let her know that I need to speak with her."

Taking a hold of Mateo's hand, we head off into the crowd, hopefully disappearing out of reach from the wicked glare that has caused the ominous thoughts to resurface.

I can feel the tiny hairs on my neck rise while goose bumps begin to form on my arms. Right, it all came back to me now; he not only lacks self-control and respect but does so without regard. I shake off the eerie feeling and continue towards my destination.

While exiting the ladies' room I sense that someone is staring at me again. I'm not sure if I want to know who is scrutinizing me this time but I must say that it's rather difficult to ignore. As I turn to face the impolite gawker and potentially shame him for his insolence, I quickly discover that this deviant male is nowhere to be found. Weird. I'm almost positive that I sensed someone close by.

Ugh! Just try to enjoy yourself tonight and stop thinking negative thoughts I tell myself. Fifteen minutes later and I finally locate Aemilia in the mist of three young gentlemen. She's busy being chatty with one of Ethan's friends who is currently eating out of the palm of her hand. Deciding that it's time to end her charade of flirting, I clear my throat to capture her attention then motion for her to come over.

"Where the hell have you been and what is going on between you and Ethan?"

Malice flows from my lips as I exhale sharply to control the frustration that has started to develop. I have finally run out of patience given the circumstances that I've endured. First, she drags me to this party against my will and under false pretenses, then she proceeds to antagonize the one male who actually feels the need to tolerate her many phases of petty selfishness.

You would think that it would end there but no, she proceeds with the silent torture by abandoning me while I sustain borderline sexual harassment from the creep that I've been avoiding my entire adulthood! And to make matters more interesting, I've got a strange feeling that someone has been following me the entire evening, but I have yet to discover the perp. So yeah, I more than a little pissed but lucky for her she knows me better than anyone and quickly defuses my foul mood with her tattered coyness.

"Oh that. I had a temporary moment of regret that's all. And as to where I've been – mingling darling. Have you seen all of the available bachelors? I can hardly contain myself, let alone stand there waiting for one of them to offer me a drink."

She turns to look at her surroundings, smiling while offering her flirtatious body language. As for me, I've had enough of her half-truths.

"Aemilia, I have no idea what that means and do not have time for riddles so give it to me straight and stop playing the victim."

She hesitates before sharing her true motives. "Damn it, alright. But you better not judge me, no matter what I say."

"Of course not, so spill already because I have something to tell you."

"Ok. Ethan and I have been hooking up for the past couple of months." She confesses boldly before continuing to try and justify her foolish actions. "Look, I know he is with Nicole and all, but we have both agreed to set feelings aside and that this was only about our physical attraction."

What the hell is wrong with her? I sense that she is nervous because she instantly starts to bite her lower lip. Placing one hand on my hip, I chuckle and scowl at her rudely.

"Oh, you are a real piece of work my friend! The two of you definitely deserve each other. What in the world did you whisper to him before you stormed off?"

Not sure that I really wanted to hear the answer, but I actually find all this amusing. Aemilia and Ethan hooking up, again. Ha. Classic!

With her left eyebrow arched, she begins to elaborate on her scheme of nonsense.

"Oh, I bet that pissed off daddy's little girl huh. Well if you must know, I told him that when he got tired of playing house with the little prom queen to come look for me so I can demonstrate what a real woman has to offer." And on that note, I pivot.

"I refuse to offer any words of advice because I have a feeling that you are just going to do whatever you want anyway."

"And you're absolutely correct so let's stop wasting time. Now tell me, what is so important that you felt the need to interrupt my conversation with that hot piece of man dime?"

She motions over to the tall handsome male standing by a set of french doors that lead to the kitchen and conveys the *give me a minute* glance. His smile widens, as he continues his conversation with his comrades.

"Well, when I was catching up with Leona, Derek stepped away to grab us some drinks and when he returned guess who he was accompanied by?"

"I know…. I'm sorry you had to find out this way. I was going to tell you, but I got um, distracted. How are you feeling?"

She has a regretful frown on her face and begins to rub my upper arm. Why does she feel apologetic that she didn't tell me?

"Wait, what? You saw him? When?"

"After I whispered into Ethan's ear I headed for the bar and saw him standing in a corner by himself looking fierce as ever. I wasn't even sure it was him at first, so I decided to investigate further when I got momentarily sidetracked by...someone. By the time I gathered my wits he was gone." She explained, looking puzzled and lost in thought.

"Well, he had me feeling uneasy and awkward, so I found a way to excuse myself and find you. His presence is extremely unsettling."

"Huh? I remember a time when you would do anything to be in his presence, and now he is unsettling? You're right, you are not yourself tonight."

"Whatever Aemilia," I lean in closer, "Look, I came looking for you because I'm going outside for a while to let Mateo run around. Do you care to join me or are you currently still occupied?"

I ask a question that I already know the answer to, but it was worth a shot. I really don't want to be by myself right now but looks like I might not have a choice.

"I'll meet you out there in a bit. I just have to finish something really quick then I'm all yours."

I roll my eyes at her when she catches me and starts laughing while heading straight to her previous destination. As I begin making my way towards the double glass doors that lead to the outside patio, I feel the same gaze lingering on me. This time I don't even bother to acknowledge whoever is making me feel uncomfortable. I just keep walking with my pink champagne in one hand that I haven't bothered to touch and Mateo's little palm in the other.

Once we're outside, I move towards a group of tables that are decorated with white garden roses and greens. Taking in the scenery, I finally start to relax. The weather is chilly and carries a breeze that moves my hair lightly across my back and away from my face. I notice that a few people have gathered onto the dance floor, waltzing to a new classical romantic piece: Liebesträume –Love Dream by Franz Liszt.

I envy how carefree the other couples are with each other. Sharing conversations and celebrating this moment together under the gorgeous moonlight. I shouldn't feel sad for myself though because I chose to be alone, so it's my own fault. Get it together Simone; he is never coming back so stop fooling yourself into thinking that you two had an undeniable connection.

Shaking these senseless thoughts from my head, I take notice that my son has decided to sit on the grass. He begins playing with a set of hot wheels that we brought him for entertainment. Walking over, I help him to his feet and sit him down in a nearby chair so that he doesn't get his clothes dirty.

Mateo seems content in his own world and pretty soon he will get sleepy and the night will end. Speaking of the night ending, where is Aemilia? She was supposed to be out here a long time ago. Well, if I had to guess what she was up to then I'd say that she is probably caught up with Ethan or some other male, talking their ear off or getting into more trouble than necessary.

My mind begins to wonder off again and I'm back thinking about the one individual that has never left my thoughts. The only male that I've ever loved, unrequited affection of course. I gave him my heart and he took it with haste like an insatiable thief, except in his case he wasn't stealthy about it.

After a few moments I decide to take a sip of my drink. Wow, this champagne is a bit strong for my liking. Guess it's been a while since I've had a cocktail so of course it's going to have a bitter after taste. I scan the courtyard again for any sight of Aemilia and come to realization that she might not be joining me after all.

Taking in the scene, light playful music, and the crowd I steal another taste from my beverage. Within a matter of seconds, my body starts to feel heavy as I slowly move to my right and place my glass down onto an empty table. Without warning I lose my balance but somehow manage to grab onto a chair and steady myself.

My head is swimming with turmoil and before I know it the sight of my son begins to fade. Next thing I know, I'm gravitating towards the floor and I've got no desire nor strength to put up a fight. Consumed by pure darkness I have no thoughts in this moment of vulnerability, only peace. My body feels relaxed and calm when I should be hurting from the fall.

Open your eyes. Open…. My eyes flutter open for a few seconds and I catch a glimpse of a male embracing me in his arms. He caught me before I fainted, and my world came crashing down. This must be a dream because it can't be him. Not here, not now and not like this.

"Simone, can you hear me? Please open your eyes. Look at me Simone."

His frantic voice engulfs my ears as I utter his name incoherently, "Jovianus."

The last thing I remember is someone lifting me into their arms and then everything goes pitch black.

Chapter Fourteen

~Treachery~

The abrupt storm continues to pour as it forcefully pounds against the glass windows of the chalet. I take notice that the room temperature has slightly dropped, producing a nippy draft in the study. A muffled whistle caused from a gust of wind followed by a lull escapes from the chimney flute sending chills down my spine. My body suddenly quivers as goose bumps resurface on my arms and legs which are still covered in damp clothing.

I've been sitting at the writing table motionless for the last hour retracing my steps and going over every detail of this fruitless mission. My instructions were straightforward; locate the asset and secure the evidence. Freyja's vision was stored in my memory like a photograph, so I negligently continued my quest and removed all doubts from my mind, determined to fulfill the assignment.

Conversely, I wasn't expecting to be followed by a corrupt proxy. I could sense his lingering presence the moment my plane landed in the States, yet he managed to remain cryptic of his whereabouts long enough to reach his objective.

Flagging down a cab at this hour was easier than I imagined.

"Where to?" The cab driver asked politely.

"Maple Street in Regent Square please." I call over his shoulder as I close the door to the back seat.

Following my instincts, I ordered the driver to cut corners and purposely diverted off course, delaying my arrival by thirty minutes. Feeling confident that I no longer had a tail, I instructed the driver to drop me off at the beginning of the street. Grabbing my crossbody handbag from the back seat, I close the door behind me and open my wallet in search of some cash. Reaching through the front passenger window, I hand over enough bills to cover my fare.

"Thank you. Please keep the change." I graciously produce a gentle smile.

"Thanks. Now you have yourself a wonderful evening."

Nodding, I wait for the driver to leave before I decide to walk through the gloom neighborhood that was once illuminated by a streetlamp. While tugging on my sweater and wrapping the scarf closely around my neck, I look up into the sky and allow my eyes to absorb the light waves radiating from the moon which will double the effectiveness of my vision in the night.

A shift in temperature causes my hair to dance about as I descend towards my destination. After about five minutes of walking in silence, the house finally comes into view. I hesitate to cross the street and risk being noticed so I decide to dematerialize in the backyard.

Careful to remain unseen, I swiftly make my way to the nearest window and glance inside. The kitchen comes into view which is dim and lifeless validating that either no one is home or rendered unconscious into a deep sleep.

Quickly dematerializing inside the dining area, I quietly make my way towards the foyer in search of any type of documentation that identifies the potential asset. I commenced by investigating a spare room located to my right. Slowly sliding the door open, my curious eyes begin to explore the unoccupied room which is filled with three sculpting tables, modeling compounds, multiple bags of clay and carving tools. I step inside and stride towards the closet hoping to catch a break.

Cautious not to make any sounds I begin to sift through art supplies, books, and jars of brushes when I spot a wire basket settled in the far-left hand corner. Piles of outdated mail rest on the top rack addressed to Linda and Brian De Luca which remain unopened. I randomly grab two envelopes from the middle of the stack and leave the rest untouched while stuffing them inside my bag. Leaving the room, I descend towards the hallway where three more living quarters are visible.

Glancing through the second entry, I take notice that several toys are scrambled across the wooden floor making it too risky to enter. A small framed bed is nestled in the center of the living area opposite of the two windows that are covered in white roller shades. The walls are decorated with colorful crayon art that was more than likely crafted by a toddler. Twinkling string lights hang from above which illuminates the revered space. I highly doubt this room could offer the answers I seek and decide to continue my search elsewhere.

The next door reveals a cozy powder room that is adorned with black and gold furnishings. I grow anxious by the minute as I swiftly proceed to the end of the foyer. My first step turns out to be perilous when the wooden floorboards decide to creak from the sudden weight shift. Flustered from the unexpected blunder, I scan my surroundings to see if anyone was disturbed by my clumsiness.

Arriving at the fourth and final room, I confirm that the door is closed and possibly off limits which has me on the edge. As I carefully place my sweaty palm on the door handle, I am immediately overwhelmed with images of the female in question. The features of her face continue to replay in my mind over and over like a broken record. Could this room finally reveal what I've been searching for?

I proceed to turn the knob until it clicks open granting me access. The hinges squeak a bit as I peer my head inside and scope out the private quarters. Once inside I notice that the bed is made, *and the room is meticulously organized with no one currently occupying the space. Without hesitation, I begin to search the drawers located on each nightstand. As I continue to rummage through this female's personal belongings I come across coupons, a bible and junk mail. Nothing useful emerges as more papers, bills and note pads appear from both compartments. Just as I'm about to give up, I notice a brown box slightly sticking out from underneath the bed.*

Squatting down I swiftly retrieve the small container and open the lid anxious to reveal its contents. A handwritten note with foreign musical symbols smeared in gold ink is the first article to appear. Moving the creased letter aside, I come across two birth certificates and some pictures. Focusing on the photographs I recognize the young woman in the photo. She is sitting on top of a huge boulder, accompanied by a young toddler on her lap. I am instantly drawn to her and realize that she is the woman from Freyja's vision. There are at least a dozen photographs in the box featuring several different mortals. Wondering why these items would be tucked away in a shoe box, I set off on studying them and store the images in my mind so that I may transmit them back to Freyja.

As for the birth certificates and handwritten note, I decide to fold them in half and shove them into my purse. At that exact moment, I hear a loud thud followed by broken glass ricochet from the front of the house. Caught off guard I instantly dematerialize to the backyard.

With my knees bent low to the ground I hide between two shrubs and remain silent while assessing the current predicament that I'm about to face. Additional banging and breaking of items continue from the inside of the home. Taking a quick glance from the bushes I concentrate on the moving shadow through the open curtains.

A male figure is lurking in the kitchen, combing the drawers while unleashing chaos and dismantling everything in his path. A thick jacket with a hoodie that is slightly unzipped at the neckline covers his broad shoulders as he moves with acuity. His long-braided ponytail swings back and forth as he effortlessly flings broken objects across the floor.

Fully aware that I am no longer safe, I attempt to depart when the intruder does the unexpected and turns his attention onto me. I freeze out of fear which causes the both of us to lock eyes for a few seconds allowing me to seize a glimpse of his face. A large raised scar runs through his lips, down his chin and ends at the center of his throat. His irises are light brown with specks of yellow that are filled with determination but immediately flash to black when he blinks. A wolfish grin slowly forms on his lips for a hint of a second when I panic and begin to run as fast as the wind can carry me.

Within a matter of minutes, I end up at the nearest bus station drenched in sweat with an over accelerated heart rate. Standing there on the platform with my hands shaking I start to hyperventilate. I bend down and rest my hands on my knees as I try to catch my breath. Focus, I need to focus right now and get to the sanctum, fast.

Knowing what I must do, I decide to avoid the public highway and take the back roads to the cabin located in Ligonier.

Sensing a change in the precipitation I promptly head off towards safe passage when the downpour begins. After about fifteen minutes of running at lightning speed, I arrive at the cottage which is settled on a two-acre lot surrounded by a cornfield. The property is invisible to the naked eye and bound with a protective spell that can only be disengaged by a seer.

Exhaling sharply, I close my eyes as the rain lands on my face and chant the words that will lead me to sanctuary, "Vent et le Feu."

The iron gate that isolates the property from the rest of the world unlocks and the chalet is revealed. Pushing my way through the entrance, I nervously fast track inside without ever looking back.

As I sit in the dark, contemplating my misfortunes, my anxiety finally prevails. Before I can register what is happening, I find myself hurling as bile begins to spill from my quivering lips. Clenching my stomach in agony, I come to terms that I lack fortitude thereby evading the actuality that I have placed our lives as well as others at risk.

At this point I'm torn between taking my own life and ending this disgrace or continue living with the fact that I am a failure. Not only is this situation dire but also delicate in nature thus the reason why I am apprehensive.

Deciding to end this charade of self-pity, I pick up the land line and begin to dial the number that I've been trying to avoid since my arrival. The phone rings twice before I'm greeted with that sweet familiar voice.

"Gersemi," she abruptly speaks my name, "Thank the goddess that you are safe."

Without thinking I gush into the receiver and begin to quietly sob while confessing my misfortunes.

"I regret to report that we have been compromised sister."

"Gersemi, are you hurt?"

"No." My hushed tone is barely recognizable as I shake my head while clasping the handset tightly with both hands.

She speaks impetuously, "Are you in one of the safe houses?"

"Yes, in Ligonier." I continue to quietly sob into the receiver as tears line up to stream down my numb cheeks.

"Ok. I need you to compose yourself so that you can explain to me what happened. No one can penetrate the spell so know that you are safe." Her voice is soothing and border line hypnotic as she murmurs words of comfort through the receiver and patiently waits for me to gather my wits.

"Everything comes with a price." My words are but a breath as I attempt to control my emotions.

"Gersemi, please tell me what happened."

"I saw him. I saw him, and he saw me." My words are followed by weeps and fear as I repeat the same phrase.

"Who Gersemi? Please tell me who you saw!"

"Remus. I saw Remus from the Nadöb tribe. He followed me here which means he also knows." Hush thoughts drift into the unknown as Freyja contemplates the risks of this precarious notion.

"That's impossible. Are you sure that it was Remus? You have to be sure Gersemi."

"Yes, I'm sure." I nod my head again as if she were standing in front of me while clasping the handset tightly.

"Then we have been compromised indeed." Her voice is stern and full of uncertainty. "Please tell me everything."

Going over the details; I first begin with my instincts that I thought I was being followed and conclude the discussion with me hiding in the bushes while Remus ransacks the home when our sights regrettably intersect. After sharing images of the pictures that I found in the box and the foreign symbols inscribed on the handwritten note, I sense confusion from the other end of the receiver while we try to understand the significance of these new findings.

Given that Freyja remains speechless leads me to believe that this matter is now beyond her understanding and that she will have no choice but to seek guidance from an elder. We will be forced to expose the safety of this being as well as ours. Deciding that it was time to disrupt our prolonged silence, I interject her misplaced thoughts with a probing question.

"What do you think these strange markings mean?"

"I'm not sure. I've never seen writings as such. This could be a form of an antiquated dialect, perhaps from another era that no longer exist."

I gather that she is overwhelmed by the knowledge that we've possibly stumbled upon something far more dangerous than we originally anticipated.

"Is it possible that this being is able to read or even understand these outlandish inscriptions?"

"At this point, nothing is off limits."

"Freyja, one more thing."

"Yes."

"The two birth certificates that were recovered from the home – one of them identifies the individual as Simone De Luca with the place of birth originating in Pittsburgh and cites Linda and Brian De Luca as her birth parents, however the other document seems to be blank."

"And for good reason I imagine," a few more pauses. "You see, I believe that document would not be safeguarded unless it contained highly restricted information that would otherwise be detrimental to that individual or their origin. Seems to me that these facts were purposely concealed with a powerful spell that could have only been performed by a compelling and rare witch."

"Are you speaking of Noita the seer?"

"Indeed. The same Nadöb Seer that was rumored to have revealed this so-called prophecy. The one who vowed silence and has continued to remain mum on the matter. All leads continue to point to Noita; she was after all Renan's confidant. I'm starting to think that she wasn't just a seer and had a bigger role to play on the matter than we have been led to believe."

"What do you propose we do with this information? What about Remus?"

"If Remus is involved then I believe that the Nadöb tribe might be plotting against us." She remains quiet and discontent possibly lost for words when she finally gains the courage to speak again.

"Gersemi, I need you to remain where you are until further notice. I can sense that this creature will likely seek your help very soon. All is not lost sister, just a small setback."

"Yes, of course." I manage to form a smile as the dial tone buzzes on the other end of the receiver and I try my best to relax.

*****

Moisture particles from the condensation continues to fog up the windshield as I place the lit cigarette between my lips and draw the smoke into my lungs while slowly exhaling. My feet are kicked up against the dashboard, crossed over one another as I lay back into the leather seat and watch the rain spill its wrath. I have parked this compulsory rental on the side of a random street in Regent Square as I impatiently wait for the call that will conclude my evening.

Everyone has scattered from this lifeless neighborhood like fleeting roaches and its only midnight. The best time to unwind is at night, far away from scrutiny and disapproving stares. Where one can lurk undetected and prey on the weak while having their way with no recollection of the prior events that took place. But for reasons unknown this sorry ass city has no action whatsoever, so here I am waiting around at his beck and call. Dogs can be heard barking in the distance as I roll down my window to catch some fresh air and flick my cigarette bud onto the wet pavement.

Quickly rolling up the glass, I take a glance at my phone to ensure that I haven't missed a call. Where in the hell is this asshole at? He was supposed to call me over an hour ago. My tolerance level starts to diminish when my phone suddenly vibrates and rings simultaneously. Skimming over the screen and confirming it's the call that I've been waiting on, I quickly press the green button, hold the phone to my ear and reposition my body frame on the seat.

"About bloody time." I snap into the receiver, angry that my time was wasted on something so insignificant.

"I was held up." His voice is monotone and calm.

"So was I, but here I am waiting on your fruitless call like a gullible teenage girl."

"Well then, let's get on with it."

Placing another cigarette between my lips I roll my thumb on the spark wheel of the lighter and light the tip while inhaling poison directly into my lungs. My phone is settled between my ear and shoulder while I continue to take a second drag from the cigarette.

"What was the outcome of your," a brief pause, "assignment?"

"I followed the sibyl as instructed and ended up in Pittsburgh." Another pause as I switch hands with my ione. "By the time I arrived she was already outside in the backyard watching me, then fled to who knows where."

"She was aware that you were following her?"

"The she-devil and her clan are witches so yeah; she probably knew I was trailing her the whole time."

"Why didn't you pursue her?" His tone has gone from monotone to cynical laced with irritation.

"And how do you propose I do that? With a skateboard?" I snicker with a sarcastic pitch. "Oh wait, maybe with my rollerblades that I carry on my back." More inhaling as I watch rain drops trickle down my windshield.

"Even if I tried there was no way I was going to catch up with her."

A few more silent pauses followed by disappointment. "So, tell me, what did you find? Anything interesting that I can work with? Who is he?" Now he sounds like he's running out of patience, eager to learn who is possibly responsible for the uproar and chaos among our race.

"There is no he. The mortal that lives in the house is a female and possibly a child."

He then begins to laugh hysterically with a less than a pleasant tone. After a few moments he suddenly stops. "Really? All of this clamor over a human female? And how do you know this?"

This is what you call *downright crazy*.

"After ransacking the home, I found some photographs of a young woman and a child. Most of the documents like letters, etc. were addressed to a female named Simone De Luca."

"Hmmm... interesting. Do proceed."

"Well, at first I wasn't sure, so I followed the most dominating scent to the opposite side of town and ended up at a private residence. The narrow street was lined with cars; the house was full of mortals celebrating who knows what. I crept towards the home and settled in the dark, waiting and lurking." Taking another drag from my cigarette I slowly exhale the smoke through my nose before continuing.

"After a few minutes, I was able to locate the young woman from the photograph through the glass windows. I knew I couldn't just walk into the house so I waited for someone weak minded to show up that I could manipulate. Just as I'm about to turn around, an idiot steps next to me and lights a cigar. Within a matter of minutes, he was back in the house to conclude my bidding."

I chuckle into the receiver as the memory of tonight's events reemerge. "Little did I know that this stupid ass was acquainted with her, so it was easy for him to complete the task. I watched and waited as she toyed with the glass until she finally walks outside onto the patio and took a swig."

"It's done then?"

"I presume so."

"What do you mean you presume?" His deep voice has been raised by two octaves as he spits fuming words into the receiver.

"I didn't stick around to find out."

"Please do enlighten me. I'm starting to run out of patience and do not have time for mind games."

"Well for starters, after she took a drink and started to faint, Jovianus shows up out of nowhere and caught her before she hit the ground. He then began to scan the area and I was not about to stick around and risk being seen."

"Oh really, you poor thing. Well, since we are being honest how about we start with the real reason as to why you fled?"

"Fuck off!"

"Hmmm, I wonder if you trembled when you saw him tonight like you did seven years ago after he slit your..."

I don't even give him a chance to finish that sentence and cut him off abruptly as my mood has gone from ill temper to violent.

"You're a real cocky asshole over the phone you know that? Here I am risking my life for you and how am

I repaid? By mockery and deceit. I don't see you out here playing detective. Besides, we both know that a fight with Jovianus is not something to take lightly. In case you forgot, he is without a doubt the most dominant male among our species so yes, I fled because I know when and how to pick my fights. My life is way more valuable than some human wench who is more than likely dead at this point so stop riding me."

I allowed his words to piss me off more than I imagine they could as my scratchy voice roars in defeat.

"Who are you kidding? The reason why you are playing detective is because this matter benefits the both of us and because you owe me your life, and I do intend to collect." His ridicule can be felt as if he were in front of me.

Oh, how I despise this jackass. At this point I have already stepped out of the vehicle and into the pouring rain, pacing back and forth like a madman while flicking my unfinished cigarette directly under my boot.

"Are you finished? Because if you are, I have somewhere to be."

A few seconds' pass before he responds with a calm and collected tone. "How certain are you that this poison reached her blood stream?"

"There is no freaking way anyone could have survived that much toxin, especially not a mortal."

"But what if the rumors are true? What if she is half immortal, half human; her powers could be far greater than all of us combined – limitless even."

"I could care less who this wicked harpy is or where she's from. No one can survive the poison from the conium plant regardless of how powerful you are. No one!!"

"I need to know for certain that her life has ended and not simply rely on speculation."

"What would you have me do?"

"First I have to know why Jovianus is in the states; I'll work that angle from my end. You will need to get close to him without being noticed while keeping a safe distance. I'm almost certain that if you find him, then you will more than likely locate the asset, or at the very least learn of her whereabouts."

"What then?"

"If you find that the human remains alive then your task would be to eliminate the threat and leave the country as swiftly as possible."

"What of the child?"

"I guess I didn't make myself clear. Eliminate the threat at all cost no matter who is involved. Anyone who resides at the residence where you so carelessly revealed your identity needs to be eradicated. Do I make myself clear?"

"And Jovianus?"

"What about him?"

"Do I factor him into this equation?"

A few more pauses..., "Well, he would have sealed his own fate should he stand in your way. This needs to be handled swiftly with no witnesses."

"Even if it means placing my life in danger?"

"A sacrifice that I'm willing to make. Now stop being a coward and get creative. The next time we speak I want to hear that this matter was taken care of. I'll handle the rest."

The line goes dead almost instantly. I stop pacing and settle my back against the side of the truck as the heavy shower begins to slowly diminish. He has got to be joking about Jovianus. Taking him down alone would be an impossible mission. The last time we had a disagreement I ended up with a dagger in my throat faster than I could count to three. How am I supposed to threaten the life of our future leader?

I bellow into the air, "FUCK," as anger and frustration fills my ego. Deciding that it's time to let off some much-needed steam, I hop back into my rental and begin scanning the streets for a possible victim as I fade into the darkness.

Chapter Fifteen

~Quandary~

When I finally wakeup, I find myself alone and secluded to an unfamiliar living space. The room is awfully quiet and dark apart from the moonlight's reflection beaming through the sheer drapes. My sight remains a bit hazy and I feel groggy for reasons unknown.

There is also an immense heat radiating from my inner core while clammy hands paddle against the bed linens as I attempt to sit up. The sudden movement triggered a dizzy spell which momentarily prompts a panic attack. Where the hell am I? Disoriented and confused I proceed to close my eyes hoping to garner some peace when images of tonight's incident slowly begin to flood my thoughts.

I recall taking a sip of my bubbly champagne and within a few moments a numbing sensation began to course throughout my body, slowly shutting down all of my senses. Then out of nowhere my legs buckled and the last thing I remember is being consumed by total darkness.

After involuntarily twitching my eyes open for a few seconds, I saw him appear before me. A tall, porcelain male with a mop of dark brown hair and a set of sapphire blue and golden-brown eyes standing out against the night. For the first time in four years, my heart was whole again.

He caught me in his arms right before I hit the floor and I murmured, "Jovianus."

At this point I'm not sure if I remain conscious or if it's merely a dream because it seems too surreal. There is no way in hell that Jovianus is here with me after all these years. I was in his arms. I saw him!

Within seconds my mood has soured, and self-reproach takes on a new form. In the mix of all the chaos I seemed to have lost sight of the most important individual. My sole reason for living – my son. Frantically removing the sheets from my body, I proceed to inch towards the edge of the bed in search of my sweet baby boy.

"Mateo!" I roar in horror.

Just then I'm greeted by a soft whisper that's embedded in a deep voice from the far-left corner of the room.

"He is right here with me."

Dismayed by the familiar accent, I slowly turn my head to confront the gaze that has been heating my body to its core. My sight remains foggy as I'm only able to distinguish outlines of two figures whose features are masked by darkness. I remain silent as the male who spoke carefully leans over to the side and suddenly the dark space is illuminated by a florescent light.

Seated in a wingback loveseat are Jovianus and my son. Mateo is sitting on his lap with his head resting on Jovi's chest. My heartbeat kicks up two notches as I take in his appearance. His masculine built, and broad shoulders are easily recognizable through his attire and hard to ignore. When he speaks again, I am instantly drawn to his voice, like gravity with an infinite range.

"We've been waiting on you to wake up."

I notice that his solemn eyebrows are cast downward with his lips set in a brim line and eyes averted towards the wooden floor. As I cautiously shift my gaze to his face our eyes inadvertently collide.

A tainted smile forms on his lips while his abnormal eyes beam with longing. The connection is instantaneous like an electric current transmitting voltage pulses through our bodies and fusing us back to life. My body responds without direction and I feel the need to exonerate him for leaving me.

"We?" I murmur in confusion, but he doesn't respond nor acknowledge my question.

We both stay silent, enjoying each other's presence as desire fills the air. His gaze is unwavering causing my heart to beat erratically. I don't understand what is happening to us, but I can't deny that it feels right. He must feel it too because he hasn't tried to disrupt our moment of solitude.

But it ends all too quickly when Mateo yawns and whispers, "Mommy."

Our bond is broken as I swiftly turn my gaze and greet my son with a gentle smile, "My love."

I was about to get up and take him into my arms when out of nowhere Mateo turns his body slightly towards Jovianus and closes his eyes. I notice that his glasses are barely holding onto his small button nose as he wraps his arm around Jovi's waist. His grasp becomes firm but comforting around Mateo's back and legs as if to hold him in place. I'm not sure how to feel about their interaction and remain motionless while I watch my son fall fast asleep.

My eyes then shift from Mateo to Jovianus in suspicion as countless questions begin to emerge. Why is Jovi here in the States and at Ethan's party after all this time? And why is my son sitting on his lap with ease?

He quickly senses the apprehension as the stroppy silence carries on and proceeds to breach the barriers of my weary judgments.

"Are you feeling any better?"

I begin to question my self-worth when I finally muster the courage to articulate words, as if finally granted permission to do so.

"I uh," I continue stammering along the way, "where am I?"

At this moment I feel more vulnerable and nervous than when I learned that I was pregnant. Diverting my gaze, I begin to look around the room again hoping to identify any piece of article that will give away my location, but quickly realize that I haven't got a clue.

Meanwhile Jovianus takes it upon himself to encourage empathy when he carefully stands up, readjusts Mateo's body so that he is cradling him and graciously begins making his way to me. The bed dips a little when he sits down while my son remains cradled in his arms. Our bodies are in such close proximity that his masculine scent overpowers all of my senses when he speaks.

"You are in one of Ethan's guest rooms. I carried you here after you... fainted."

Each word is cautiously vocalized as if he has suddenly become upset. I don't ever remember seeing him this way and decide to remain guarded until his true intentions are revealed.

"What happened to me? How long have I been asleep?" My soft whisper gives away the grief and heartbreak that I'm experiencing.

But his gaze never waivers when he leisurely speaks the next few lines.

"Simone, I believe you were drugged. We all think that someone slipped something into your drink when you weren't looking. I was about to walk over and properly greet you when you started to faint. I then rushed to your side and caught you in my arms before you hit the floor. Derek provided a quick examination and determined that you either had too much to drink or had your cocktail spiked. He said that we didn't need to take you to the hospital and that we should let you sleep it off. That was over three hours ago."

"Oh," was all I could manage with my mouth still partially opened, lost in thought.

I'm grateful that Derek is in med school and knew exactly what to do which avoided an unjustified detour to the hospital. A trip that would have opened old wounds and flooded my mind with painful memories of my parents passing.

"Where's Aemilia?" Where is that backstabber and why isn't she here with me?

"She has been by your side this whole time up until a few moments ago. I assured her that I would take care of you and that she didn't have to stay."

Why would he feel the need to take care of me? He didn't care for my wellbeing when he left without saying goodbye. He didn't care about the aftermath or repercussions that would follow soon after, so why now? I can feel my concern slowly being replaced with resentment as I proceed to ask prying questions.

"Why do you have my son instead of Aemilia?" I narrow my eyes at him as anger starts to boil over.

His smile widens from ear to ear which only infuriates me even further. What part of all this is funny to him because I surely don't find it amusing? Oh damnit, stop asking so many questions and just take your son from him already if it's bothering you so much.

"Simone, I think you should lie down for a while longer. You seem a bit agitated and if I'm not mistaken the drug effect has not completely worn off just yet."

He continues to beam at me with a crooked smile playing on his lips. I notice that his firm jaw line is covered in beard stubble which gives him a five-o clock shadow.

Shaking off his charming appeal I decide to focus on his treacherous betrayal instead and finally give in to my alter ego that is swarming with rage and allow her to take over. Who the hell does he think he is, barking orders at me? You're over thinking this Simone, just blow off some steam and let him have it. Remember that he left you with no explanation and now he reappears into your life, bossing you around. Giving into my natural instinct, I stand from the bed and place both of my hands on my hips while turning to face him.

"Who do you think you are...," and I don't get to finish my sentence because at that exact moment a light knock sounds and the door creaks open. Aemilia's head pokes in before she steps into the room.

"Simone darling, how are you feeling? We thought you'd never wake up." She darts towards me and pulls my body into her arms.

I'm glad to see her but still confused that she left me alone with Jovianus. She knows how I felt about him and failed to mention that he was here. I bet she knew all along and deliberately hid this from me.

"I'm fine I guess, just have a pounding headache and obviously still confused about many things." I motion my eyebrows towards Jovianus and Mateo.

She begins to snicker and hugs me again while smoothing out my hair.

"Well, we can talk about this some more tomorrow when you feel better. I think you should get some rest and I'll be back later to get you."

"What? No! I'm ready to go home, I've rested long enough." I sigh as my shoulders slump and I turn to face Jovianus.

Extending my arms out, I request for my son to be released, "Let me get him off your hands. I know he can get a little heavy."

I thought my tone had conviction, but I guess he took it as if I was asking for permission instead, which I was not.

Slowly standing to his full height with an innocent smirk on his face he retorts my claim with a proposition.

"You still seem a bit shaky. How about I keep him a bit longer until you're ready to leave? We wouldn't want you to drop him now would we?" He states as a matter of fact while towering over me.

We? Did he just say, *we?* When did he place himself into the *we* equation? I turn to look at Aemilia like *is he freaking serious* and give her my *warning* expression.

"Aemilia, how about we leave, like now please?" I'm practically begging because I'm full of mixed emotions and unsure of myself. Could he be right? I do feel a little queasy and my head is a bit floaty.

I see a sheepish grin on Aemilia's face as she chooses her words carefully while stammering along the way.

"Sure, I uh, can you give me like 30 minutes? I was in the middle of something and need to finish before we leave. I'm sure Jovianus wouldn't mind keeping you company for a little while longer."

She has got to be kidding me. First, she doesn't even tell me about Jovianus and leaves me under his care without my knowledge and now this. Don't make a scene, let her down easy and go *full on Simone mode* later.

"Well, I guess I don't have a choice, do I?" I scowl at her with a boisterous tone.

My sarcastic comment was meant as a rhetorical question, however as Aemilia attempts to respond Jovianus decides to intervene with a more implausible outcome and clears his throat to capture our attention.

"I was just about to head out myself, so I don't mind dropping you and Mateo off on my way home." He blurts out with a hint of caution.

Both Aemilia and I turn to look at each other and speak at the same time.

"No, that won't be necessary. I can take a cab home."

"That sounds like a great idea. What a wonderful gesture."

He then looks at the both of us and confirms Aemilia's plans instead of mine. "Ok, then it's settled. I'll go get my vehicle and wait for you out front."

"No, it's ok really. I can take a cab. I'm sure you have other plans and I don't want to inconvenience you."

With a half-smile he proceeds with his manner of persuasion.

"Simone, you can never inconvenience me. Besides, I would feel more comfortable if I took you home myself and inspect your place for any signs of trouble. You were drugged by someone here at the party; whether that individual was a stranger or acquaintance, it just doesn't sit well with me."

He is more concerned for me than I would have expected which only intensifies my resentment. I was about to protest yet again but was unexpectedly interrupted by another light knock.

Ethan's body comes into view from behind the door and wastes no time with piteous commentaries as he strolls in and takes me into his arms.

I can sense a hint of distress when he finally breathes, "I thought you were hurt. Thank god you're ok."

"I've been better," is all I could muster at the moment given the events that have unfolded tonight.

He gently pulls away and places both of his hands on my shoulders to ensure that he has my undivided attention.

"Just so you know, we are going to find out who drugged you and beat him senseless. I don't care who this fool is because I'm almost certain that his intentions were malicious as they were dishonorable."

"Wow Ethan! Did you really figure that out all by yourself?"

Aemilia's criticism knows no bounds as she unsurprisingly resumes her rants of attack on Ethan, yet again. "Isn't it obvious that his sole objective was to take advantage of her? Why else would this twerp feel the need to drug her? Please do feel free to tell us something that we don't already know!"

With a smudge grin and arms crossed over her chest she patiently waits for Ethan to defend himself but before he could get a word out Jovi decides to speak up.

"Exactly my point; I have offered to take Simone and Mateo home while ensuring their safety. I'm sure we would all sleep better tonight knowing that she was out of harm's way. Wouldn't you agree?" He validates his plans on taking me home to avoid any further objections on my part, knowing that I respect Ethan's opinion and will have no room for argument if he agrees.

"You read my mind. And who better to take her home than you? I'm the host of this party so unfortunately I'm unable to leave till the last guest departs." He then turns his attention to me and offers an alternative solution.

"You're more than welcome to stay here if you'd like." I notice that he is now shooting daggers at Aemilia for making him feel stupid.

And just like that, the fate of my life is left in Jovi's hands without me having a say or opinion about the matter. It's not like I don't trust him because I do. I have no doubt in my mind that he would place his own life in danger before I am hurt.

That is not the issue here, the concern pertains to our solitude and being in each other's presence by ourselves after all this time. I'm not sure that I'm ready, and I don't believe that he is either. If I object, then I am forced to either wait for Aemilia to conclude whatever trouble she has gotten herself into or stay here under Ethan's care where the incident occurred. And I am not comfortable with any of those options.

"Thanks, but I'm really tired and would like nothing more than to just go home. At this point I don't care who takes me so long as I arrive in one piece."

There, I gave in. It's a little past midnight and I really don't care if Jovianus is the one who drives us home. I just want to be in the confines of a place where I feel safe. I warily turn to face Jovianus and notice that his charismatic mood has not diminished despite my discourteous behavior. It's infectious and difficult to ignore, so I return his polite smile when I accept his offer.

"Well, since you insist on carrying my son, can you please take him downstairs and wait for me while I grab my purse and his belongings?" I ask politely but with a twist of agitation.

"Of course." His response is instantaneous, complacent with the outcome that resulted in his favor.

I watch in despair as he vanishes through the door with my precious cargo in tow. Why am I ok with this? I feel like such a bad mother, leaving him with a stranger. Well, technically he isn't a stranger, to me anyway. Sighing, I find myself still staring at the empty doorway where Jovi and Mateo have disappeared through.

Shaking off my troubled thoughts, I turn around to find Ethan caressing Aemilia's shoulder while whispering sweet nothings into her ear. Wow! She just insulted him and here he is caressing her body. Whatever! I am not about to ask because these two definitely deserve each other.

Clearing my throat, Ethan immediately removes his hand from Aemilia's arm and walks over to me showing no signs of remorse for being caught with the *she-devil*.

"I really am glad that you're ok. You're in good hands with Jovianus. He won't let anything happen to you. Get some rest and I'll call later to check on you both."

He then kisses me on my head, hugs me tightly and walks out the room, leaving the door halfway open. I half smile because I sure am lucky to have him in my life. Too bad I can't say the same about Aemilia. I immediately turn around to confront my so-called friend and hopefully uncover the details of her hidden agenda.

"Trader! Don't you stand there and tell me that you didn't know about Jovianus' presence in the states? You know about our past and what he meant to me. How dare you hide this from your best friend?"

"You mean; what he means to you not meant as in past tense."

"Stop correcting me!! You know what I mean Aemilia!" I raise my voice a few octaves because now I'm livid.

I'm pissed because she is still playing games and I don't find any of this amusing at all.

"I have no idea why you're acting like you didn't know. Did you forget that you ran into him when you were with Leona and Derek? You told me so yourself!" She then folds both of her arms across her chest in frustration.

"What are you talking about you loon! I told you that I ran into Franco not Jovi. You've gone mad. Why in the world would I associate Jovi with disgust?"

"Oh, makes perfect sense now. I was referring to Jovi when you rudely interrupted me, and you were speaking of Franco. Ah. Gotcha. Well," she begins to smooth out her dress while gliding her hand through her silky hair, "It was a case of miscommunication on both of our behalf's so get off my case. Look, it's been a long night and I have a hot date waiting for me in the piano room. Go home, get some rest and I will call you tomorrow morning."

She quickly kisses my cheek and begins making her way towards the door. My subconscious jumps in to question my motives before I can overreact to Aemilia's dismissal. Who are you really mad at? Get your priorities straight before you start pointing fingers.

"Fine! But this conversation isn't over," I yell over her shoulder.

She already has one foot out the door when she fades into the dark hallway. This conversation isn't over for damn sure. I quickly find my purse and Mateo's brown backpack near the window. Grabbing both and swinging them over my shoulder I walk out the room and head downstairs. I should have listened to my instincts and stayed home because I knew this night wouldn't end well.

By the time I reach the front of the house, I notice that the crowd has dwindled down. The lights inside the house are dim while gentle music continues to play in the background. Surrounded by unfamiliar faces and a handy bartender, I instantly begin to wonder what became of the perpetrator that drugged me. Is he still here, waiting for me to leave or is he lurking around my home?

Shaking the scary thoughts from my mind I proceed towards the valet area where two young males with vest remain. Just as I'm about to ask one of them if they've seen a tall broad male with spectacular eyes and a child, I witness a Black QX80 pull up and park. He gets out of the driver seat and gracefully walks over to the passenger side to open my door. With a halfhearted smile, I try my best to avoid eye contact. Once I'm in, he closes the door and slides into the driver seat.

Within seconds we both begin to hear light snoring coming from the backseat. I turn to find my little Mateo fast asleep with his glasses halfway off his nose and his mouth partially open. He is lying down sideways with a seatbelt across his lap and a small pillow to hold him in place. As I attempt to lean over and remove his glasses Jovi leaps in.

"Stay. I've got it." He smiles, cautiously leans over, and reaches towards the backseat while carefully removing the little frames from Mateo's nose. He then turns back and places the glasses in my hand, careful not to touch me.

A swift, "Thanks," leaves my lips as I proceed to place the small frames in my purse.

I can feel him staring at me, but I somehow manage to continue avoiding eye contact. As I'm placing my seatbelt across my chest, he begins to clear his throat.

"So, where to? I mean, where do you live?"

Finally looking up, our gazes meet for a brief moment when I decide to end this ingenuous display and turn my attention back towards the dashboard. His demeanor suggest that he is troubled and in that moment I decide to remain cordial.

"Regent Square on Maple Street please." I then turn my gaze towards the window as we head onto the interstate.

A light drizzle begins to descend from the dark sky, landing droplets of rain on the windshield. Surprisingly, the sound of the wispy rainfall begins to soothe my edginess and calms my anxiety.

The drive home was quiet which was surprising to me because I have a list full of questions that I'm itching to ask him, but reluctant to discuss. I wonder if he shares the same sentiment. Sighing out of frustration, I suddenly find myself tired and completely overwhelmed.

Turning on my street, Jovi finally ends this ghastly silence when he asks, "Which house?"

"Up here to the left. The house with the car garage in the back. You can pull into the driveway," I confirm with a soft-spoken tone.

He pulls in and turns off the engine. Just as I'm about to reach for the handle, he opens my door and lends me his hand. Obliging, I place my palm into his as he helps me out of the vehicle and that's when I'm quickly reminded of his charm and gallant manners, something that most men lack.

The light rainfall begins to hit my face and body as Jovi tends to my son. Gently removing his seatbelt, he lifts Mateo into his arms while gently adjusting his sleeping body. Closing the door behind them, I quickly begin making my way up the sidewalk that leads to the entrance while digging through my purse in search of my keys. I find them just as we approach the door then immediately stop. It's totally dark because the veranda light is out.

He then realizes that something is amiss, "What's wrong Simone?"

"The light is out. I.. I don't remember it being off when I left this afternoon. I'm almost certain that I flipped the switch on before leaving."

We both look down and spot broken glass on the cement just below the light post. I step to the side and lift my heels, inspecting the shards of glass underneath my shoes when I notice my door is slightly open. Just then the rain picks up pace and turns from a light drizzle to a full-on downpour.

"Get back into the vehicle. Here are the keys. Take Mateo with you in the front seat and lock yourself inside. Do not open the door until I return. Do you understand?" His voice is menacing, even commanding mixed with anger.

With Mateo in my arms I quickly rush to the SUV while keeping a close watch of my surroundings. Unlocking the door, I place Mateo inside first then quickly slide in when I become aware that he has not detached his sight from us. With his eyes affixed unto mine I simply nod, signaling that we are safe and out of harm's way. My mind is running at a hundred miles per hour with endless thoughts of a possible ambush.

Sitting there helpless and exposed, I begin to speculate of all the possible outcomes as he takes two steps up the sidewalk and squats to inspect the broken glass. He then shifts his attention to the light post above while the rain soaks his clothes and hair, but he doesn't seem to notice. Slowly standing up, Jovi begins to carefully examine the door before tapping it open. Oh no, what's he going to do? I anxiously witness as he walks through the entrance of my home. This doesn't feel right for so many reasons. Shouldn't we just call the police? Why would someone force their way through my home?

Seconds turn to minutes which seems like hours when Jovi finally emerges from my backyard. I see the outline of his figure through the foggy windshield and rapid rain as he walks straight to the driver side, which leads me to believe that we are not staying. Reaching over and unlocking the door for him, he slides in, remote starts the engine and begins to put his safety belt on. Just before we drive away, I muster the courage to ask him the one question that continues to torment my thoughts.

"Was I a random target….. or is someone after me?" My voice is shaky which causes my nerves to get the best of me.

Involuntary tears slowly begin to stream down my cheeks. As he turns to address me, I notice that his hands are balled up into fist. Danger is written all over his face when he finally speaks.

"As long as you're with me, no one and I mean no one is going to hurt either of you. I'm going to get to the bottom of this if it's the last thing I do."

Reaching for my shoulder, he gently pulls me and Mateo close into his chest then kisses the top of my head. Without warning I begin to quietly weep while nestled in his arms. All too soon I become overwhelmed with the chilling thought that I could have been at home when the break in occurred. Why is this happening to me?

I suddenly feel him relax a bit and the tone to his voice changes when he speaks again.

"You and Mateo cannot stay here tonight, it isn't safe. I've already called the police and a patrol unit is on their way to examine the scene and collect any evidence that may have been left behind. Another officer will meet us at my place to take our statement."

"What did they take?" My voice is hoarse with sobs filling the gaps between each word.

"I'm not sure. It looks like your home was ransacked, as if someone were looking for something. The most important thing is that the both of you are out of harm's way. You must rest now; we can figure out the rest tomorrow."

I shake my head in agreement and managed to choke out one word, "Ok."

My voice cracks once more as we sit in the same position for a few more minutes, enjoying each other's warmth. Moments pass when I finally decide to remove my body from his embrace. As I'm making the attempt to settle back into my seat, he catches my face in between his palms. With my cheeks cradled between his hands, he lightly wipes at a falling tear with his thumb. Our mouths are inches apart as we gaze into each other's eyes, searching for the spark that once ignited our affection.

We both feel that same pull again as our breathing pattern accelerates. Sure, our chemistry is undeniable but after all that has happened tonight, I cannot allow these vulnerabilities to cloud my judgment. He left me when I was in dire need and today proves that he is only here out of sympathy. I quickly break eye contact and look away, wiping the tears that remain on my cheeks. But he knows me all too well and tries to recover from my rejection by keeping his hands loosely on my face and attempts to speak words of ease.

"Simone, I will never leave you again. Not as long as you want me to be around. That, I can promise you."

I'm speechless and unable to respond because my heart is torn between loving someone who abandoned me and the one who used to love me unconditionally.

Chapter Sixteen

~Refuge~

After driving in silence for about 20 minutes with the sound of the heavy rain purring in the background and the constant vibration of his phone, we finally arrive in Highland Park.

Jovi pulls the SUV into a logging path driveway that leads straight to the front of the residence. The two-story home is nestled in the woods of Cecil Township with no neighbors in sight. Surrounded by a dark lush forest, the building structure is more modern with a contemporary design and is covered with hand burnt cedar siding. Bright lights are beaming through the floor to ceiling glass windows from the inside.

The outside of the house is also equipped with outdoor lighting, providing a welcoming view. I notice a large white framed gateway slowly opening on the lower level as he steers the vehicle into the garage. Once the lock is secured in place, he turns off the engine and swiftly opens my passenger door. Without thinking he gently takes Mateo from my chest and cradles his motionless body into his arms.

I don't even bother to protest and allow him to assist me while I rummage around the back seat for my purse and Mateo's bag. But my quest is short lived when he interrupts my concentration by clearing his throat to capture my attention.

"Don't worry about your belongings, I will come back and retrieve them for you. What I really need right now is to get the both of you inside where it's safe," he commands in a low but ominous tone.

Wondering what brought on his sudden mood I look up into his eyes and begin searching for the kind and gentle being I once knew.

As our eyes meet, I'm greeted with a wholehearted smile that is mixed with agony and confusion. I know that he means well, but what I don't understand are his motives in the matter. He somehow seems different and I can't figure out what has changed. Without further objections I comply with his request and almost instantly lower my gaze.

"Ok." I respond in a silent hum and nod in agreement while getting out of the vehicle.

As he begins to fumble with his house keys, Mateo decides to squirm in his arms with his eyes still shut. Fully aware that I can't risk him waking up at this hour I immediately take the keys from his hands and assist with unlocking the door.

I don't even get a chance to step inside as he suddenly halts me before entering.

"Give me two seconds. I have to turn off the alarm before anyone else can enter."

"Oh," I sigh sheepishly while crossing my arms over my chest out of habit and because I'm starting to get cold.

He pauses for a brief moment as if to say something but then almost instantly stops and instead steps through the doorway.

Five loud beeps ring, and he reappears with Mateo still in his arms. He then extends his right hand to me, a polite jester; one that involves physical contact. I hesitate at first, unsure if being here alone with him is the right place to be, but then quickly shut down that notion and begin to question my own motives. Where else would I be? I know I can trust him just as I once did before.

He senses my indecision and immediately retrieve's his hand and settles on holding the door for me instead. I instantly regret my actions because he doesn't deserve this

307

from anyone, especially not from me. So, I push my arrogance aside, allow my intuition to take over and accept his invitation by stepping through the entry. He walks in after me as I slowly begin to wander along the dim hallway.

Feeling his warm presence close by, I abruptly turn around and almost collide into his chest. Damn it, why am I being so clumsy? Taking a few steps back I divert my gaze towards the dark concrete floors when I hear his soothing voice.

"Come this way. I have a guest room on the second floor that you both can stay in until all of this is sorted out." He half smiles and leads the way to the geometrical stairway as I begin to follow suit.

As we ascend to the first set of porcelain stairs, I notice that the dining area is visible from below. Small led lights are aligned at the bottom of each step, illuminating the full staircase. A spiral crystal chandelier hangs in a cluster at the center of the stairwell. Black and white photographs of Jovianus and his siblings fill the walls that contain a history of memories.

I instantly become distracted as I focus on the beautiful faces in the frames which tells a story of love and devotion. Before I know it, we are at the top of the second floor when he leads me down another corridor and through a set of french doors before stopping at the end of the hallway.

"So, this is it, the guestroom that you will be staying in tonight and uh... for however long you decide."

The edgy look on his face gives away that he's nervous. Feeling pleased that I'm not the only one, I respond with a simple, "Thank you."

As I cautiously enter through the door, a light instantly comes on which momentarily jolts me, stopping me in my tracks.

"It's just a motion sensor. The light will come on automatically when someone enters the room, but I can turn it off if you wish," he politely offers with a hint of caution.

"No, that won't be necessary. It doesn't bother me much. I just, didn't expect it."

As I take another step, my eyes immediately begin to explore the unfamiliar yet spacious room. Zooming in on the colossal bed, my body suddenly feels heavy as sleep begins to take over. Turning around I notice that he hasn't stepped into the room nor has he taken his eyes off of me.

My curiosity finally prevails, and I find myself asking questions that I'm quite sure I don't want the answers to.

"What's wrong?"

Come on Simone, do you really want to know what he's thinking? Does it really matter at this point? You've pretty much made up your mind about him so stop stringing whatever this is along.

"It's nothing." He smiles tentatively and carries on with the conversation while leaving his worries behind. "May I come in or would you prefer to take Mateo from here?"

I promptly answer, "Of course, please come in," puzzled that he would feel the need to ask me permission to enter a room in his own home.

"What side of the bed do you want me to place him?"

"Oh, on the left, facing away from the windows please."

I instantly begin to pull back the slate duvet so that he can lay Mateo down. As he places his body on the bed, I carefully begin to remove his shoes and damp clothing from his tiny frame. Jovianus instinctively assists, taking the shoes from my hands while delicately lifting his body so that I'm able to remove his pants and shirt. Mateo squirms a little bit more before getting comfortable underneath the blankets as he continues on his quest of dreams, unaware of tonight's events.

After tucking him in, I straighten up, take a few steps back and marvel at his innocence. My arms automatically cross over my chest again as the cold air breezes over my skin, reminding me that my clothes remain wet from the rain. I wasn't aware that Jovi was watching my every move when he disrupts my train of thought.

"Where are my manners? Would you like a clean pair of clothes? I'm sure I can dig something up from Clodia's closet."

"Sure. Dry clothes would be nice."

Without thinking I begin to inspect my damp attire and find myself fidgeting, perhaps out of habit.

"Ok. Wait here and I'll be right back." He turns and heads out into the hallway.

While he's out searching for women's garments, I sit on the bed next to Mateo and force my mind to retrace my steps of the evening.

Who did I come into contact with after Derek brought us our champagne? I don't recall leaving my drink unattended. Hmm, I wonder if Derek or Franco would have seen anything; unless it occurred while they were at the bar. But before I'm able to dwell on that thought, Jovi reappears in the doorway with a set of fresh clothes neatly folded in his hands.

I stand up and walk towards him as he hands me a white t-shirt, gray striped socks, and a pair of what looks like men's boxers.

"My apologies, but it looks like Clodia's closet and dresser lacked the most important item – clothing." He grins and continues to clarify his wardrobe choice. "It's been a few years since our um…I tried to find something tasteful; I hope you don't mind?"

That fleeting explanation sparked old memories to resurface.

Pushing those thoughts aside, I swallow hard before responding, "Thank you, these will do just fine," and return his smile while avoiding direct eye contact. Placing the clothes on the edge of the bed, I begin to fidget again as we both stand in equal silence.

Then, from the corner of my eye I see him slowly place his hands inside of his pockets and begins making his way towards the door. An overbearing need to stall his departure unexpectedly emerges and without warning I find myself calling his name, "Jovianus."

He responds almost instantly, "Yes," and stops a few feet from the door while turning around to face me. His hands remain in his pockets like he is unsure of himself which only intensifies my anxiety. This moment of longing feels painfully subjective and all too familiar.

How is it possible that this undeniable connection that we share not only brings us together but somehow manages to pull us apart? Quickly overcoming my doubts, I carefully take a few calculated steps in his direction until my body is a few inches from his face.

Our eyes are now affixed onto one another as I warily lift my arms and gently wrap them around his neck. My heartbeat kicks up two notches and my hands begin to shake while I pull him into an embrace and speak softly into his ear.

"I just want to thank you for everything you've done for us. I don't even want to consider what could have happened had you not been present."

And although my voice is but a whisper, he was still able to detect the despair in my tone.

It doesn't take long for his body to respond when I suddenly feel his muscular arms slide around my lower waist and he tenderly pulls me closer, fusing us into one. My mouth remains inches from his ear; any sudden moves and my lips will be begging for an ambush.

"Simone..." My name trails off as his chin glides right above my head and my name tenderly rolls off his tongue. "I will always be here for you and regret every minute that I wasn't."

I don't respond and decide to remain mum on the topic as discontent takes a new form. Unknown to him, he was the author of my undoing when he left four years ago, but right now is not the time to discuss our many offenses.

Our grip tightens as we both get lost in this moment of desire. This feels right in so many ways, however, I know I shouldn't take it for granted.

Deciding that it was time to end our display of affection, I gently pull away but not before planting a soft kiss on his cheek. I quickly recover my posture and take a few steps back, giving us both space to process the exchange. This time I don't try to avoid eye contact and meet his gaze full on when I speak.

"So..., I have an embarrassing request to ask of you before you leave."

He responds almost instantly, "Anything," while I fumble with my words.

"Aemilia helped me get into this dress and I'm afraid that she isn't here to unzip me."

He chuckles before asking, "What's embarrassing about that?"

"Well, the zipper is in the back of my dress, it's damp and also tight so, this can be a little challenging to accomplish on my own," I confirm shamefully.

"You don't have to be embarrassed around me." He politely beams, momentarily causing that chin dimple to reappear.

And although I return his smile, it's not lost on him that I'm a bit nervous, so he decides to take the lead.

"Come over here," he motions with his index finger.

Looking up, I respond by cautiously walking back towards him while turning around and picking up my hair so that he may locate the zipper. This is weird, but for some reason I suddenly don't feel anxious anymore.

After a few heartbeats, I feel his big palms tenderly land on my hips as he carefully pulls my small frame closer to him by forcing me to take a few steps back. My body is now covered in goosebumps as his warm breath lightly skims along my neck. I silently gasp for air when he begins to gently tug at my gown by separating the rows of plastic teeth from the zipper track and slowly undresses me.

The room has gone completely silent with only the sounds of our intense breathing to fill our ears. I feel relaxed and calm at his feather like touch. Why does this feel so familiar I think to myself?

315

Shaking the erotic thoughts from my head I remove one of my hands from my hair and place it on my chest to hold the dress in place. Since the gown has no sleeves, I was not able to wear a bra. The only undergarment covering my body is a pair of white laced panties which I forgot until now. Damn it.

Jovi clears his throat and even pauses several times while unfastening my dress before finishing.

"There. Not a hard task."

His enticing voice sends chills down my spine as he proceeds to take a few steps back.

"Thank you." I slowly let down my hair and turn around while still holding my dress in place. He smiles and attempts to say something when a ringing sound interrupts our private moment. We make eye contact for a brief second when I look away and he begins to dig into the pocket of his pants in search of his cellphone.

"It's Ethan. Will you excuse me? I'm going to take this outside. I'll be back as soon as I can."

He quickly heads out the door, eager to take Ethan's call. I just stand there, staring into the empty space before me from where he once stood as I contemplate about our intimate exchange.

Deciding that it's time to change, I head to the restroom that is located inside the bedroom. Removing the dress, I hang it over the towel rack and allow it to dry overnight. Sliding into the t-shirt and boxers that Jovi brought, I instantly capture a whiff of a masculine cologne. I didn't realize how much I missed his scent until now.

As I proceed to explore the living quarters, I weight my options on whether to fall asleep now or wait until he returns. He could be a while, and there is no telling if Ethan is also playing detective.

My eyes begin to search the room for any type of entertainment when I notice a huge wood armoire by the floor to ceiling window. Over to the center, the wall is lined with several built-in wood shelves that contain numerous magazines, a collection of law books, encyclopedias, and various novels. I could watch television for a while or read until sleep finally takes over.

With so many things running through my mind, I finally come to the conclusion that reading at this hour is probably not a great idea and settle on watching tv instead. Just as I'm walking over to the armoire, I notice red and blue lights flashing through the windowpanes.

Cautiously peeking through the shutters, I observe two vehicles out front. One of them is a police car and the other is Ethan's, both are parked in the driveway. It's still pouring outside so the window glass is slightly fogged, making it difficult to distinguish any additional details.

317

Where are they? I open the shutters just enough to allow me to see more clearly and I spot three men chatting in the distance under the covered veranda as the man in uniform begins to write on his notepad. Both Ethan and Jovianus are using hand gestures to communicate with the police officer. I instantly become nervous by the silence of the hushed discussion that is currently taking place outside.

What did the officer uncover? I wonder if the two incidents are connected, if so, then who is behind this scheme? These unanswered questions have me biting my nails right off, a bad habit that I picked up a few years ago.

Deciding that I had enough of this agony, I settle on going to sleep and finally get some rest. Today was a walking nightmare so I will pray for solace and deal with the consequences of tonight's events tomorrow.

Walking over to the light switch, I turn it off and head towards the bed. I can still see red and blue lights flashing in the background with only the sound of the pounding rain against the window. Pulling the duvet cover out from underneath the feathered pillows, I cautiously slide my body onto the mattress which lands me right behind Mateo.

Curling my arm around his waist, I close my eyes and begin to search for the woman clothed in white. I've been dreaming of her more frequent than before, but I don't recall any details. All I remember is that she brings me joy and tranquility which is what I need right now.

Before I can count to ten my mind and body is suddenly filled with purpose. A bright blue light with specs of white dots becomes visible in the far distance and she reappears. All it takes is her beautiful smile and my mind is lost once again.

*****

After Ethan called me to check on Simone, I filled him in on everything that had taken place as I was dropping her and Mateo off. He instantly became alarmed and insisted on coming over to discuss the details and wanted to be present when the officer arrived.

I was glad that he decided to come over because he asked questions that I wouldn't have thought of. After the police official left, he was eager to see Simone, so I led him upstairs to her room. He gently knocks a few times with no response and decides to let himself in. But before he could enter, I stopped him and signal towards the motion sensor. Ethan nods in acknowledgment and examines their surroundings from the doorway instead.

There on the bed nestled in the middle are both Mateo and Simone. I have her bags suspended over my shoulder, ready to deliver their belongings but it seems that we took longer than expected. Carefully placing the items in the hallway, Ethan immediately closes the door and takes a few steps away from the bedroom before turning around to face me.

"She's had a lot to deal with today. I don't understand what's going on here but I'm sure as hell going to find out."

His words are more than just a threat as we descend downstairs and I lead him into the kitchen. I open the fridge and grab a bottle of water, handing him one as well. We both take a few sips as the conversation continues and I stay focused on the topic. My mind is occupied with so many questions, but I resist until I've completed my own investigation.

"I agree. So, what are we going to do about her living arrangements? She can't go back home. Not until we figure out what's going on. It can't be a coincidence that she was deliberately drugged, and her home ransacked all in one night. We need to get to the bottom of this as quickly as possible."

Ethan becomes withdrawn, and I know that he now believes this fiasco is far from over as do I. There's a high possibility that she could be a target which has the both of us on alert.

"No, I get it and totally agree. She can either stay with Aemilia or me so long as she doesn't go home for the time being." He then raises both of his arms and folds them over the back of his head while slowly pacing back and forth in my kitchen.

"Well, I was thinking more along the lines of either staying with you or me. I don't want Aemilia becoming the next target if that's what's going on here."

Ethan suddenly stops pacing and turns to face me while lowering his hands.

"Guess you're right, but I thought your trip here was temporary. Aren't you heading back to Baie-Saint-Paul soon?"

His assessment is head on. Those were my plans originally, however, I failed to take my heart into account. There is no way that I'm leaving Simone this time. By some miracle, the goddess has granted me a second chance to make things right and that's exactly what I intend to do. The winds of time have unexpectedly changed and something new has sparked within me.

"Initially that was the arrangement, but it seems that my stay has been extended indefinitely."

"Alright. How about we discuss this with her tomorrow and break the news. Let's allow her to decide so long as she is with either one of us. Regardless, I know she will be safe under our care."

"Sounds like a plan."

We both make our way to the front driveway, hoping to place these unfortunate events behind us. It's now sometime after 2 a.m. and the rain has begun to fade into muffled drizzles as the moon reaches its highest peak. A light breeze is carried over my skin causing me to shiver. He halts right after unlocking his door and turns to face me when he speaks.

"I think it's worth mentioning that it's good to have you back. I know with time she will come around; just don't lead her on and leave again. The both of you have moved on and she has been through a lot as it is. I'm not sure that she would be able to handle another heartache. What she needs is stability in her life and not another distraction."

Him labeling me as a distraction is truly ironic given that this was the same sorry ass excuse I gave her when I left. I understand his concern and totally respect him for taking care of her while I was away because I'm sure it wasn't easy for either of them. But what he has failed to understand is that she wasn't the only one affected by my departure. I also paid a heavy price, one that continues to torment my fretted heart, and be as that may, I refuse to dive into that conversation. That discussion is being reserved for another time.

"Times have changed Ethan and I don't plan on allowing history to repeat itself. My sole interest at this point is her and Mateo's safety. Everything else can wait."

I mean every word; Simone and Mateo's safety are my top priority and I will do whatever it takes to protect them both.

"Good. I'll call you tomorrow morning."

He gets into his car and departs, satisfied and content with our little pep talk. I wait outside in the light drizzle until his vehicle is out of sight then walk back into the house. So many thoughts are crossing my mind at once that I cannot fathom the why's or how's. Simone was drugged and her house looted; this is not how I envision our union to be.

And Ethan, he never ceases to amaze me. After all, I was the one who decided to leave without a single explanation. But this time it's different. Different because after laying my eyes on her for the first time in four years, my affection for her has only been amplified. Different because I finally know what I want, and I will do whatever it takes to keep it in my grasp.

I have already broken two cardinal rules since my arrival in the States; having any type of interaction with Simone and allowing mortals into our private residence.

What would the council members and tribe leaders think about me now? Well, it doesn't matter because I will no longer sit back and allow someone else to dictate the course of my life, regardless of the consequences.

Satisfied with my declaration, I scramble to my feet realizing that the sun will rise in a few hours. I'm fully aware that last night's troubles are far from over, therefore I will seize the moment and treasure every minute that I'm able to share with her.

A shower and breakfast are both underway.

Chapter Seventeen

~Grievance~

It's **Sunday morning**, 7:30 a.m. to be exact as I sit in the kitchen impatiently waiting for Simone and Mateo to wake up. I'm extremely nervous and unsure of myself because I'm terrified to admit that her disapproval of my actions in the past will not be pardoned so swiftly.

It's not like we can pick up where we left off. She has clearly moved on with her life as Ethan blatantly pointed out last night. And to make matters more complicated, for reasons beyond my knowledge, I have this overbearing need to protect her and Mateo. It's puzzling and irrational yet I was ready to carry out any actions necessary to keep them both out of harm's way regardless of the outcome.

With a stiff neck and tense muscles, I slowly sip my black coffee and quickly find myself agitated with displaced thoughts that continue to ponder on all the *what if* situations and hypotheticals that correlate to last night's incident. As I think back to how Simone's body laid motionless and exposed while the culprit waited for a chance to ambush her, I quiver with rage.

How is it possible that I didn't notice anyone suspicious? I had my eye on her from the moment she walked through the door and kept a close watch throughout the evening, but apparently that wasn't enough. Everyone that she was in contact with seemed to have some type of close friendship with her.

So, this individual must be someone she knows well. How else would he or she have gotten the opportunity to poison her? And why Simone? Why her out of all people? She seemed as confused as we were to find herself in such a dire situation. While I grapple with the thought that someone, whether a friend or foe, would want to deliberately hurt a kind and gentle soul such as Simone, I secretly make it my mission to even the score with her assailant.

My mood suddenly shifts from angry to a sense of possessiveness as a violent surge of jealousy unexpectedly slaps me across my face. It's a deadly emotion, from its raw introduction all the way to its merciless wrath.

The urge to protect what is rightfully mine overpowers my logic. Rage begins to feed my inhumanity while I struggle to remain calm. Taken aback by this strange and unfamiliar sentiment, I quickly retract this haunting transgression that is begging to emerge and try to rationalize my reaction. But there is no justification because I haven't earned the right to feel this way. She doesn't belong to me and has already given herself to someone else.

Removing these troubled thoughts from my mind, I stand and walk over to the home audio system that is housed in the office nook and begin to shift through my collection of music. Classical tunes always seem to lighten my mood when I feel apprehensive. Within a matter of minutes, *Overnight* by Chilly Gonzales comes into view.

I keep the volume on low while the piano keys hum in the background. Since sleep is not vital to our overall health and is only required every so often, I was able to get a whole lot done in the wee hours of the morning.

I've made a few calls, showered, and even left the house for about 45 minutes to shop. Trader Joe's had all the necessary foods that a toddler could dream of and I was able to buy some items for breakfast, just in case she didn't feel like eating out.

As I begin making my way towards the refrigerator, my phone decides to ring. Looking into the receiver I confirm that its Ethan and quickly answer the call.

"Hey Ethan."

"Am I calling too early?"

"Not at all. I've been up for a few hours already. Didn't sleep much."

"Same here." Silence lingers for a bit as we are both unsure how to approach the delicate situation we are forced to face.

"How's Simone holding up?"

"Um," I begin to pace around the kitchen with the phone held close to my ear, "she's still asleep so not sure yet."

"Ok. Ah…what time would be good for us to come over and chat about her current dilemma?"

"Who is we?"

"Aemilia and myself of course."

"Right." I chuckle a bit before continuing, "You both can come after eight thirty. This should be enough time for her and Mateo to shower and eat."

"Sounds good. See you then."

I slide my phone shut, place it onto the kitchen counter and make another attempt at reaching the refrigerator when I hear two sets of footsteps approaching from the foyer. Seconds later, Simone and Mateo appear in the kitchen hand in hand. They have both showered and seem to be in a relaxed mood as our gazes meet. I greet them both while leaning against the kitchen island and cross my arms over my gray t-shirt.

"Good Morning."

"Morning," she smiles and stops by the porcelain sink still wearing my borrowed clothes from the night before.

Her wet crimped locks are partially tangled as they hang mid waist, leaving droplets of water on the stained concrete floor. Mateo's wavy hair has been hand brushed to the side and is dressed in fresh clothing.

Adjusting his glasses with one hand he continues to stare at me. At that moment, I notice that one of his iris's is a different color from its remainder. The bottom half is dark blue while the top has a splash of chestnut brown. That's odd. I didn't notice it last night at Ethan's place but then again, it was late in the evening which would explain why this feature did not stand out.

Clearing my throat, I continue to interrogate their sleeping arrangements and bury that note for some other time.

"Did you two sleep well?"

A slow cautious smile forms on her lips as she breaks away from our brief contact.

"Actually, this is the best sleep I've had in months." There is a hint of shyness in her tone.

Confusion crosses my face at her response given the events of the night before. She notices my reaction and decides to clarify before I jump to any conclusions.

"I sometimes experience lucid dreams with nightmarish hallucinations, but last night was an exception."

Unable to contain my curiosity, I proceed to inquire about her personal life as if we never broke stride.

"What are these dreams usually about?"

"I really don't want to get into that topic right now."

"Right." Clearing my throat, I decide on changing the subject, "So I see that you found the clean towels and extra toothbrushes I placed in the room for you both."

"Yes, we did. Thank you."

Uncrossing my arms, I remove myself from the counter and place one of my hands behind my back. "There's fresh fruit on the glass table to your right," I motion in the direction by the pantry. "And the refrigerator has just been stocked in case either of you are hungry."

"Thanks, but we don't want to trouble you anymore than we already have. I think it's best if I take a cab to Aemilia's and try to figure this out on my own."

Panic settles in as she swiftly begins to slip through my fingers.

Without thinking, I launch into a spew of jumbled words, pleading along the way as I attempt to persuade her in staying.

"Please, it's no trouble at all. Besides, you two haven't had a proper meal."

She doesn't seem convinced with my tireless efforts. Mateo on the other hand escapes from her loose grip, strolls over to the kitchen table, slides open a chair and settles in. I slowly take measured steps in her direction and halt my advance by a few feet. The seductive aroma of sweet jasmine radiating from her skin and hair fills my senses, reminding me how much I crave her touch.

With a calm and collected tone I make one final attempt at reasoning while maintaining a commanding presence.

"It would be an honor if you two would accompany me for breakfast."

"Jovi….." My name trails off her lips while our eyes remain locked onto one another.

We exchange stolen glances for a split second only solidifying that we are two individuals who ache to be resurrected. Feeling determined, I quickly formulate a plan to change her mind. She only just came back into my life and I couldn't bare it if she left right now. There is much to discuss.

"Both Ethan and Aemilia are on their way over here. At the very least, stay until they arrive and then you can leave with one of them if you'd like."

She hesitates at first but then finally agrees, "Ok."

This grueling space between us is difficult to navigate as the memory of her velvet lips enters my mind. I quickly snap out of my trance because I know that I mustn't act on impulse, otherwise I will jeopardize any chance of a possible reconciliation. A victory grin immediately forms on my face as I turn around and head towards the refrigerator.

"I was about to make some egg omelets before you walked in. Would you like some?"

"Actually, I'll have some cereal and almond milk if that's alright."

"Sure. What about Mateo?"

"He'll have toast with some fruit and orange juice."

"No chocolate-milk?" She comes up behind me as I set off in search of the items she requested.

"Uh no. He can't have any dairy. His stomach doesn't cooperate, and it will only make him sick."

After locating all of the requested items, I close the refrigerator with my leg and begin making my way towards the breakfast table.

"Ok. Orange juice it is then." My grin is wide from ear to ear as we embark on a playful conversation.

She seems to be in a blissful mood while searching the cupboards for the plate sets and cutlery. Meanwhile, Mateo has been sitting at the table with the same set of hot wheels from the night before in total silence. He has managed to line up all three cars onto the table and hasn't stop staring at them. That's odd, for a child his age he should be running around senseless or babbling meaningless words that no one understands.

"He's rather quiet for a child his age. Is he shy?"

I just finished popping soft slices of bread into the toaster as requested when I take notice that she has found her way around the kitchen pretty well.

Placing three bowls, silverware and tall glasses on the table, she turns her body slightly in my direction with a bit of hesitation.

"Um.. yeah. I guess you can say that."

"What do you mean?"

Unable to conceal my curiosity, it becomes apparent that I've developed a need to continue inquiring about matters that I'm not privileged to. She hesitates a bit when I realize that I've overstepped my boundaries and quickly launch into an apology.

"I'm sorry. You don't have to answer that. It's not my place to ask personal questions."

I hear her hesitate and then respond. "No, it's alright. It's just that I'm not used to people taking interest in him that's all."

Settling between the two of them, I position a stack of toast in the middle of the table along with three boxes of cereal. She fills each glass with orange juice and begins to place fruit in a bowl for Mateo. After a few minutes she summons the courage to speak, weary to share personal information about her son.

"He's autistic and," she pauses for a few beats before continuing, "Lacks social skills."

Unsure how to react to her comment, I respond with an, "Oh. I see."

"But he does communicate to an extent. Like with Aemilia and Ethan, but that's pretty much it."

"That's a good sign. I'm sure he'll get better as time passes."

Our gazes meet for a brief second when she smiles politely and turns away. I grab a bowl for myself and fill it with fruit while Simone loads hers with oats and honey cereal.

A mixture of berries is settled in a glass container that Mateo continues to pick out of even though he has his own personal stash right next to him. It's the funniest thing to watch and I can't help but wonder what my life would have been had I never left the states.

Well, for starters there would be no Mateo because celestials are unable to procreate with mortals given that our reproductive systems are not compatible in nature.

And not to mention the fact that the tribe leaders would have intervened at one point or another, regardless if I would have left willingly. So, as it stands, the outcome would have probably been the same. I honestly believe that my choices, whether right or wrong have led me here. Right here at this very moment and I wholeheartedly believe that everything happens for a reason.

She glances over my meal before pouring almond milk into her cereal.

"So, no dairy for you either huh?"

"I'm a vegetarian. Did you forget?" I frown at her comment because she would always give me a tough time about my eating habits which is not something that anyone could easily overlook.

"Guess I did." She quickly takes a spoonful of oats into her mouth, lost in thought. I take a drink out of my orange juice when the doorbell rings.

Pushing my chair back, I stand, "It's probably Ethan and Aemilia. I'll be right back," and place my napkin on the table.

She smiles and continues eating as I exit the kitchen and head towards the front entry.

Peeking through the camera located on the intercom I confirm that it is indeed Ethan and Aemilia. After turning off the house alarm, I open the door and step aside, allowing them entry to my home.

"Please come in."

Ethan gives me a quick pat on the back while Aemilia approaches and plants a swift kiss on my left cheek.

"We were just about to eat breakfast. Would you two care to join us?"

Ethan is the first to respond while I lead the way towards the kitchen, "I think we are good. Just anxious to see them."

Meanwhile Aemilia stays mum about the subject leading me to believe that maybe they spent the night together. I just smile and try my best not to give away any indication that I'm onto them.

As we enter the kitchen, I find Simone standing by Mateo's side, assisting him with his toast while her half-eaten cereal remains abandoned on the table. Aemilia swiftly walks over to her and they both engage in an affectionate embrace with apprehension marred on each other's face.

"Ethan told me what happened to your house last night. I'm so sorry Simone."

"Don't beat yourself up over it. This could have happened to anyone of us." Her gloom expression does nothing to conceal her discomfort about the subject while she sways from side to side.

"But it didn't, did it? It happened to you instead."

"Stop it Aemilia. Don't do this. Not right now." Her voice unwillingly breaks at the end which was unexpected.

Ethan then walks over, pulls Simone into a hug and kisses her forehead, "You had us worried sick."

This burden is far too much for her to carry and she has finally had enough. Although she tries hard to keep her emotions in check, tears slowly begin to stream down her cheeks.

Ethan then whispers, "Don't cry, you're stronger than this," and keeps her body close to his while providing emotional support. "What this schmuck failed to take into consideration is that you're always surrounded by people who love and care for you. I promise that we will get to the bottom of this and everything will be back to the way it was before."

She wipes the remaining tears from her cheeks and gently squirms out of Ethan's hold. Aemilia remains standing by her side, rubbing her shoulder in a soothing manner.

I on the other hand do nothing as I lean against the wall with my hands safely tucked away in the pocket of my jeans. Silent and observant is what I will be; waiting for the opportunity to demonstrate my trust without invading her privacy.

I must admit that it's extremely hard for me to watch her endure pain and not being able to provide consolation. It takes all of my strength not to walk over and take her into my arms. To whisper words of encouragement; promises that I will never leave her side again. That I've been a fool to think that I was better off without her. But I won't. Not today. Because today I will be a friend. Someone who supports her in every way possible whether she is right or wrong.

Patient is what I will be. I only just came back into her life. She needs time. Time to digest the fact that I'm here to stay and that nothing or no one can come between us again. So, as I sit back and watch her two most trusted friends console her, the unthinkable happens.

While leaning against the wall with my hands jammed in my pockets, her brown-haired boy walks up and just stands there, staring at me again. Sensing that he is either troubled or adrift I immediately recover my posture and bend down to his level.

With a welcoming tone I greet him with a, "Hi!"

He doesn't respond right away and instead lifts both of his arms in the air. Without further hesitation, my body responds almost immediately as I pick him up and walk over to the breakfast table where his band of colorful sedans await. The room doesn't feel stuffy anymore and I can feel a sense of serenity spring to life from within. Everyone slowly begins to fade while the events from yesterday become a distant memory.

As we both set off on our journey to race the shiny wheels that currently occupy our hands, I hear a few gasps followed by a male's voice.

"Guess he found a new best friend Aemilia." And everyone begins to giggle, including Mateo.

Unknown to him, he was the icebreaker to a much-needed discussion that is essential to their wellbeing. With Mateo still on my lap, I hear chairs being pulled from the table informing me that we are no longer secluded to our own world. Slowly lifting my head, I take notice that

Simone is sitting directly across the table from me with a wary frown of disbelief.

Aemilia is sitting next to her just glaring at us in amusement while Ethan settles beside me, ready to take a plunge into this difficult conversation that will soon be behind us all. This topic is inevitable. Problematic even because no one has any idea where to start or how to handle the matter.

Clearing his throat, Ethan dives right in, "So, did you notice anything strange or out of the ordinary last night? Anything that you can remember?"

"Um, no. I spent most of my time with Leona and Derek before heading outside with Mateo."

"And you didn't see anyone possibly following you or accidently bump into you?"

"No one comes to mind, no." She pauses for a brief second and turns to face Ethan with confusion on her face. "Well, I did run into Franco. Derek returned from the bar with him and he stayed for a bit to chat."

Ethan immediately sits further back into his chair, a bit alarmed while squinting his eyes.

"You know, I never fully trusted him. What if he finally got tired of your rejections and decided to act? You have to admit, it makes sense."

"Please, Franco wouldn't hurt a fly if it was growing on his ass."

Aemilia's objections about Franco makes him sound like a creep which means he fits the profile.

I guess his obsessive behavior only got worst after I left. Wouldn't doubt it if Franco is behind all of this. What would he get out of it anyway? Surely there is no pleasure in hurting the one individual you desire, even if that being doesn't feel the same. Taking a mental note; the next time I run into Franco, I'll be sure to express my disapproval of his persistence and ill-mannered deeds towards Simone.

Quickly changing the subject, I launch into my own means of cross examination hoping to identify the offender.

"Does Franco know where you live?" I am hoping the answer is no. Please say no.

She immediately responds, "Uh... no," and shakes her head with revulsion.

"Anyone from work? Maybe an unsatisfied customer?"

"I can't think of anyone."

She then stands up, crosses her arms, and begins to fidget while slowly pacing back and forth. I can tell that she has become uneasy with all the prying questions which hasn't solved anything.

Ethan then interjects by snapping his fingers,

"Didn't you have lunch or dinner with that one fella that you met at work? What's his name again, Stefano?"

"His name is Santino and yes we had dinner in a public place. But it was only once, and we haven't seen each other since."

Her reaction to Ethan's question only irritates her further which pushes my jealousy over the edge. What are the odds that this Santino character would be the same mortal that I rammed on the ice rink four years ago? No way, not a chance.

There's still a bitter taste in my mouth caused both by envy and spitefulness as resentment floods my heart. So, she's going on dates while a nameless prowler is stalking her who she may or may not know. Great, now I have two prime suspects of which I'm all too eager to investigate and fill the gaps of her past. Unknown to me, my timing was off causing a series of events to unfold.

I blurt out without thinking, "What about Mateo's father?"

Both Ethan and Aemilia look at me like I just committed a crime. I give them the harmless *what* look and turn my attention back to Simone.

"What about him?" Her question comes out harsh and confrontational.

I quickly come to my senses that this is a rather sensitive subject, one that should not have been brought up but hardly regret doing so.

"Well uh, I haven't heard anyone bring him up. Do you two have a written agreement regarding Mateo's guardianship? This could very well be the product of someone close to you that you're probably overlooking."

She exhales sharply right before lashing out at my candid informal intrusiveness.

"Mateo's father has not been a part of his life nor will he ever be. So, to answer your question, no he is not a threat because he has no knowledge of Mateo's existence."

Before I can try to defend myself, Ethan jumps in and attempts to defuse the already complicated topic by justifying our invasive approach. From here on the conversation takes a turn for the worst and no one was ready for the aftermath.

"Look Simone, the truth of the matter is that you can't go home anytime soon. Not until the police completes a thorough investigation and confirms that you weren't a target. You could very well have a stalker on your hands and not even know about it."

Her voice has quickly spiked two octaves as she uncrosses her arms and approaches the table in an aggressive manner.

"So, what am I supposed to do in the meantime? Hide like a fugitive? I'm of no importance so trust me when I say that no one is stalking me. This could easily be a mistaken identity situation."

"Your life doesn't have to stop. All I'm saying is that until all of this blows over, you should stay with either Jovi or myself. I don't feel comfortable with you going home just yet."

"Ethan is right. There's a possibility that you weren't a random target and the perpetrator is just waiting for the opportunity to ….," my thought trails off because I am unable to finish the sentence.

The idea of someone lurking in her home waiting to ambush her sets me on fire. How can I address my concerns without appearing to be intrusive?

Aemilia finally speaks up as she stands from her chair and joins our voyage of concern.

"Darling, I'm afraid they are both right. If you want, you can give me a list of items you need and Ethan and myself can go to your house and retrieve them for you."

"Well, someone definitely needs to go over and at least secure the house. The officer told us last night that after he left, he was unable to fasten the doors because they are both broken."

As Aemilia and Ethan go back and forth about her safety, I sluggishly raise my voice to capture their attention.

"Um, I've made a few calls this morning and had someone go over to your house to change both doors, locks and even install a security system."

"On a Sunday......"

Ethan seems surprised that I was able to find someone to complete this type of request on such short notice being that it's a day of rest, for mortals anyway. Never underestimate the power of having friends in low places and one who owes me a huge favor.

"Jovi, why would you do that without my consent?"

She doesn't seem pleased with my act of kindness, so I decide to provide further clarification and avoid any objections.

"We can't have you go back to your home exposed and defenseless. Your doors were kicked open and no one was alerted…" But I don't get the chance to finish my explanation because she cuts me off brusquely.

"This is not something that you or anyone in this room gets to decide. You're back for like two minutes and now you're committed to making decisions in my life? Where were you four years ago when I needed you? Because you sure as hell weren't here!"

"Simone!" Ethan stands but only manages to get one-word in.

"Don't Ethan!" Her booming voice echoes throughout the room.

Sensing tension, Mateo begins to slowly slide down my leg and quietly walks over to his mum. I do my best to remain calm. Careful not to raise my voice and lose control.

Pushing my chair back, I stand and halt Ethan from interfering as I raise my palm outward, "No, it's ok Ethan. Let her speak. This is good. She's scared and frustrated. A lot has happened and it's not healthy to hold it in."

With a wicked grin and bitter stare, she slowly walks over to my side of the table, halting her advance by a few feet. As I begin searching for that gentle and compassionate being, a harsh and unpleasant persona takes over.

"So, enlighten me Jovianus, why are you back? You didn't bother informing anyone that you were leaving nor that you were returning. What business do you have in the States this time?" Her tone is laced with malice and anger, making a spectacle of my past. I find myself at odds with telling the truth.

"The answer is not that simple."

"The truth is always simple."

"Truth comes in many forms and sometimes that truth isn't yours to share."

"You know what, I am getting tired of your baseless justifications."

"I don't want to do this right now." My message is curt and straight to the point, "I'm not your enemy Simone. The enemy is out there, waiting for the opportunity to hurt you and I will not stand aside and allow that to happen."

"Oh really? Why do you care what happens to me now? You never wrote a single letter. Never called to check on me. You made me a promise and broke it the moment they left your lips."

"That's not fair."

"You know what, fuck being fair. Life isn't fair!"

I can tell that her thoughts are displaced but that doesn't stop her. No indeed. She would rather continue on this path of destruction and has every intention of pulling in everyone around her no matter the cost.

This is out of character and my patience is running short. I'm no longer able to distinguish the difference between adoration and aversion.

So, I continue to plead, hoping to end this frail discussion, "Simone, please stop," but it doesn't work.

"I'm not your problem. I never have, and I never will be so please do us all a favor and drop the disguise that you care because you don't."

"That's enough!" My orotund voice catches everyone by surprise as I toggle back and forth with my emotions.

Bewildered and defeated, I close my eyes and make an effort at reason. Her once shrill voice is instantly replaced with a loud buzz, like a beetle humming inside my ear.

Breathe. Just breathe Jovi. Remember that you're not furious with her. You're enraged with yourself because everything she said has some truth to it and you weren't ready to hear it. You did all those things to her and you only have yourself to blame. Stop hiding beneath the cloth of lies and prove to her that your love was not a notion or belief. It was real, untainted, and full of conviction. Surely you didn't erase that part of her memory. She couldn't have easily forgotten how you two felt about each other.

And just like that, my fury vanishes without a trace. Blinking my eyes open, I find her standing in the same position, shocked at my outburst.

Gently maneuvering in her direction and careful not to smother her space, I begin sharing my most inhibited, private thoughts and bring them to life.

"You're right on all accounts but one."

With my eyebrows cast downwards, I continue explaining the best way I'm able to without disclosing too much information.

"All those things that you just said have some truth to it, but that doesn't mean that I didn't care, and it wasn't without consequence because you weren't the only one who suffered from my departure."

My tone remains soft and harmonious as I continue to pour the remnants of my soul on display.

"I did make you a promise and unintentionally broke it. And although we knew that me leaving was inevitable, I still left abruptly and without warning. I never bothered to call or write and before I knew it, my long days bled into years and yet, not a day went by that I didn't think about you."

I then reach for her hand and place it into mine, pleased that she didn't flinch at my touch while she remains captivated by my willingness to share something so intimate.

"I initially came back with the intent to attend a party and depart the very next day. What harm can come of that I thought to myself?" I stifle a timid smile, "But what I failed to take into consideration was my heart. As it turns out, it was not as easy to see you and walk away as I thought it would be, and now I'm finding it impossible to leave."

Aemilia and Ethan remain frozen in place like two statues; unmoving and at attention, as if our life were a soap opera.

"There is no explanation as to why I left other than for my own selfish pursuits and for that, I am sorry. But I do want you to know that a part of me died that day and I've been lost without you ever since. These feelings, these emotions within me are not temporary like a rush of adrenaline. They are perpetual and unconditional like the sun in our solar system. Without them, my life wouldn't exist. And although we've been apart this whole time, nothing or no one has been able to change that fact."

Tears are now streaming down her cheeks as I make a final attempt to mend our shattered friendship.

"Can you ever find it in your heart to forgive me?"

Her response is not what I expected when she whispers, "It's too late," and retracts her hand from mine.

Without hesitation she exits the kitchen with Mateo in her arms and doesn't bother to look back. It doesn't take long for Aemilia to run after her, leaving Ethan behind. We both just stand there for a few minutes, unsure what to say or do. Shocked at how things turned out, I open the chair next to me and take a seat because I no longer have the strength to stand on my own two feet.

Not sure how much time has passed when Ethan finds the courage to speak up

"At least you tried. Give her some time to digest it all, she'll come around."

I don't say anything other than a simple nod with my hand partially covering my mouth as I rest my elbow onto the breakfast table.

I never lift my head when Ethan confirms that he will work on convincing Simone to stay with him until all of this blows over. And when he leaves, I don't bother to walk him out nor thank him for taking care of the one individual that matters the most to me.

Watching them leave my home through the kitchen window was harder than I anticipated. I might feel hopeless, but I have not been defeated.

All is not lost. Not yet anyway. Not for me.

Chapter Eighteen

~Aggress~

I **find myself sitting in silence**, folding Mateo's freshly washed clothes on the living room sofa as I focus on the task at hand. It's late afternoon as the sun slowly begins to set on the horizon, casting a variety of dark red and pale orange hues across the sky. I'm distracted by the beautiful skyline as the wind carries a mild breeze, causing the sheer curtains to sway to the silent rhythm.

I've been home for the past four days with Aemilia by my side to provide comfort and reassurance whenever needed. Since my arrival, I haven't opened the ceramics store because I currently lack reason. Given that I never bothered to change my number, Jovianus has been calling and texting non-stop since my abrupt departure from his home.

And to make matters more interesting, Mateo has been restless from the moment we walked through our door which is unusual because he would rather be home than anywhere else.

So yes, my life has officially been turned upside down overnight, literally.

While placing the empty basket on the wooden floor, my cell phone rings. I quickly glance at the screen and confirm that it's Jovi again. I don't have the energy to continue with our dispute or hear anymore apologies, so I settle on overlooking his call. I know that a text message will likely follow soon, so I swipe at the *ignore* call option instead. When I left his house late Sunday, we were not on good terms because things remained unsettled between us. I have so many questions with no answers.

Not only was I in love with him, but he was also one of my best friends. We spent every minute of the day with each other and when we weren't together, we were either communicating through the phone or video chatting. There was nothing that he couldn't or wouldn't tell me and vice versa. We were inseparable from the moment we met, but that all changed when he decided to abandon his former life and fast forwarded to his new one. The only reason I knew he was alive was through Ethan.

I tried contacting him several times after the fact but was quickly greeted with, *this caller is no longer accepting calls*, yada.

I'm frustrated, confused and angry; how am I supposed to suppress these feelings if he is the root cause of them? Did he really expect me to accept him with open arms after all this time? A part of me wants to forgive him because deep down inside, my heart still yearns for his affection, but this is not something that can simply go away overnight. I know that it will be impossible to move forward without honesty.

So, when I confronted him about his sudden departure, he decided to dodge my questions with vague responses. At that point, I couldn't take it anymore and walked out of his house.

Since I've been ignoring his calls these past couple of days, he has decided to contact Aemilia directly to check on me. All of her responses have been the same, *she is doing great. Give her time and I'm sure she will come around.* I've told her many times over to stop responding but she insists that he is just worried and deserves to know.

Finishing the laundry, I stroll over to my bedroom and begin undressing Mateo for his afternoon bath. Aemilia is buried somewhere in my closet, trying on several outfits I'm sure. She has a date with one of Ethan's friend's tonight whom she met at Nicole's graduation party. All of her wardrobe is shoved into my closet with half of them dangling off the wooden hangers.

"Have you figured out what you're wearing tonight?" My toneless voice is barely loud enough for her to hear as I remove Mateo's shoes and white socks.

"I think so. Just need a few more minutes." She calls out in frustration, possibly due to the fact that she can't make up her mind on whether to be provocative or conservative. I find her fashion choice exhausting and overwhelming at times.

Standing up from the bed, I look over in her direction. "Alright. I'm going to be in the next room taking Mateo a quick bath. Let me know if you need my help." Haha…like she would even consider any suggestions that I might have.

"Ok. Thanks."

She quickly dismisses me as I head over to the restroom with Mateo covered in his tiny bath robe. Tightening the drain cap and turning on both the hot and cold water, I slowly pour raspberry scented bubbles into his bath. As the tub fills to a safe depth, I turn off the water, remove Mateo's light blue robe and gently place him inside the tub. Wasting no time, he locates his two small power boats that glide on contact and switches the *on* buttons. Grabbing the tear free shampoo, I pour a small drop onto his head and slowly workup a lather while massaging his scalp when I hear my phone buzzing against the nightstand in the next room. This time it's not a call, but another text message. I remain seated on the restroom floor, debating on whether I should check my phone to make sure it's not someone important like Ethan or Leona. Trying to ignore the buzzing, I distract myself by rinsing Mateo's hair. Once finished I sit back and watch him play in silence for a few minutes. The phone has stopped buzzing, but the unknown is eating at me, causing my curiosity to give in.

"Aemilia?" I cautiously call out to her.

Her response is filled with skepticism, "Yes….."

"Can you check who that is please?" I can hear her heels thud against the wooden floors as she makes her way to fetch my phone. After a few seconds, she responds and I can tell that she is annoyed, but not sure if it has anything to do with me or her date.

"It's your favorite person in the whole wide world, again." Her voice just got a little higher as she spoke the last word.

"What does the text say?" All of his prior messages have mostly been sweet quotes from some of his favorite poets. Every now and then he will sneak in a, *"Hey, just checking on you to see if you needed anything,"* or my favorite, *"I understand if you never want to see me again, but I would do anything just to hear your voice one last time, so please pick up."*

"You really want me to read it out loud right now?" Sighing I respond with enthusiasm, "Yes please."

"Ok…" She trails off and begins to read his text message:

"His life has been nothing but a farce, amid unrequited pleas, and tormented beliefs; Until a star, from afar, emerged from the depths of his weary dreams, and transformed his soul into a worthy being."

She doesn't say another word and instead walks over to the restroom with my phone in her hand as she leans in the doorway. I'm sitting down on the tile floor with my hands crossed around my chest as I stare at the wall behind Mateo. I don't bother to turn around and acknowledge her presence, so she wanders in and decides to sit on top of the toilet seat.

"Simone honey, you can't ignore him forever." Her voice is modulated and soft as she continues to stare at me, probably wondering how I will react.

I still haven't looked up as I continue to stare at the wall, shocked at his persistence. I don't know how to feel about it; however, I do know that I never stopped loving him. But that doesn't change the fact that he left me and has yet to be completely honest about his sudden departure.

"Sweetie, I know that you're angry with him and you have every right to be, but I also know that you're hurting inside and that you still love him. And don't try to deny it because I know you better than anyone. Just… give him a chance to explain that's all I'm saying." I turn to look at her and we both smile at one another.

"I know." I pause, "You're right. This silence between us isn't going to solve anything." Turning my attention back to Mateo I continue addressing her. "I'll finish bathing Mateo then I will give him a call."

"Good." Aemilia stands up, hands me my phone and does a quick spin which causes her frock to float above her knees. She is wearing a tan tiered dress with a dark rose pattern that drops at the neckline. Her hair remains straight and hangs down her back in layers. She looks incredible!

"How do I look?"

"Like your about to get into some real trouble." I suppress a laugh and give her my stamp of approval.

"Then I'm right on track." We both laugh and Mateo giggles, joining in on our private conversation, unaware that his auntie Em is up to no good.

"Well, I'm about to leave. Are you sure that you're ok staying by yourself for a few hours?"

"Yes, I'm sure. Go have fun and don't worry about us. I'll lock the doors and turn on the house alarm. Plus,

Ethan is just a phone call away if I need him." She frowns at my last comment but otherwise continues to beam.

"Ok. I'll be back before midnight. Call me if you need anything. I mean it, ok?" She bends down, kisses me on the cheek then leans in and kisses Mateo on top of his head. "I will. Love you."

"Love you too." She walks out the restroom and disappears through the hall. I hear the alarm beep twice and the front door lock at the same time. I'll turn the alarm back on after Mateo falls asleep, I think to myself.

I finish taking Mateo a bath and quickly dress him in some blue and gray striped PJ's. Somehow, I've managed to wet my t-shirt and jogging pants, so I return to my bedroom and change into a cream-colored tank top with light green boy shorts. Mateo walks in behind me with *The Lion King* movie in his hand, alerting me that he wants to watch a cartoon before falling asleep.

So, I pick him up, place his tiny body on my bed and pull the duvet over his crossed legs. Taking the movie from his hands, I turn on the tv and insert the cartoon into the blue ray. Mateo's eyes are glued to the screen as he waits for the colorful pictures to appear. Pressing play on the remote, I quickly return to the bed and sit on the edge as I grab my phone and dial the number to the one individual that I've been avoiding. Surprisingly, he answers after the first ring.

"Simone?" His voice sounds exasperated, like he has run out of breath or something.

"Hi." My nerves got the best of me, cutting off the air supply to my brain and losing my train of thought for the moment.

"Is everything ok?"

"Um yeah, everything is fine. I uh...I just finished taking Mateo a bath and decided to stop avoiding you."

"Well, I...," he continues to stammer, "I... I'm glad that you called. I've been going crazy over here."

Shaking my head, I switch the phone to my other ear and settle beside Mateo. "Jovi, ... we can't continue this...whatever this...." He cuts me off unexpectedly and doesn't allow me to finish.

"Believe me when I say that I had no choice in the matter when I left. The guilt that I have, is leaving you without saying goodbye and not keeping in touch. Things can go back to the way they used to be, if you trust that I did what I thought was the right thing given the circumstance."

"No, they can't. We cannot move forward as if nothing happened because it did happen. Things have changed since you left. I have someone else to think about other than myself. Any decisions I make will also affect him. Besides, if we aren't going to be honest with each other then what do we have?"

"Honesty? You want honesty from me yet you're not willing to be honest with yourself."

"What are you talking about?" Confusion and anger consume my thoughts while he begins to point fingers. This is going nowhere fast but decide not to press for a response and quietly pledge to be patient.

"I don't want to argue with you. That's not why I've been calling."

"Then why have you been calling?"

He hesitates at first, causing the other end of the receiver to go silent while he finally gains the courage to speak. "The truth is that I miss hearing your voice, and I haven't been able to stop thinking about you since I saw you at Ethan's party. And it's become unbearable since you left my house."

Silence followed by light breathing over the receiver echoes as I carefully consider his words. What is he saying? That he misses me like a child misses their favorite blanket or something more?

"And that all I want is for you to be happy and safe." His voice is low and husky but with a hint of urgency.

"I'm as good as anyone can be considering the circumstances. So much has happened these past couple of days that I haven't had enough time to digest it all. I feel confused, angry and sometimes even sad."

"I can only imagine what you're going through and wished that it never happened."

"Jovi..." His name trails off my lips as I am lost for words.

"Simone...I... I really wish that I could go back in time and change the way things ended, but I can't. I want to be here for you now and be whatever it is you need me to be. Whether that means being a friend or just someone you call when you need to talk. Either option places me back into your life and for me that would be enough. All I'm asking is for you to please give me another chance."

How can I be friends with someone that I'm still in love with? How does someone do that? Silence has taken over our conversation as seconds continue to trickle by.

"Please, say something." He continues to plead. "I am prepared to do whatever is needed to make this work."

I know that now might not be the best time to bring up the past. There will certainly be another opportunity for this, and the sole question remains; can I or will I forgive him for leaving me four years ago? Can I move past this one obstacle that is keeping us apart? What

363

my heart and mind desire are two totally different things. Closing my eyes with the phone over my ear, I begin searching for answers deep within my mind.

Looking over my shoulder, I confirm that Mateo is still focused on the movie and at that moment I decide to listen to my heart instead. "Will the day ever come when you are in a position to thoroughly explain your reasons for leaving?"

"Yes." His response is instantaneous. This one word has so much meaning and it's all I needed to hear. A possibility. The truth of the matter is that I also want what he is so willingly offering. A chance to have him in my life again. A life that I share with my son Mateo.

"Then my answer is also yes."

He sighs out of relief, "Does this mean that you agree to forgive me?"

"I will certainly try."

"You have no idea how happy you have made me."

At that moment Mateo starts laughing in the background as he stands on my bed and begins jumping which causes me to giggle a bit. "I'm sorry. I've got my hands full over here and thought the movie would put him to sleep, but it seems that it has quite the opposite effect on him."

"No need to apologize. Were you getting ready for bed?"

"It's only a little after eight and I haven't gotten much rest lately so no. I'm not going to sleep anytime soon, not until Aemilia gets home anyway."

"Are you by yourself with Mateo?" He seems a bit alarmed but otherwise remains calm.

"Yeah, I guess so. Aemilia is kind of out on a date but she promised to be back before midnight."

"Is that right?" After a few pauses he continues, "Well, since we are friends again, would you care to have the companionship of an individual who is seeking forgiveness until Aemilia returns? We could do whatever you'd like."

How did this conversation end up with him coming over? That truly does sound nice and I sure could use the company. Maybe I could even sleep a bit while he is here, but I don't want to sound desperate. How can I agree without actually agreeing?

I start laughing as I respond, "You don't have to trouble yourself. What's more is that you'd be bored with me and a three-year-old."

"Nothing about you or Mateo is boring." His words have more meaning than I know he intended them to.

"It's late Jovi. Don't you have to work tomorrow?"

"My work does not require me to be in the office and can be accomplished at any hour of the day. Besides, it would make me feel better knowing that you are safe until Aemilia arrives, otherwise I will insist that we stay on the phone until she returns."

"Ok. It's your funeral."

"I'm just going to change and then I will be on my way."

"See you soon then." The line goes dead as the phone remains glued to my ear. What just happened? Damn. Should I be worried or pleased with this outcome. Keep calm, he's just coming over to keep you company because he cares about you as a friend and nothing more.

Shaking my head, I leap off the bed and stroll over to the stereo by the television. Skimming through my collection of music, I locate the track that will help clear my head. Within a matter of seconds, the keys to the piano sounds over the built-in stereo system and *Colorblind* by the Counting Crows begins to play in the background. Mateo jumps off the bed and trails behind as I make my way towards the kitchen.

Flicking the light switch on, the kitchen quickly becomes illuminated by a bronze metal track that is equipped with four light fixtures. Walking over to the counter, I open the cupboard that is nestled above the oven to retrieve two stemless glasses which are typically used for wine. As I reach for the handle to the refrigerator, I take notice that one of the stainless-steel doors is covered in tiny fingerprints that belong to Mateo. Hmm, I thought I had cleaned these off yesterday but guess he somehow managed to recreate his work of art again.

Snickering to myself and shaking my head, I proceed to open the refrigerator and search for the carton of orange juice while balancing one of the glass cups between my chest with one arm and holding the other in my left hand.

After locating the carton, I place one of the glass cups on the clear top shelf, grab the orange juice and begin to twist the white cap off while pouring the auburn liquid into the glass that is occupying my left hand. At that exact moment, an earsplitting racket like something has crashed resonates from behind me, enlisting fear, and anxiety all at once. Without warning the glass slips out of my hand, lands on the floor, and breaks into countless pieces. The carton of orange juice has also managed to escape my grip and splatters across the floor, soaking my socks and even lands on Mateo's face.

From here on, everything seems a blur as the events unfold in slow motion. Mateo begins to scream at the top of his lungs and falls to his knees while covering his ears with the palm of his hands. I quickly turn around to face whatever wrath is being unleashed behind me and take notice that my house has been breached. Sharp thick glass that was once part of my door is sprawled across the floor like a bed of clear crystals. The frame remains partially intact by a single gold hinge as it sways from the impact.

A tall muscular male is standing in the doorway with a large lop-sided scar that runs through his top lip, down his chin and ends at the hub of his throat. His dirty blond hair is pulled back into a ponytail and his upper body is covered in a dark colored jacket with a hoodie that is slightly unzipped at his chest, exposing his pectorals.

Within a matter of seconds, the vicious male begins to make his way through my kitchen. I can hear the shards of glass scraping the floor as his scuffed boots gain momentum and he lunges at me. My first instinct is to protect Mateo, so I attempt to throw my body on him, but fail at the task when I'm knock back against the refrigerator and land on the broken glass and orange liquid. Numb to the pain that has taken up residence on my lower back and head, I try to retreat when suddenly I feel a big cold hand wrap around my delicate throat. The intruder then lifts me up with one hand, pins my body to the wall and slams my head several times against the gray wallpaper. Struggling to breathe, my hands automatically go up and over his hold hoping to loosen his grip. Lifting me up higher, he tightens his grasp, leans in close so that we are both at eye level and begins to address me as if he knew who I was.

"How can someone as small and frail as you be a threat to anyone?"

His low, disembodied growl sends chills down my spine while my feet unwillingly dangle midair. My desperate eyes plead for mercy as I struggle to breathe. Images of Mateo flood my thoughts while I gasp for air.

Changing tactics, I remove my hands from his hold and begin to push against his chest attempting to place some distance between us, but it doesn't work.

He then snickers, "Look at you. You're like a flimsy little butterfly, trying to flap your broken wings against a silk spider web."

Drawing attention back to his face I notice that one of his irises are dark brown with specs of yellow while the other is a yellowish brown like that of a cat. When he blinks, his pupils unexpectedly expand, causing the shade of his irises to transform to a deep lifeless black.

"It's pathetic," his menacing snarl is inches from my ear as he continues to choke the life out of me.

In an instant, the course of my fate worsens when he reaches for my tank top and rips it off in one swift motion, revealing my bare breast. With his free hand, he sets off on groping me while I whimper in displeasure. His forced smile doesn't reach his eyes. I can smell the musk of cigarette radiating from his breath as he continues to unleash his abuse both physically and psychologically.

"I knew you were a myth." He briefly chuckles and resumes assaulting me, "You are nothing but a worthless human parasite," then spits in my face all while grinning as I continue to fight for my life.

Blood is rushing to my face while agonizing tears slowly trickle down my warm cheeks. My son's shrieks and presence has been silenced by the pressure around my neck causing my sight to become hazy. I can feel my strength slowly fading into the distance. All my senses have become numb and dull just like a cold bitter morning. The fight to live has vanished while my eyelids involuntarily close, causing my hands to go limp and my mind to surrender. The intruder leans in real close to my ear one last time, inhales sharply and hisses with sarcasm. "But guess what…. myth or not, I'm still going to kill you."

Within a matter of seconds, my mind goes blank and I am instantly lost. Lost forever.

Chapter Nineteen

~Demiurge~

My body shivers as a cool breeze glides over my balmy skin, causing goosebumps to rise on my frail arms and legs. To my surprise, I'm fully clothed in a silk creme gown, similar to a stola that hangs just below my ankles.

With my hair pulled to the side in a loose braid, I stand alone and barefoot, in an unknown dark place. Looking around in search of a door or exit I quickly come to realization that the empty space before me is infinite.

There is no beginning or end to its structure as my eyes continue to scan the area. The gray textured tiles beneath my feet are embedded with ancient gold calligraphy that stretches out for miles, displaying a continuous glowing trail of foreign musical symbols. It's surprisingly quiet and there is no sense of life or time in this unknown dwelling. The only sound filling my ears is the rush of crashing waves that only one could sense through the cavity of a seashell.

I can also hear my own breathing as I inhale the salty, sulfur like aroma through my nose. An assortment of speckled diamonds twinkle from above uninterrupted like the wind underneath a bird's wings. This must be where all the people who cease to exist go after they die. I feel confused and anxious as I slowly turn around to examine my surroundings when suddenly I am greeted with a familiar voice.

"Don't be alarmed Simone. You are safe now." Her soft-spoken tone echoes throughout the abandoned darkness confirming that I'm not alone.

My curiosity is unexpectedly aroused as I grapple with the idea that I could very well be dead. Stammering, my shaky voice calls out to the vacant space overhead.

"Where... where am I?" Suddenly she appears in the distance, her body radiating a bright yellow beam from where she stands as her canary gold robe sways from a light draft. A fish tail braid embellished with a silver lace hangs straight down her back while icy blue lights pour from her eyes. I just stand there, mesmerized by her beauty, wondering if a creature as such could really exist in my world.

"You are where I want you to be." A warmhearted smile forms on her perfectly shaped lips, providing both comfort and relief at the same time.

"And where is that?"

"Sanctuary."

"Am I," swallowing hard I pause and reconsider my word choice as my hands slowly drape around my neck.

"Dead?"

Unable to stop myself from being straightforward, I impatiently await her response. I feel sick to my stomach for allowing the dreadful thought to even cross my mind, but I have to know if I remain alive by some miracle or if I've finally met my fate.

She chuckles succinctly before speaking, "Actually it's quite the opposite," and begins to walk towards me in a gentle calculated stride. The gray textured tiles flare up beneath her bare feet with each passing step, leaving an afterglow behind like stones that have been set on fire.

"You are more alive today than ever before." She is confident in her response which makes no sense given that I'm in a strange place with garments only worn in ancient roman times.

"Forgive me for not understanding, but a few moments ago I was strangled to death and then I somehow ended up here with you. How is it that I'm alive again?"

The sarcasm in my voice was unintentional and insolent, but otherwise well received. As she approaches, our eyes remain locked on one another, unwavering and cautious. The stream of light flowing from her icy blue eyes softens but otherwise doesn't disappear. She continues to speak while circling me like a predator enticing their prey.

"Right now, you are alive because I stopped time which has caused you to travel from one dimension to another, thus physically placing you in my presence."

"What does that even mean?"

She stops ten feet from me and raises her hand towards the assortment of lights from above.

"It means that you are unquantifiable like the living organisms from beyond. A component to the universe that adapts and modifies to life itself. Your soul is eternal, and your mind is an unstoppable element, unique and inclusive to your own willingness. You exist and will continue doing so because of who you are and what you're made of."

I am confused beyond measure. This is a paradox with less clarity than before. My anger only spikes as I begin to lash out from fear and intimidation.

"I don't have time for riddles! Just tell me who you are, why am I always dreaming about you and what is happening to me?"

My taut voice is menacing and steadfast as I stand my ground. Now we are both circling each other, like an assumed waltz as we analyze our every move.

"Simone, you have to understand that your mere existence poses a threat to all, especially those who do not understand and are afraid of what you might become. This is the reason why your foes plot against you. You have to…"

I cut her off mid-sentence because her perceptions of who I am have been fabricated. A forged fable in leading me to believe that I am of importance for reasons that she has failed to clarify. No living being is unquantifiable. It's impossible and irrational as we both stop to an immediate halt.

"You still haven't answered my questions. Don't you get it? Someone has been chasing me for the last couple of days and has somehow succeeded in killing me for reasons that I cannot fathom. And here you are yet again with more bedtime stories that are illogical!"

I'm yelling out of frustration and anger. Yelling because none of this makes sense. I don't want to be whatever she says that I am. And I'm not interested to find out. But in the mix of all the confusion and shock, I have somehow managed to carelessly upset the only individual who has become my personal refuge in a time of need.

A penetrating and shrill sound rings out like a warning, "SATIS," which stops me in my tracks.

The icy blue light flowing from her eyes has doubled as she quickly diverts her gaze towards the endless night illuminating the uninhabited space. Silence trails for a few heartbeats when she finally turns her attention back to me and resumes speaking in a composed and dominating tone.

"Make no mistake, you were created for a purpose. And you must now play your part, otherwise you will be the demise of all living beings. There is no choice in the matter – you will comply." She delivers a direct order that is laced with an impossible objective.

But to my surprise, it has no effect on me as she closes the distance between us. My blood remains pumping with rage that is not directed at her but instead aimed at my current predicament. A dilemma that is dictating the course of my future whether I choose to accept it or not.

Reaching for my face, she cups my chin with two fingers while addressing me in a faint voice. She seems weary for reasons unknown as our gazes unite.

"Your past has already defined your future and you are all that you should be. There is no need to look further because all that you seek has already been gifted. You are the key to our survival."

As she withdraws her hand from my chin, she proceeds to reach for the tips of my cold fingers. In that instant, an intoxicating force emerges, forming an indescribable bond between us. A sudden massive energy begins to course throughout my body while unspoken thoughts are exchanged, fusing our separate minds into one. My eyelids involuntarily slide shut as distorted images begin to flood my psyche.

A turquoise ocean appears from afar with rocky shores and an endless coastline. Complex cliffs take refuge behind the smoky clouds while several giant mushroom trees with sprouting branches hover above the ground like flying saucers. A mystical blue magnetic storm emerges from above and transmits an electric current onto this paradisiacal terrain, thus breathing a new life onto all living organisms. The creatures, plants and animals including the inanimate objects are all neurologically connected in a spiritual sense.

It's all coming together now – who I really am, my purpose, all the why's, when's and how's. The past, present and future but most notably, what all of this means and the importance of my mere existence as well as hers. She interrupts my concentration, causing me to lose sight of the vision.

"Can you see it? Do you understand now?"

"Yes." My response is but a murmur lost in translation as I open my eyes.

"Your energy is resilient more than ever. It's been dormant; caged up like an untamed animal that has been yearning to break free. This energy is boundless, and it will do as you command. It is now your personal refuge."

"But I'm afraid."

She straightens her back and tightens her grip.

"Don't ever be afraid of who you are. It is in your nature to carry this burden. It has been written that you will not fail."

Her icy blue eyes transform to a deep ocean blue and the stream of flowing light completely diminishes as she continues to speak.

"Close your eyes. Quickly. We are running out of time."

I do as she commands and close my eyes. Our fingers remain intertwined as she resumes her soothing lullaby.

"Now, I want you to focus on my voice and open your mind. I need you to clear it of all qualms and allow it to completely consume you so that it may become whole again."

She begins to utter something unintelligible in a dialect that I've heard before. At first, it's silent and measured but as the hymn continues, it becomes urgent and dynamic causing a sense of peace and tranquility to wash over me. It lifts me up and fills my soul with purpose as my body is transported through thin air by an invisible source.

I can feel limitless energy at my fingertips and at that moment it becomes abundantly clear that I am a weapon. A defense mechanism and exception to the rule with a difficult objective that hangs in the balance of mother nature itself. It's no longer a want but a need, and what was once a burden has now transformed into a responsibility.

*****

Opening my lethargic eyes, my first reaction is to reach for my constricted neck but stop short when I find myself inhaling with ease. Air remains flowing through my lungs as I continue breathing. My bare back is still jammed against the wall with the intruder's palm pinned to my neck but there is no pressure or aggression in his hold. The violent male's grasp has not tightened nor made any advances to end my life. I can feel something thick and wet dripping from the side of my lip. Lifting my left hand up to my mouth, I gently wipe with my index finger and reveal a discharge of dark red blood. My heart begins pounding in my chest as I become fully aware that he remains frozen in time.

Time. She has given me a head start to do as I will and free myself from this horrid nightmare. Unsure when this momentarily lapse will end, I know that I must be prepared to face his wrath when time catches up. Just as I'm about to squirm out of his hold, he snaps out of the trance.

Disoriented and angry, he tightens his rough fingers around my throat and resumes his physical abuse. No longer resisting his cruelty, I close my eyes and instruct my body to surrender. Whomever sent him here to end my life obviously fears me more than him. I'm no longer surrounded by darkness but rather light as her voice sings into my ear with clarity.

"No one can hurt you unless you allow them. You are the sun, and now it is time to shine."

As I continue searching for my inner self, I sense my body being knocked around, but I feel no pain or discomfort. I can hear cursing in the far distance followed by more abuse.

"Powerless commoner. Why haven't you stopped breathing?"

But nothing matters at the moment. He has become a faint memory, detached from life itself. Instead, I decide to focus on self-control because at the rate that my strength is increasing, I'm certain that he'll be no match for my fury. His brutality has become my new ally. A supporter that feeds and fuels my inner savagery which is about to make an appearance as it fills my soul with the necessary elements to set my mind free.

"You are ready Simone." Her soft whisper ends my search when my eyes stop twitching and I open them.

Taking in my surroundings, I confirm that my body is now laying on the dining room floor with him mounting me. Cowardly hands remain wrapped around my tiny neck while my head continues to take abuse as it repeatedly makes contact with the porcelain tile. He takes notice that I remain very much alive and goes in for the kill by pulling out a silver blade from his jacket and proceeds to aim for my heart. But his quest is short lived when I effortlessly block his attempt with my forearm. His struggle has apparently become strenuous while I consciously prepare myself for the violence that will soon follow.

"What the…..." He hisses through clenched teeth as shock and disbelief crosses his face while he continues to tussle with my opposition. My voice is strident and menacing as I sit up with my forearm still blocking his advance.

"SATIS!"

His head snaps back out of shock and I can see a reflection through his eyes of an icy blue light radiating from my own pupils. The assassin is caught off guard by my abrupt movement, causing him to roll back on his heels for a hint of a second. In that moment of doubt, he becomes helpless and immobile when I place the palm of my right hand on his chest.

A bright glowing light projects a force so powerful that it instantly hurls his body across the kitchen, landing him on two metal chairs and breaks them in half. A loud thunderclap echoes throughout the house causing the glass from every window to shatter into a million pieces.

My head is swimming with pain while my ears are muted by a piercing sound so loud that I'm unable to process the consequences of my actions. At that precise moment, the front door is kicked open and Jovianus appears while I witness the intruder slither away through the back entry. I fall back and land on my side, wasted from the drawn-out attack. He eagerly reaches my broken frame, leans down, and places his arms underneath my head while mouthing inaudible words as I struggle to keep my eyes open.

Warm blood continues to trickle from my nose as it slides onto my upper arm. The last memory I have of the incident is Jovi removing the shirt off his back and covers me with it when he leaves my side in search of something or someone.

Chapter Twenty

~Incursion~

Standing on the front doorstep of Simone's home with a dried flower bouquet in one hand and a wine bottle in the other, I begin to feel confident that maybe there is still hope for us after all. Being absent from her life for an extended period of time has placed a tremendous amount of stress and doubt, therefore I must prove to her that what we felt for each other was real and hasn't changed.

As I raise my finger to the doorbell, I hear a male's hostile voice coming from the opposite side of the door. Frowning out of confusion, I quickly eliminate any negative thoughts from my mind and assume that the voices being heard are coming from the television. She's probably watching a movie in the family room and doesn't realize that its loud. Stay calm.

Reaching for the doorbell again, I hear another loud thud followed by brazen profanity which stops me short from pushing the glowing button. Fear takes on a new form as my worst nightmare becomes reality that the perpetrator has possibly returned to finish what he started.

My mood swiftly changes as I eagerly pound my fist on the door while frantically calling her name, "Simone," hoping to garner a response. The level of my anxiety unpredictably spikes when she doesn't reply. Then out of nowhere, a loud explosion resonates from within the home causing the windows to shatter and sends broken glass flying straight towards my face.

Quickly ducking to avoid direct contact, I discard both the bottle and flowers then proceed to kick open the door. My heart briefly falters when I catch sight of her naked broken body lying lifeless on the dining room floor. Her face and arms are smothered in fresh blood from an unprovoked attack. I quickly rush to her side and kneel by her head as blood drips from her battered nose and lips.

Placing my left palm underneath her head to provide support, I speak words of comfort as her eyes flutter open then closed again. My oversized hand slides down her cheek while I beg the goddess to spare her life and take mine instead.

I instantly remove my white t-shirt off my back and cover her upper body while glancing at the kitchen in its entirety. The back door has been kicked open, partially hanging on by a broken hinge. There are two busted chairs with blood stains and countless pieces of glass scattered across the tile floor. Dry blood is smeared on the damaged wallpaper and counter tops.

He must have dragged her around the kitchen like a ragdoll while she fought for her life then fled like a coward. That son of a bitch! In an instant my blood thirst for violence reappears after being confined for so many years which sends a thrill of satisfaction through my body.

The reckless and destructive Jovianus has finally made an appearance and I have no intention of concealing his identity. When I find her assailant, and that's not if, it's a matter of when, I guarantee that he will be begging me to end his life.

Changing tactics, I set off in search of Mateo as I begin scanning the living area and hallways. My calls are desperate and unyielding as I attempt to find her sole reason for living

"Mateo! Mateo! Where are you?"

Running through the hallway, I begin pushing every door open and quickly examine the area. After searching three rooms including a powder room only to find them empty, I slowly begin losing my mind as I try to digest the endless possibilities of what has occurred to them both. Please, please let him be safe.

Entering the last door to the left, I catch a glimpse of a tiny body squatted down behind a nightstand. His hands are covering his ears while his head is tucked between his knees as he rocks himself back and forth. I gently approach him with my hands up in the air and softly call out his name again.

"Mateo, it's me Jovianus."

Her terrified son warily lifts his head with shielded eyes as his fragile body continues to tremble from fear. I slowly bend down, careful not to make any sudden moves and lower my arms as I continue to implore.

"Mateo, there is nothing to worry about anymore. I'm here now and you're safe."

He stares at me for a few moments then leaps into my chest and wraps his arms around my neck. There are no sobs or cries, which is what I wasn't expecting considering the circumstances. As his body continues to shake from fear, I speak words of comfort to ease his frightened state while wrapping one of my arms around his waist and lift him up.

Rushing outside to my SUV, I unlock the doors and place him in the back while I fasten his seatbelt. Fetching my phone from my back pocket, I rush to plug the wire to my headphones and immediately press the play button. Moonlight Sonata from Beethoven resumes its peaceful lullaby. I place my device into his palms and proceed to speak in a soothing manner.

"I'm going to get your mum from the house. Do you think you can take care of this phone for me while I'm inside?"

He shakes his head in approval as I place the black band over his head and adjust the pads that are pressed against his ears.

"I'll be right back, ok?"

I kiss him gently on the forehead before locking the vehicle and rush to her side. As I approach her fragile body, I take notice that my t-shirt slowly rises and falls confirming that she remains breathing, but not sure for how long. I know that I must get her and Mateo out of here as fast as possible.

Jumping into action, I kneel behind her and gently place my hands on her waist. Carefully turning her away from me and moving her into a sitting position, I place the palm of my hand above her chest to keep the shirt from sliding off. She mumbles something inaudible as I pull her small frame backwards, closing the gap between us.

My bare chest is now flush with her back as I gently remove the shirt from her upper body and pull it over her head while sliding each delicate arm inside. Placing all my weight on the back of my heels, I manage to stand with my arms wrapped around her torso. Sliding my hands underneath her legs, I begin pulling her body into a cradling position and proceed to carry her outside.

Unlocking the door, I gently place her in the front seat and move it into a sleeping position. While stretching the seatbelt over her lap, she opens her hazel eyes for the first time since I burst through the front door. Our gazes unintentionally meet, unraveling a frayed and undying passion that was thought to have been obsolete.

At that moment, I become fully aware that the love I feel for Simone is dangerously vigorous and far more lethal than my own demise. It's a gentle sin that defies our most sacred decree, causing disgrace and imposing death to all who violate it. But to no surprise, this risk is the least of my worries as I inspect her bruised body and furtively pledge to kill the imposter who has purposely harmed her.

With our mouth's inches apart, she attempts to articulate words through her lacerated lips. Her voice is hoarse and low as she struggles to speak.

"Jovi... please tell me you found Mateo."

A single tear manages to escape from her eyes and slides down the left side of her cheek. The palm of my hand automatically cradles her face while my thumb swipes at the clear droplet.

"Shhhh. He is safe and was unharmed."

So many angry thoughts are crossing my mind at once that I'm unable to fully digest the extent of what has transpired here today. I feel helpless because I'm unable to take away her pain and suffering. And to make matters worse, I feel somewhat responsible for this attack because had I been more persistent about her safety, then this would not have happened. Why didn't I pressure Ethan in making her stay with him or at the very least kept a closer watch from across the street. I couldn't live with myself if something were to happen to her.

As I continue to examine her injuries, she interrupts my shattered thoughts with another inquiry about Mateo.

"Where is he?" She closes her eyes for a brief moment as additional tears begin to trickle over my thumb.

I whisper back, "In the back seat, listening to some music from my phone," hoping to enlist peace in an already havoc situation.

She then shifts in the leather seat in search of comfort as she continues with her inquiry.

"Not Mateo. The man...the man with the scar across his lip. Where is he?"

Confusion crosses my face, causing me to pose her previous statement as a question. "A scar across his lip?"

"Yes," she gently shuts her eyes and grunts out of pain as she continues to explain, "It trailed down to his throat. Did you see him?"

Remus? No. No, this can't be right. What in the world is Remus doing in the States and why would he purposely target Simone? Unless this is his way of getting back at me; our troubled past isn't a secret to anyone. But why now? Why wait this long to get retribution? Unless someone else put him up to the task.

I'm struggling to make sense of this new information because it can't be true. Well, one thing is certain, if Remus is her assailant then I will definitely be sentenced to death because there's no way that I'm going to allow him to walk away with his life intact. My rage has finally reached a level of no return and I'm finding it difficult to concentrate on the task at hand.

"Don't worry about him. I'm taking you to the hospital and calling Aemilia to keep you company while I file a police report. Everything is going to be ok. I promise."

I gently kiss her on the head and close the passenger door. Dashing to the driver side, I hop in and start the engine while we descend to the nearest hospital. It's dark out as we begin driving down the steep hill towards the interstate when she begins to mumble again.

"What was that?"

Her voice remains faint while she speaks, "Please stay away from him Jovi. He's dangerous."

Dangerous? I silently chuckle to myself because she has no idea that I am by far deadlier than the spineless Remus and anyone for that matter. Glancing in her direction, I smile while maintaining a calm and collected tone.

"You don't need to worry about me. There are far more dangerous things out there than a cowardly male who attacks women. I will not stand idle while the man who assaulted you roams this earth free of guilt."

She then places her warm hand over mine that is nestled on the console and shakes her head.

"No. You don't understand Jovi. He...he isn't from this world..."

Her words are suppressed by a violent side impact to the driver door that shoves my body against the steering wheel with brute intensity.

As the seatbelt begins to constrict against my bare chest, my neck and head are both forced backward then forward causing instant whiplash. The driver window immediately shatters and disseminates glass across my lap and into Simone's direction. The blow is overwhelmingly hard and forceful that it veers my vehicle off the incline road and straight into a tree, however, my quick reaction enables me to swerve in time and avoid a direct collision.

I can see dirt and rocks sailing through the thin air in slow motion from my rearview as they strike the decklid at the same time. My hands remain glued to the steering wheel as I slowly begin to experience tunnel vision and ease my foot off the brake pedal. The firm tires finally grip to the asphalt, allowing me to gain control of the SUV once more.

Adrenaline is circulating throughout my body while I come to terms that Remus is in fact behind this gutless assault. His bold attack knows no bounds, reminding me that he is unstable and will go to great lengths to complete his mission. He could be anywhere, and I am not about to place Simone nor Mateo's lives at risk. So, I decide to continue driving down the steep hill towards the hospital and out of harm's way.

During this unexpected commotion, Mateo has finally reached his limit and begins to cry uncontrollably. With the tires screeching in the background, I look over to my right and validate that Simone is shaken beyond measure. Her eyes remain tightly closed with her hands balled up into fist confirming that she is holding on by a thread.

I attempt to speak words of comfort, "We're ok. Everything is going to be alright. I'm going to get you both to safety, I promise."

But fail horribly when she doesn't react to my comment. Her eyes are open, and laser focused on the empty road ahead as if she were lost in a nightmare. I continue to speed through the neighborhood and run past two more stops signs hoping to reach the hospital in time to save their lives from a psychopath who may or may not have a death wish.

As I accelerate towards the entrance of the highway, a huge dark truck with blaring headlights intentionally smashes into the passenger side door. My SUV loses complete stability and begins to skid sideways for a few seconds when it turns and strikes head on with a utility pole, causing the airbags to deploy from every outlet.

The impact is far more painful than the first as my head smashes against the steering wheel and I lose total control of my body while I'm lifted up and off my seat. Disregarding the ache in my head and torso, I reach down my leg, pull out a switch blade from my ankle and begin slashing through the airbags. I witness as gray smoke escapes from the engine through the hood of the vehicle and releases a foul odor that is mixed with gas and other toxic fluids.

Looking over to my right, Simone's fragile form comes into view. Her body buckles and bends forward then backwards like she is possessed from within. The seatbelt is the only item holding her in place while her eyelids flutter from side to side with rapid movements. Puzzled and distraught from the incident, I blink my eyes several times and shake away the blurriness that has begun to settle.

At that moment, I notice that her door is smashed inward, causing her legs to be wedged between the crushed dashboard. Realizing that another impact would set the engine on fire, I set off on a mission to get them both out of the vehicle before Remus completes his mission.

Meanwhile, the constant sound of my horn remains high pitched throughout this ordeal, drowning out all other noises.

The heavy-duty truck then reappears from afar. At top speed, he begins making his way towards us and I know that there is a high possibility that this impact will be fatal to either Simone, Mateo, or both.

Chapter Twenty-One

~Transgression~

Thinking fast, I cut the seatbelt from my lap, reach in the backseat, and unbuckle Mateo. Pulling his small frame into my arms, I hastily kick open my crushed door and rush him out of harm's way by safely tucking him behind a set of shrubs.

Returning to the vehicle, I duck my head inside and attempt to free her legs from underneath the dash when my body is suddenly hurled backwards onto the concrete. The attack was so unexpected that I had no time to break my fall when a razor-sharp pain quickly begins to spread to my arms and legs.

As my chest tightens, I find myself gasping for air and immediately sit upright to relieve some of the pain. Stunned and disoriented, I attempt to stand when my sight is suddenly blinded by two scorching lights. Its Remus!

Acknowledging that this collision is inevitable and that there is nothing I can do to possibly prevent this incident from happening; I decide to spring into action and make a final bid to save her life. Summoning all my strength from within, I impulsively launch my body over hers like a protective shield right before the impact only to witness an uncanny outcome. The glaring lights which I thought was a product of the pickup truck turned out to be some form of illusion that was being projected directly from the palm of Simone's frail hands.

The heat and power of this beam is so intense that it effortlessly flings my body through the front windshield. I land face first onto the rigid pavement which only amplifies my injuries further. At that exact moment, Remus's truck is thrown back about a hundred feet. It flips over several times then finally lands upside down near a large oak tree. The crushing sound is deafening, similar to a massive boulder sliding down a cliff then splitting in half from the impact.

I can feel shards of glass scraping against the palm of my hands as I sluggishly push myself upright into a standing position. My mind is partially disconnected as I stand at the foot of my vehicle, wondering what the hell just happened. Just then, I detect movement coming from the inside of the truck which remains a few feet from the incident.

Adjusting my sight, I catch sight of Remus crawling out of a broken window, attempting to escape. His mouth and nose are both smothered with blood as he struggles to stand while stumbling a few times before holding his weight onto the medal railing. The truck's headlights are flickering off and on while the tires remain spinning in the air.

As I turn my attention to Simone, who remains seated in the passenger seat of my vehicle, I note that her sight is affixed on Remus. My sudden movement causes her to snap out of the trance as she turns her mask of eloquence on me.

When our gazes meet, I am taken aback by the icy blue light pouring from her eyes and all traces of assurance instantly vanishes. I become immobilized and unable to formulate words while questioning everything that I've ever known to be true. How is this possible?

Just as I'm about to take a step in her direction, she lowers her gaze from mine and places her left palm onto the dashboard. I witness the panel bend at her will all while unbounding her crushed legs. No freaking way!

Without hesitation, she removes the door from its hinge and starts to make her way towards Remus in a measured stride with only one mission in mind. Vengeance.

She intends to avenge her assailant. But to what extent? Simone is no match for Remus. He is a trained killer, weighing more than two hundred pounds who has murdered countless victims with his bare hands.

Realizing that there is a high probability that I am either hallucinating or that she is possessed, my mind tussles with one question that conquers all. Should I join her quest in killing Remus or stop her? How do I impede her actions without placing her own life in danger? Better yet, how do I stop someone that is under the influence of someone else and not get myself killed in the process? One thing's for sure – I'm not about to sit back and contemplate all the possible outcomes while she marches to her death.

While taking a step forward, I'm momentarily distracted by an object in the dark sky. Looking up, I confirm that the disturbance is a flock of white birds. They are flying low and way too close for my liking. Within a split second, they make an unexpected turn and begin making their way back one by one as they continue to circle us from above in a synchronized formation.

Suddenly without warning, she raises her hand and releases another harmful blow that flings Remus's injured body against a tree. He lands on the ground with a loud thud, and moans from agony that is brought upon from the scorching light.

She never breaks stride as her palms illuminate the pavement underneath her feet with every passing step. Deciding that I must intervene, I begin to trail her while keeping a distance and attempt to stop this madness.

"Simone," my call is stern but soft spoken that emulates a plead. She continues walking, ignoring my request at all costs as she inches closer to Remus's unconscious body. I resume calling her name as I catch up and we begin walking side by side.

"Simone. Will you please stop?"

Agitated, she halts and turns to face me while forcing her palms downwards. Her icy blue eyes are focused on something behind me, as if she were deliberately avoiding eye contact.

"My name is not Simone."

"What?" I shake my head out of bewilderment.

"I said, my name is not Simone." Her voice is calm but commanding as if she was under the influence of someone else.

"Simone, just listen to me for a second..."

She abruptly cuts me off, "NO!"

But before I'm able to explain why I don't want her anywhere near Remus, she turns those icy blue eyes on me.

"You listen to me! You should learn to properly address your adversary if you plan on distracting them. Either you're with me or against me. Which of the two are you?"

Her voice is low and tight while conveying an unjust assessment of my actions. Surprised at her hostility and the delivery of her ultimatum, I can't help but wonder if she is purposely trying to antagonize me. Without warning, discontent slaps me in my face as I take personal offense to her remark. Taking a step forward in her direction and careful not to cross any lethal boundaries, I lash out with an unruly tone and capture her undivided attention.

"I am with you! I've always been with you, that's why I'm here!" My arms are extended outward while my eyes are filled with rage and pain.

"Then let me be, so I can finish what they have started."

Her hands begin to tremble uncontrollably. Who the heck is *they*? I'm under the impression that she is unaware how to control this power and seems to be struggling with her inner self, so I lower my voice to a soothing tone, careful not to rouse her any further.

"I can't let you do that."

Balling her hands into fist, she leans in close and whispers, "Oh really? And how do you intend to stop me?"

Sarcasm and mockery leave her lips while offering a challenge. Whatever has consumed her mind is about to lead her to her death and I will not allow that to happen. This is a reckless task. One that could very well end badly if I'm not careful. My dignity is cornered as I struggle to look directly into her eyes and proceed to refute her opposition with a feeble proclamation.

"So now you threaten those who love you? Is that how this works?"

She takes a step back, confused at my statement and unsure of the meaning behind this one word.

"Yes, you heard me correctly. I am in love with you. I always have been and nothing or no one can ever change that. Don't you understand – everything that I've done up until this point has always been to protect you. That is why I cannot stand aside while you march to your impending death. I couldn't bare it if something happened to you."

Her head begins to shake like she doesn't believe it while her icy blue eyes dull to an ocean blue. As I take a step forward, a *swoosh* sound echo's directly from behind her.

Acting on impulse, I grip her body tightly against mine and spin her around and away from the sound. Within seconds, I feel a sharp stabbing pain in my right shoulder when another *swoosh* sound resonates from behind me.

At this point, I become fully aware that Remus has awaken and that Simone's life is in grave danger. This time I was able to avoid his deadly advance as I instinctively shove her body onto the pavement floor. I then witness the dagger slowly glide past my torso, missing its target by a fraction of an inch.

Without further contemplation, my body automatically responds to his threats and a devastating need to protect what is mine conquers all my senses. It's a survival instinct that is primitive and comes second to none. I have yearned for this opportunity to arise for many moons. The day when we meet on equal grounds and fight till death. Away from prying eyes where only one of us will walk away from this perilous battle.

Not only is it risky because I will be killing one of my own, but the reasoning behind my actions will not be justified. I will be violating two of our most sacred decrees; murder and treason, because I plan on bestowing the same respect onto him that he has conveyed upon Simone. The only difference is that he will not have the pleasure of surviving this ordeal. Only one thought comes to mind. Kill Remus!

As I turn to face this despicable being, I begin to charge at him with all of my strength. I'm not surprised to find him smiling as he also sets off on lunging himself at me and we both embark on a much awaited one on one combat. His fist instantly connects with my mouth the moment our bodies clash. But the strike has no influence on my welfare. I am bigger, faster, and far more lethal.

Without much effort, I launch my body over his and kick him in his lower back. This blow catches him by surprise, causing his knees to buckle from underneath. He has now lost the upper hand as I turn around and strike him in the throat. While attempting to end his life with my bare hands, he swiftly maneuvers to my right and yanks the dagger from my shoulder. I advance and land another jab to his torso, causing him to lose his balance for a split second.

But that doesn't slow him down as he gains momentum and charges at me with the dagger all while swinging the blade violently. Raising my forearms to my face for protection, I endure several gashes but otherwise hold my ground.

Changing tactics, he decides to aim the blade at my abdomen, but his quest is short lived when I reach for his wrist, bend it backwards and he unwillingly drops the weapon. He somehow manages to escape my grip and begins to retrieve like a frightened dog with his tail between his legs. I'm not about to let this pariah escape. This will end tonight!

An angry bellow escapes my lips in a desperate attempt to capture his attention.

"Remus!" He comes to a swift halt and turns to face me with a sinister expression on his face.

"My most cynical foe. Quit fucking around and let's end this already!" Both of my arms are extended outward that radiates an ill-disposed warning as my chest constricts from the heavy breathing.

"No! I'd rather watch you suffer a little longer, like your sorceress harlot!"

"You should have left our unsettled quarrels between us and maybe I would have thought about sparing your life. But instead, you decided to get back at me by coming after her. A mistake that will cost you your life!"

He chuckles and wipes the wet blood from his nose with the back of his hand.

"You never fail to surprise me. I had no previous quarrels with you until you decided to meddle in my business."

I slowly begin to close the distance between us while distracting him with my inquisitiveness.

"And what business might that be?"

"Why killing the helpless mortal that you so desperately defend. Tell me, since when did you care about a human's life more than our own?"

Ignoring his inquiry about my relationship with Simone, I pursue the most disturbing fact of all.

"So, I see that you're now in the business of killing human beings among other things."

"Oh, I'll kill just about anyone for the right price."

"Are you implying that someone ordered a hit on Simone's life?"

"Why else would I be here?"

"You lie!" I snarl at his claim that he has fabricated to justify his biased deeds.

"So now I'm the liar? A manipulator? Deceiver? But how are you any different?"

No sooner are we circling each other, ready to pounce when the opportunity arises.

"I can assure you; we are different in more ways than you can count. I for one am not someone else's puppet."

He chuckles, "You should know better than anyone that I have no reason to falsify these claims. What would I gain by baring false accusations?"

"Then speak their name and I pledge to end your life and theirs quickly."

He begins to laugh hysterically, "My life is already spoken for and it is not yours to take."

"Make no mistake Remus, you forfeited your life the moment you laid your eyes on her and we both know what happens when you touch what's mine."

"Ah, well aren't you two fast friends. At last, the truth comes out. And here I was thinking that it was a coincidence, but it turns out that you actually have feelings for this creature. What would the council members think about your… indiscretions?"

"This isn't a game Remus. Speak their name. I will not ask again!" My tone is loud and thunderous as I move closer to my target.

"Tell me this, why do you care what happens to her? They have little respect for our race yet here you stand vowing revenge on my life for hers. Have you forgotten that they tried to exterminate our species? Do you need a trip back down memory lane? Perhaps a history lesson of how we got here?"

"Stop trying to weasel your way out of this encounter. My personal interest is none of your concern. You've made your bed Remus and now you get to lay in it."

He notices that I've cornered him between the tree and his truck, so he makes a second attempt to escape but fails when I block his passage with my body.

"I can promise you that it will be you against the world. You see, a little bird told me that the council members want her dead, for undisclosed reasons of course. And who am I to question their motives or desires? Unfortunately, I'm afraid that her time on this earth is up. If not by my hands, then by someone else's."

"The council would never order the death of a mortal. They would not break the treaty that we've worked so hard to set in motion. So, tell me, what does she have that you want?"

"Other than what's between her legs, she has nothing to offer me."

"Then why are you hell bent on ending her life?"

"Poor Jovianus. The great almighty future leader who has been loved and loathe by the citizens of our tribe. So dangerous. So lethal and yet he too has a weakness."

"Spare me your criticism and accept your fate. Today is not the day that you gain victory. Not against me."

"Oh, I can assure you that this is a war you will not win."

"Then I shall strike all those who oppose me. Starting with you!"

With the dagger lost and no weapon to protect himself, Remus acts on impulse and picks up a discarded brick that was left on the side of the road. Hoping to stall my advances, he propels the brick with all his strength and aims at my head. My agile movements dodge his attack which only drives me closer as I lunge my body over his, landing me at his back.

Swiftly wrapping my upper arms over his face, I pull his body down over my knee and prepare to break his neck when he breathes his last words.

"How does it feel to betray your tribe for a worthless cause?" His voice is strained and measured as he continues to struggle with my grip.

"It feels…. rather delightful." I hear his neck break then crack, causing his arms to go limp and motionless.

Then without warning, the flock of eccentric birds circling above cease their peculiar display by breaking formation and begin to depart one by one in a single file.

They swiftly disappear into the darkness and fade, leaving no trace or recollection of their presence.

Reaching down, I check his chest and neck for any signs of life but quickly confirm that he has met his fate by my hands. I thought that by killing him I would feel some type of satisfaction, but it turns out that I still feel empty inside. Like my mission is far from over, especially if what he said is true.

I was so consumed with seeking revenge on behalf of Simone that I lost sight of her whereabouts. My eyes quickly begin scanning the area when I notice some movement from the corner of my eye. A white t-shirt, specifically my t-shirt that I carefully placed over her body is partially exposed from behind the left rear tire.

Standing up, I tug at Remus's collar and drag his lifeless body over to his vehicle. I leave him close to the driver window and begin searching the pockets of his jeans. His skin and the inside of his truck reeks of nicotine so I know there has to be a lighter somewhere.

I quickly recover a gold trim lighter from his back pocket that contains a small skull icon towards the bottom and William Shakespeare's signature engraved on the side. Hmm…that's an odd looking lighter. Taking a closer look, I notice that it is made by S.T Dupont. What is he doing with such a fancy item? Whatever the case might be, I take a mental note of the brand and flick the lighter to life while I toss it towards the leaking gas that is dripping from the engine.

Escaping the scene before it lights up, I head towards Simone and Mateo and take cover behind my wrecked vehicle. It doesn't take long before Remus's truck bursts into flames as I cover her ears from the deafening sound of the blast. After about thirty seconds, I stand and extend my hand to her with Mateo cradled in her arms.

"The police will be here any minute, so we have to move fast."

Carefully placing her palm into mine, I lift her to a standing position.

"Go on down the hill and I will meet you in a few minutes."

She nods and begins making her way down the steep incline. I then crank my sputtering engine and set its course towards the already burning truck. Jumping out right before it makes contact, I catch up with Simone when I hear another loud bang. She doesn't jump or look back as I reach for Mateo and take him into my arms once again. Sirens can be heard in the background as we both begin jogging in silence through the back streets of Regent Square.

Coming to a slow stop, I decide to make our escape a little less complicated and steal a car that is parked on the side of the street. Luckily, the vehicle didn't have an alarm as I hotwire it to life and we descend towards the back roads, away from the horrid memories that will soon begin to torment our fretted minds.

"My house is no longer safe. It's best if we both keep a low profile for the time being until I can figure out why Remus was after you. Is that alright?" She stays silent for a few moments.

With her eyes focused on the road before us she responds, "Where will we go?"

"I'm not sure, a hotel or one of my cottages outside of Pittsburgh. Both you and Mateo need some rest. Everything else can wait."

She doesn't speak and instead nods her head in agreement with Mateo fast asleep in her steady arms.

Keeping my eyes on the road and giving her some personal space, I can't help but wonder if she was in control of her actions this whole time or if someone else was behind this scheme. She showcased a side of herself that is contradictory and illogical. The strange part of this whole ordeal is that she specifically stated that her name wasn't Simone. And not to mention the fact that her wounds have now magically healed themselves. What is she hiding?

My private thoughts are interrupted by her modulated voice.

"We have to call Aemilia." Knowing that I will not have all the answers tonight, I decide to focus on the task at hand instead.

"Does Mateo still have my phone?" She begins searching his body, finds my cell tucked away in the seam of his pants and attempts to hand it to me. I politely decline and offer another solution

"Can you please text her? I need to focus on the road in case something else decides to blindside us."

Quickly calling out my passcode, she unlocks my phone and begins texting while we ride in silence into the unknown.

Only one thing is certain, and it undoubtedly comes with a heavy price; one that I am too eager to pay.

I will stand by Simone regardless of her true origin. Even if it means that I must stand alone.

Chapter Twenty-Two

~Unscrupulous~

"**R**ing!" "Ring!" "Ring!" "Ring!"

After a few buzzes, his voicemail chime's in with the automated message that he is unavailable at the moment. I smash the end button with my thumb and impatiently dial his number again, hoping that by some miracle he will answer. But to my dismay there is only silent dreadful ringing, then the call goes straight to voicemail for the fourth time.

Ringing is all I've been hearing from the other end of the receiver for the past couple of days. It's become a musical note that I've gotten used to, replaying over and over like a catchy song that gets lodged into your brain and can't get rid of. The continuous buzzing of several unanswered calls had me on the edge at first, but now I've gone from being uneasy to pissed off.

Removing the cell from my ear, I begin to lightly brush the metal device across my lower lip like a nervous tick lost in thought.

Hmmm…I wonder if the poor bastard finally met his fate at the hands of his nemesis. It's no secret that those two have a renowned history of animosity which was bound to resurface sooner or later. I'm positively certain that Jovianus would not have hesitated to take his life if he felt threaten. I mean, that was the intent after all. Well, maybe not this early on in the game but rather after he had carried out this simple favor that was entrusted upon him.

Why can't anyone follow proper instructions anymore? I specifically asked him to remain discreet and in return his debt would be paid. And now here we are, with no word from the emissary. I should have known this would happen. Now I'm further away from executing my plan and becoming the impartial monarch that our tribe desires. Damn-it Remus! That selfish hellion!

Abruptly pushing my chair back, I stand and begin pacing back and forth in my study, agitated over unanswered questions that linger about whether the deed was completed. Pulling out a bolivar cigar from my desk drawer and lighting it, I take a puff and walk over to the full-length window.

Numerous towering buildings come into view as I stare at my reflection, enthralled by the dark ominous skyline from the forty-third floor. Silently chuckling to myself, I blandly come to terms that this whole scheme has inevitably gone sideways. This is what happens when you place all your delicate eggs in one basket. I relied on one individual to complete, what was supposed to be an easy, straightforward task, but it quickly turned out to be more problematic than we anticipated. There are protocol's that need to be followed and its apparent that our plan was flawed from the start. Now I'm second guessing all the decisions that I've made up to this point.

Stay calm. Don't overreact. There is still time to salvage my plot without skepticism. I just have to think things through before calling this in. Swiftly formulating an unspoken plan to restore my loyalty, I make a thoughtless decision that may or may not backfire.

Taking another slow draw from the cigar, I walk back to my desk, pick up the cell and dial the treacherous number that has been haunting me since this whole ordeal began. She picks up after the second ring.

"Late is the hour in which you call." The tone of her voice instantly gives away her agitation and displeasure with my lack of communication.

"My apologies for calling you at this hour. Is this not a good time?"

"I haven't heard from you in over a week."

Her voice is outward and bleak, like a common side effect caused by a prescription drug that promises to treat the problem but instead creates further impairment. Before responding, I place my half-smoked cigar into a round crystal ashtray and stiffly swallow a few times as I mentally prepare myself to go into the lion's den.

"I was busy handling matters in our neighboring country as previously discussed."

I keep my voice measured and composed, hoping to neutralize any potential conflicts that are likely to emerge.

"Well then, you have good news to share I presume?"

"Um not exactly, I've had a bit of a hiccup."

"No! Not a hiccup. Please do share."

Not sure if she is genuinely curious or if sarcasm has become her new form of irony. Regardless, I'm nervous as heck because she isn't someone you'd want to disappoint. Not when this someone is at the top of the food chain with political power at her fingertips. So, I cautiously ease into the subject and choose my words carefully.

"I did as you asked and deployed a professional to take care of our…potential problem."

She clears her throat, "And?"

"And, um… my associate was intercepted by an unlikely acquaintance that…"

She snaps back and cuts me off before I can continue.

"I don't understand why this is of any importance. First, you don't report to me in over a week, then you decide to call, in the middle of the night with a pretext for your failures instead of reporting results."

"Can you give me a minute to clarify, I…"

"If I wanted to hear excuses then I would have named you Alibi Ike, but I didn't, did I?"

Her daunting voice attacks without warning by labeling me as a deceiver knowing that this would only enrage what little tolerance I have left. No longer able to take her criticism, I unexpectedly blurt out.

"Jovianus is our interloper," like a colluder whose intentions are vindictive and personal.

My response is not met with a rebuttal or backlash as one would have anticipated. Why? Well, because he is also a high-ranking member of our society, and not to mention our future leader. His name alone holds merit and should not be taken lightly when mentioned.

He has this commanding presence that is undeniably strategic which governs his character and reason for survival. One that must be met with caution and scrutiny in order to prevail.

Silence lingers a little longer than I would have predicted but glad that I was finally able to capture her attention and reveal how dire this situation has become.

"Are you sure Jovianus is involved?"

"Yes, I'm sure." She then bellows over the receiver, as she is no longer able to contain her disappointment with the outcome of this heinous reality.

"Then why didn't you come to me the moment you were informed about his involvement?"

"Because I was under the impression that the most important task was to eradicate our foe no matter the collateral."

"Even if it meant placing your brother and future leader's life in danger?"

Now I'm the one lost for words. She previously made it clear that this creature was to be eliminated at all cost and now she is questioning my logic as if I were incompetent? I guess she forgot that Jovianus has gone rogue and does whatever the fuck he wants when he wants and on his own terms. He has no regard for our decree, nor the council members request. But hey who cares, right?

With honeyed words and a silver tongue I deliver a convincing justification of my thoughtless, yet candid remark.

"Let's take a minute and calm down. Clearly there was some miscommunication with the delivery of my message. I certainly did not imply that he was collateral damage, besides, his life was never in danger. It would take more than one individual to defeat him and no one is that bold to go against him."

Damn, that last statement was not supposed to leave my deceitful lips but they somehow managed to tumble right out and expose my own objective. Sure, this hardship could very well go away at the snap of my fingers if Jovianus was not in the picture. Eliminating my biggest threat would definitely tip the scale in my favor, but now is not the time nor place to bring up such foolish ideas.

"I'm going to pretend you didn't just say that and focus on the task at hand."

Clearing my throat while loosening the tie around my neck, I dive into the dynamics of scheming and point out the facts of this botched mission as I sit on the corner of my desk.

"We should start by trying to figure out what his intentions are and what he is doing in the States."

"Jovianus is there on business and he has certainly overstayed his welcome. So, tell me who is this creature that Freyja spoke of? Should we be alarmed?"

"Well, I have reason to believe that the individual could quite possibly be Simone."

"What did you say?" Her tight voice expresses annoyance as I continue to explain my knowledge of this grim affair.

"It seems that Jovi's infatuation has come back to haunt us all. You know, the mortal that he was bent out of shape over when he lived in Pittsburgh. As it turns out, Simone is somehow linked to Freyja's vision or at least that's what it seems to be. Although, according to my accomplice, she seemed like an ordinary human."

"I don't understand," her reaction remains steady as she continues to refute these facts. "All first born have always been males within our species. Males represent strength and power in all aspects of life, that is why the burden of leading invariably falls unto the eldest. If this creature is the same one that Freyja spoke of then I am almost certain she is not Renan's heir. This doesn't make sense and I'm afraid we are missing something here."

"There are definitely several misplaced pieces to this puzzle of which do not add up."

"Indeed, there is."

Silence carries on for a few seconds as we both try to reason with the facts before us. Who is this individual that Freyja mentioned and what is Simone's involvement? Now I know why Jovianus was in the States to begin with, but what are his motives? How did he know to intercept? Has he been onto us this whole time or did he just happen to be at the same exact place at the right time? Coincidence? Fuck no! This isn't a fluke. Jovi is a renowned strategist; every move he makes has a purpose.

"When was the last time you heard from your contact?" She startled my concentration as I snap out of my reverie and quickly respond.

"A week ago, when he saw Jovi assisting our adversary after she was poisoned. I then instructed him to confirm whether the deed had been finalized but never heard back."

"Interesting.... well, if this female Simone is the same being that Freyja and your associate spoke of, and she remains alive, then we are in far worst trouble than we anticipated."

"Agreed."

I'm almost certain that she is withholding vital information, possibly for her own agenda, however, I can't hold that against her as I'm doing the same. You can't deceive a deceiver; not when the mastermind has nothing to lose which is far more dangerous than a half breed and an interloper whose past will be their own demise.

"Are you confident that this matter cannot be traced back to you?"

"Don't worry. If there's anything that I'm sure of, it's this. My coconspirator would die before turning his back on me."

Which is most likely the scenario at this point given that he has fallen off the radar. A sigh of relief is released from the other end of the receiver.

"Good! We can't afford any more mistakes. The stakes are too high, and we have to handle this situation with the upmost care."

"What would you have me do?"

"First, you will need to gather more information about this creature and Simone. We must understand the connection between these two mortals and why has Freyja gone to such extreme measures to undermine my authority without council approval."

"What about Jovianus?"

"His bond with this human was never severed as he led us to believe and it's a bit alarming. His loyalty lies with her. It always has been and I'm afraid that it will continue to be no matter the outcome, therefore he has become a liability. I have no use for him in this state, however all is not lost. His interference could work in our favor after all."

"Oh, how so?"

"Technically, he is aiding our natural enemy and if we expose him to the council members for what he is, then he would be accused of treason thus rendering him unfit to rule. We will make you look like the savior and hope that the goddess declares you as the next successor. Only then will we be able to carry out our plan to wage war against the mortals who continue to condemn us. It's a win-win for all."

Well I'll be damned. Didn't see that one coming. At last, she sees me for who I am although I feel like second choice right now, but her plan does seem solid. And I must admit, it's everything I ever wanted.

"Leave Jovianus to me and I'll be in touch soon."

The phone goes silent and all I hear is a dead buzzing sound, confirming that she hung up. What the heck just happened? I mean, I've always dreamed of Jovianus being obsolete, but this is even better. I get to watch him suffer and wither away while sitting at the head of the table and doing what he failed at. Waging war.

Checkmate!

ABOUT THE AUTHOR

Eli Liszt has always been fascinated with myths, folktales, and unexplained phenomenon. During her college years she became captivated with the campus library and took personal interest in literature, particularly works of poetry and fiction. After reading countless novels and becoming immersed in their fables, she decided that it was time to pursue her own passion in writing.

A native to Texas, she divides her time between Houston and Dallas as often as possible. Her hobbies include gardening, cooking, listening to classical and new age instrumental music as well as spending time with her husband and children. There hardly isn't a time when she's not writing, but as time permits, she aims to discover new authors in hopes of getting lost in another profound story.

You can find her on twitter @LisztEli or facebook @EliLiszt